CREATURE OF HAVOC

STEVE J[...]N

Fighting Fantasy: dare you play them all?

1. The Warlock of Firetop Mountain
2. City of Thieves
3. The Citadel of Chaos
4. The Forest of Doom
5. House of Hell
6. The Port of Peril
7. Creature of Havoc
8. Deathtrap Dungeon
9. Appointment With F.E.A.R.
10. Island of the Lizard King
11. Sorcery! 1: The Shamutanti Hills
12. The Gates of Death

And look out for more books to come!

CREATURE OF HAVOC

STEVE JACKSON

SCHOLASTIC

N
ALLANSIA
ICEFINGE
CHIANG
MAI
Kaad
PAGA
RED RIVER
Dark
Tower
Mirewate
DOGFISH
ISLAND
Flax
CATFIS
PORT
BLACKSAN
WHIT
OYSTER
BAY
FIRE
ISLAND
SKULL COAST
SOUTHER
BLOOD
ISLAND
THE DESERT OF
SKULLS

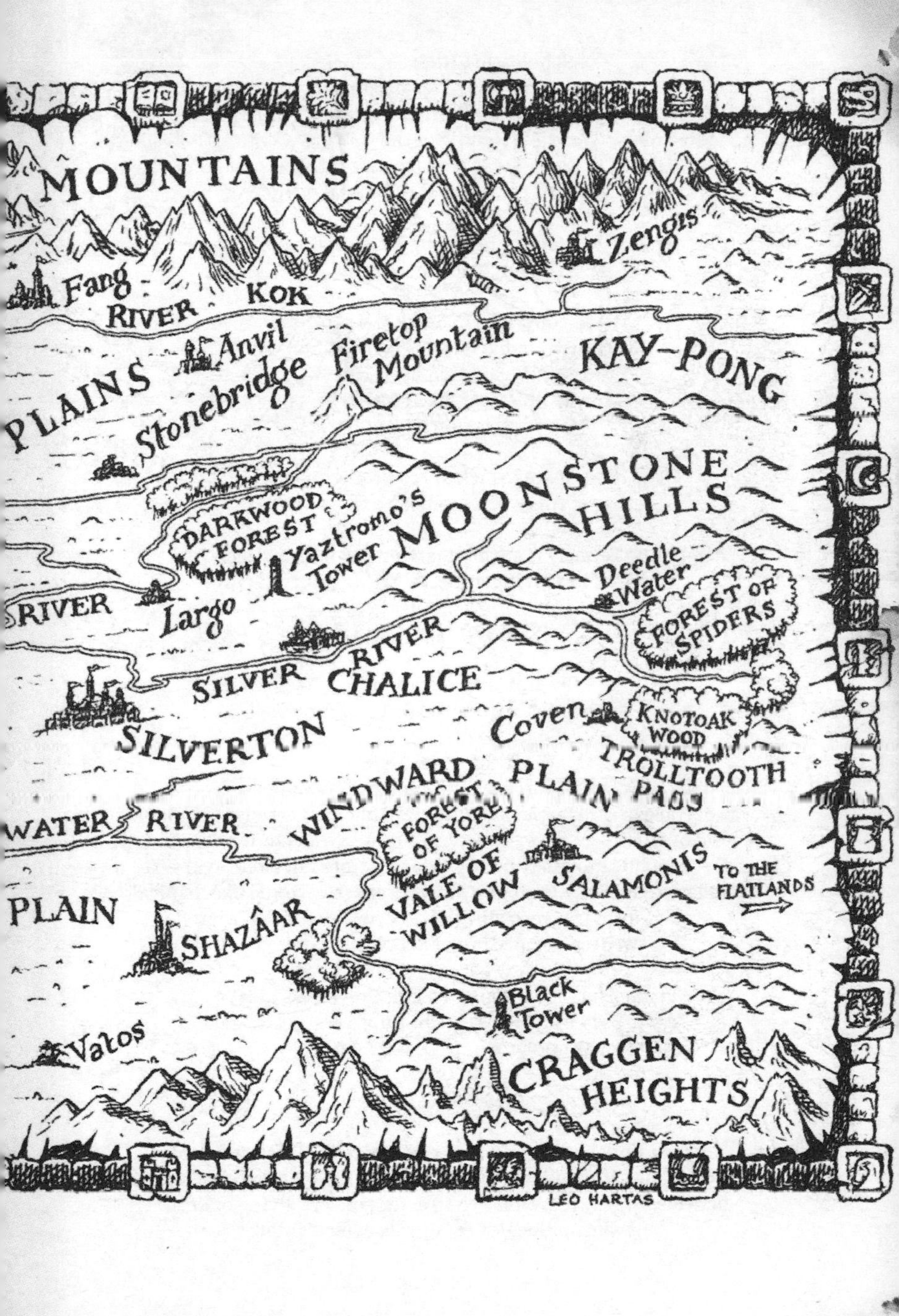
MOUNTAINS
Zengis
Fang
RIVER KOK
Anvil
PLAINS
Stonebridge
Firetop Mountain
KAY-PONG
MOONSTONE HILLS
DARKWOOD FOREST
Yaztromo's Tower
Deedle Water
RIVER
Largo
FOREST OF SPIDERS
SILVER RIVER
CHALICE
SILVERTON
Coven
KNOTOAK WOOD
TROLLTOOTH PASS
WINDWARD PLAIN
FOREST OF YORE
WATER RIVER
VALE OF WILLOW
SALAMONIS
TO THE FLATLANDS
PLAIN
SHAZÂAR
Black Tower
Vatos
CRAGGEN HEIGHTS
LEO HARTAS

Scholastic Children's Books
An imprint of Scholastic Ltd
Euston House, 24 Eversholt Street, London, NW1 1DB, UK
Registered office: Westfield Road, Southam, Warwickshire, CV47 0RA

First published in the UK by Penguin Group, 1986
This edition by Scholastic Ltd, 2018

Cover illustration by Robert Ball
Inside illustrations by Vlado Krizan
Map illustration by Leo Hartas

ISBN 978 1407 18618 4

A CIP catalogue record for this book
is available from the British Library.

Printed by CPI Group (UK) Ltd, Croydon, CR0 4YY
Papers used by Scholastic Children's Books are made
from wood grown in sustainable forests.

1 3 5 7 9 10 8 6 4 2

www.scholastic.co.uk

CONTENTS

HOW WILL YOU START YOUR ADVENTURE?

The book you hold in your hands is a gateway to another world – a world of dark magic, terrifying monsters, brooding castles, treacherous dungeons and untold danger, where a noble few defend against the myriad schemes of the forces of evil. Welcome to the world of **FIGHTING FANTASY!**

You are about to embark upon a thrilling fantasy adventure in which **YOU** are the hero! **YOU** decide which route to take, which dangers to risk and which creatures to fight. But be warned – it will also be **YOU** who has to live or die by the consequences of your actions.

Take heed, for success is by no means certain, and you may well fail in your mission on your first attempt. But have no fear, for with experience, skill and luck, each new attempt should bring you a step closer to your ultimate goal.

Prepare yourself, for when you turn the page you will enter an exciting, perilous **FIGHTING FANTASY** adventure where every choice is yours to make, an adventure in which **YOU ARE THE HERO!**

How would you like to begin your adventure?

IF YOU ARE NEW TO FIGHTING FANTASY . . .

It's a good idea to read through the rules which appear on pages 351-360 before you start.

IF YOU HAVE PLAYED FIGHTING FANTASY BEFORE . . .

You'll realize that to have any chance of success, you will need to discover your hero's attributes. You can create your own character by following the instructions on pages 351-352. Don't forget to enter your character's details on the Adventure Sheet which appears on page 360.

You should also take note of the rules for Instant Death, which are new to this adventure, and appear on page 354.

ALTERNATIVE DICE

If you do not have a pair of dice handy, dice rolls are printed throughout the book at the bottom of the pages. Flicking rapidly through the book and stopping on a page will give you a random dice roll. If you need to 'roll' only one die, read only the first printed die; if two, total the two dice symbols.

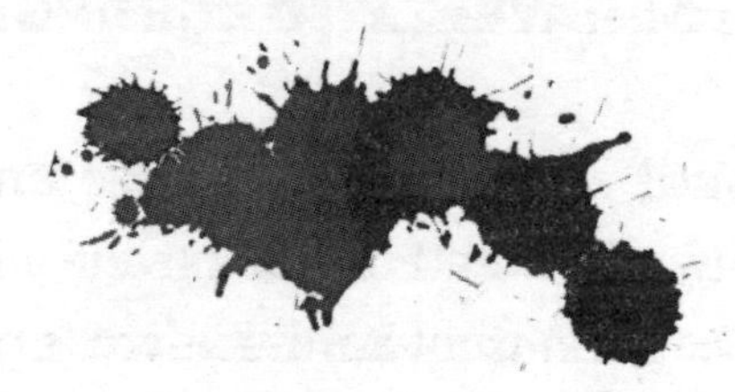

TALES OF TROLLTOOTH PASS

The *Creature of Havoc* adventure takes place in the region of Allansia where the dusty Windward Plain meets Trolltooth Pass. North of the pass, the Forest of Spiders and the Moonstone Hills hide dark secrets; this is the region that the necromancer Zharradan Marr considers his own. To the south, the town of Salamonis stands as the last vestige of civilization before the rolling hills become the mountainous reaches of Balthus Dire's Craggen Heights.

Westwards, the featureless Windward Plain leads the way towards Port Blacksand and the Western Ocean. The plain is a vital trade-route between eastern Allansia and both western Allansia and the Old World. Wares are brought to the west by merchants' caravans, which are heavily guarded by hired warriors, known as Strongarms, whose job is to see that the caravans pass safely across the Flatlands, those treacherous wastes east of Trolltooth Pass.

Once through the pass, the Strongarms leave the caravans at Chalice or Silverton and pick up another caravan making the return journey. Some prefer the peace and quiet of smaller villages like Coven and Drystone, but not even the most courageous Strongarm will stay near Dree, home of the witch-women.

DREE – VILLAGE OF THE WITCH-WOMEN

A dark village nestling in the fork of two rivers like a viper in its nest, Dree is a magnet for miscreants and black-hearted creatures. It came into being originally as the home of the exiled hag-witch Romeena Dree, who had been banished from the town of Salamonis for her hideous magical experiments. Not content with the more acceptable forms of witchcraft – curses, foretelling the future, love-potions and herbal remedies – she turned her attentions to the essence of life itself.

Romeena Dree developed a fascination for what became known as *marrangha* – the transplanting of limbs and organs from one creature to another by magical means – and was obsessed by the desire to create a sort of hybrid super-creature. Her magic was used on both men and beasts and it left many mutant mixtures of each species suffering in the gutters of Salamonis. Her vile witchcraft was branded as an unholy insult to the sanctity of life;

she was on the verge of displeasing the gods of Salamonis. Thus she was banished from the town.

She was taken in chains to a place far north of Salamonis and there released. This place was in the fork between the Deedlewater and Spider rivers, and there Romeena Dree made her home . . . and continued her experiments.

Though exiled from Salamonis, she was not without her devotees and many of her fellow hag-witches from Salamonis made the pilgrimage to visit or even join Romeena in Dree, as the growing village became known. And from other areas of Allansia witch-women joined the growing community, where they could practise their black arts freely and learn more of the developing art of marrangha from Romeena herself.

Outsiders who sailed the Deedlewater and happened across the witch-women's village were horrified at the sights they saw. Semi-creatures with dreadful deformities were left in the streets to suffer – indescribable monsters, which by rights should never have seen life at all, but were now doomed to scratch a living in the gutters of Dree. This they did by murdering and feeding off other creatures whose mutations were such that they could not defend themselves or escape. Hell itself could surely not boast that its minions were as wretched as the marrangha-spawned creatures of Dree.

The witch-women revelled in their creations. In their eyes, such suffering was inevitable and they considered their creations no more than living vegetables, unworthy of pity. The creatures were eaten as food, or kept as pets, or used as subjects in further marrangha experiments. Later, the most hideous were sold to visiting merchants and traders as curiosities and many are to be seen in the travelling circuses which tour Allansia.

Dree's notoriety spread and, the greedy eyes of opportunistic traders turned towards the village. Trading in witchcraft was a time-consuming business, since witches tend to be hermit-like creatures living alone in obscure places. If trade links could be established with Dree, how convenient it would be to buy potions, charms, curses and enchanted objects from a single place! Or so merchants thought – but setting up trading links was not easy. All visitors to Dree who were not practising witches were at first greeted warmly, but when the crafty witches felt their visitor had relaxed his guard, a simple potion was administered to enable him to be captured easily. This was how the witches acquired fresh subjects for their experiments!

The first trader to venture into Dree and survive was Ganga of Mirewater. His enterprise was to be admired and he made handsome profits from his trading. He was the first to realize that the only way to trade successfully was to enter Dree with goods the witches valued, but could not get elsewhere. He scoffed at his forerunners, who took in exotic fruits, jewels, fine silks and spices. Each one had finished up with a Clawbeast's arms, a Lizard Man's face or a Mungie's brain – if he was allowed to live at all.

Ganga took in not spices, but herbs – Sculliweed, Medusa Grass, Curseleaf, Purity Plant and the like. He took in dried Goblin livers, Manticore stings, Elf eyes and pulped Flesh Grub juice. The witches became willing partners in his trading activities and it was many years before other traders appeared with similar items of witchcraft and deprived him of his profitable monopoly. But by then Ganga had already made his fortune.

THE WOMEN OF DREE

The witch-women formed an insular community. They very rarely leave the village of Dree and usually then only in spiritual form. However, Romeena's younger sisters delighted in appearing to the world outside. These three, known as the Women of Dree, have become infamous around Trolltooth Pass for appearing to travellers and Strongarms, to warn them of something or send them on missions. Their unexpected appearance is terrifying and may lead an unwary traveller to distrust them. Certainly they are known to have sent many an adventurer on a pointless mission merely in jest. But they do seem to have some sort of maternal instinct towards mankind and they are probably feared more than they ought to be. There is no evidence of their actually causing harm to those whom they have chosen to meet, unlike their neighbours in Dree.

The rest of the world would be happy to leave Dree alone, so long as the women kept to themselves. But one or two witches have been known to leave Dree and settle in the lands of men. Usually they establish themselves in harmless occupations, as herbalists (like Vitriana in the Forest of Yore), fortunetellers (like Rosina near Coven) or cooks (like the sisters of Sheena in Balthus Dire's citadel). But occasionally one of the witch-women will leave Dree in search of mischief. This was the origin of the ill repute of the village. And more recently, with the strengthening of Zharradan Mare's power, Dree has earned the abject hatred of the peoples of Trolltooth Pass.

ZHARRADAN MARR THE NECROMANCER

It was Romeena's sisters who secretly raised the infant Zharradan. No one knows who fathered the child, but the most likely candidate is one of the numerous Hell Demons conjured up by the witch-women during their black masses. Some, however, prefer to believe that the necromancer is merely a product of another of the marrangha experiments.

Being the only man-child in a village of witch-women, the sisters removed him from the village and raised him somewhere in the Moonstone Hills. When he was old enough, Zharradan was sent east into the Flatlands to be educated. He had already shown *skill* in simple sorcery, and the witches wished him to study the magic arts under a teacher of great repute. This man was Volgera Darkstorm, and the young Zharradan was accepted as his pupil along with two others, Balthus Dire and Zagor.

The three of them studied hard and perfected the black arts with a *skill* which Darkstorm had never seen in any of his previous pupils. The three became both friends and rivals, each respecting the others' *skills*, but each striving to prove that his were the greatest.

It was during his studies that Zharradan changed his name. Zharradan Dree, as he was called, was a name that embarrassed him. Dree was the village of witches, and the name was a constant reminder of their primitive magic with its simple herbalism and curses. The only interest Zharradan had in his home was the witches' fascination with marrangha, a subject that obsessed him.

He changed his name with a single spell which he had learned especially from an ancient black-magic tome. One midsummer night he locked himself away from sunset to sunrise to complete the ritual. When he emerged, Zharradan Dree was a name which had been erased from the minds of everyone who had ever heard of it. Instead, from that time onwards, all knew of the young man as Zharradan Marr.

Marr and his co-pupils learned at a rate which astonished the ageing Darkstorm, who soon became fearful of their powers. When they sensed their mentor's weakness, the three eventually turned their allegiance from him towards themselves and they revelled in the power that their new *skills* brought. In their own minds they became powerful demigods, scornful of the pathetic world around them. When Volgera Darkstorm realized how dangerous his pupils were becoming, he tried to stop them. The result was a short, bloody battle of magic between them which ended as the 'Demonic Three' (as they called themselves collectively) cut down their teacher with a carefully disguised Rain of Knives spell.

After looting the old wizard's library, the young sorcerers fled Darkstorm's home and headed east towards Trolltooth Pass; from there they sought refuge in Darkwood Forest, where they eventually split up to continue on their own separate ways.

COVEN

Zharradan Marr disguised himself as a prospector and headed south towards the village of Coven, a half day's journey from his home in Dree. Though his disguise was merely a sham to enable him to build an underground stronghold for his future operations, he was astonished to find gold deposits in the ground. He immediately realized that with gold he could recruit an army, and soon his Yellowstone Mines were making him a powerful – and wealthy – man. His real ambition, however, was not to become merely wealthy but to rule over his own empire and eventually over the whole of Allansia.

But this he could not do alone. He had already recruited Vallaska Roue, a well-rounded human with a fiery temper, to supervise his mines. Roue was a scruffy character, but he had a will of iron and shared Marr's thirst for power. His loyalty to his master persuaded Marr to share his secret ambitions with Roue and between the two of them they laid plans of conquest. Vallaska Roue was dispatched to find suitable officers for Marr's army. Meanwhile, Marr himself was deep in thought: he had recently heard a story which was occupying his mind.

Hannicus, a wizard of neutral alignment, had arrived in Coven to gather supplies to take back to his home in Knot

Oak Wood. During his visit, he had bumped into Zharradan Marr. After some hours of talk, Marr offered Hannicus a position within his underground complex, looking after the area in which he held his office, outside the mines. Hannicus gratefully accepted. Marr realized that the wizard knew much about the surrounding regions and he pressed Hannicus for more and more of his knowledge. Among other tales, Hannicus told Zharradan the legend of the Vapours of Stittle Woad.

THE RAINBOW PONDS

Hidden deep within the dark depths of the Forest of Spiders, sheltered from prying eyes by tall Speartip trees, is an enchanted glade. Though outsiders have never seen this glade (thus no story can ever fully be believed), it is said to contain a number of beautiful rock-pools. As if designed by the gods themselves, each pool is decorated with brightly coloured flowers which bloom throughout the seasons. Tall orange lilies, scented with sweet perfumes, rise from the waters. Each pool is fringed with bouquets of colourful peacock flowers. And shining silver-bells are scattered around them, tinkling faintly as the wind disturbs their delicate silver flowers. The pools are wondrous to behold in their full splendour and are known as the Rainbow Ponds.

But the Rainbow Ponds are so called not because of their adornment by the most beautiful flowers in the whole of Allansia, but rather because of the waters contained within the pools themselves. For each of the Rainbow Ponds is a different colour. This extraordinary natural feature is said by some simply to be a matter of crystal deposits in the rocks beneath the pools. But this may not be true. The colours are so distinctively different that this phenomenon may well have been created by magic. Elvins would delight in conjuring up these gardens of colour, but Elvins are not to be found in the area. Most likely this is the magic of the Elves.

Needless to say, speculation abounds about the mysterious properties of the Rainbow Ponds. The turquoise pond, it is said, brings the gift of beauty. Bathing in the waters of the amber pool before attempting a new *skill* will ensure excellence no matter whether this *skill* be a mental or a physical one. And the ruby pool bestows charismatic powers: no one may meet such a bather without experiencing immediate feelings of affection and friendship. Perhaps some or perhaps none of these stories are true. No one can be found who has ever set eyes on the Rainbow Ponds. This in itself may be due to their enchanted nature. The pools are an oasis in the midst of a jungle of Chaos; a nirvana which, once found, persuades any visitor to remain, for ever in awe of the beauty of the Rainbow Ponds.

STITTLE WOAD

The most recent stories of the Rainbow Ponds have caused great excitement among adventurers and explorers. For rumour has it that the ponds form part of the domain of the white-haired Wood Elves of Stittle Woad.

The Elven village of Stittle Woad, or Eren Durdinath in the Elvish tongue, is a mystery to outsiders. Protected by Elven magic, no one may discover the village without an invitation from the Elves themselves. And the Elves will admit only those who swear to preserve the secret of its whereabouts.

But one thing is for sure. Eren Durdinath is to be found deep within the Forest of Spiders, and is most probably close to the spectacular beauty of the Rainbow Ponds. Occasionally one or two of the more adventurous young Elves can be found outside the forest. Curious about the world beyond their tree-top kingdom, they will roam abroad, sometimes coming into contact with other races and – very occasionally – entering the cities of men.

One such Elf, known as Leeha Falsehope, ventured as far as the town of Chalice, where he succumbed to the temptations that exist in such places. Stories spread of this mysterious white-haired creature whose manner was so delightful that the young women of Chalice would follow him wherever he went, tittering and offering their favours. The rowdy menfolk knew him as a regular in the town's drinking-establishments. They watched in amazement as he entered – and won – every drinking-contest in every inn. At a street market he once acquired a well-made mandolin, and within a short time he was a master of the instrument, delighting every audience with his amusing songs.

As his status rose to that of a celebrity within Chalice, folk naturally inquired about his past. At first he managed to remain true to his vow of silence. But this only caused rumours to circulate, not all of which were complimentary to Falsehope. Eventually he was forced to reveal glimpses of his real past. His stories so enthralled his listeners – and each 'glimpse' spread like wildfire as news around the town – that he was encouraged to tell more and more. Many of his stories he set to music and, even today, his songs are known and sung by all the minstrels of western Allansia. But finally, one night after far too much ale and maybe a little smoking-weed, Leeha Falsehope revealed more than he should have done.

In his drunken conversation with a young serving-wench, he not only revealed that Eren Durdinath existed and could be found deep in the Forest of Spiders, but his loose tongue told the story of the Vapours whose secret had hitherto been known only to his fellow Elves. After he had finished telling the story to the wench – and the large crowd of eavesdroppers who had gathered around him –Falsehope realized his folly. Desperately he tried to cover up his Words, but this merely prompted more and more questions from the crowd. The question most asked was, 'And what was the name of this village of yours?', for men find Elven names difficult to pronounce. Falsehope searched quickly for a name that would throw them off the track and from somewhere deep in his memory the name Stittle Woad appeared (Stittle Woad is in fact a particular type of dye used by Elves to colour their clothes).

The young Elf was devastated when the effects of the ale wore off and he realized what he had done. The secrets of generations of Wood Elves had been revealed to all and sundry in a common inn. He left the town of Chalice and returned to his home in the Forest of Spiders, where he lived the rest of his days in disgrace. Until the day he died he and his family were social outcasts in Eren Durdinath. Even today, the family of Erulia Falsehope, Leeha's great-grandson, must bear the shame, which cannot be forgotten, of revealing the existence of what became known as the Vapours of Stittle Woad.

THE VAPOURS OF STITTLE WOAD

High in the tree-tops of the forest, the Elves are protected from harm. This is partly due to their magical abilities and their keen eyesight, which is able to spot a likely intruder well in advance of their arrival. But partly this is a protection bestowed on them as a special favour by their gods. The Elves of Stittle Woad believe themselves to be a chosen race, a belief which has a ring of truth to it.

After their creation, the gods were astonished at the natural grace and beauty of the white-haired Elves they had brought to life. The early priests of Stittle Woad were offered a 'bargain' by their creators. The gods promised to watch over the Elves and provide a good deal more protection than they afforded their other creations. In return, each generation of Elves undertook to choose an Elf maiden to be groomed as eventual queen to rule over Eren Durdinath. Each future queen must be the most perfect child in the village, a maiden of stunning beauty, charming wit and faultless grace. And on her eighteenth birthday, she had to undergo a celebratory ritual in which she would eventually commune with the gods. This communion represented the greatest honour which could be bestowed on each generation, and the longer this communion lasted, the more pleased the gods were. During the communion, great powers of wisdom and leadership were bestowed on the princess. Afterwards, she would be recognized as queen of Eren Durdinath.

Within four seasons of her accession to the throne, the queen would always give birth. Such a birth was a religious affair, during which the queen was attended only by her priests. When the queen left her priests after the birth, she left alone. Only the priests and a handful of trusted villagers knew what actually happened at the birth. But all knew the result.

No normal child was born to the queen. Instead the gods gifted the queen with a benevolent spirit – a Vapour – with a special power. Whichever god had been present at the Elf princess's communion gave her Vapour his special power, which was to be used wisely by her as queen. The Vapour's birth ritual was unknown to all but the queen herself and her priests. But after birth the Vapour, safely stored in a glass flask, remained with the priests. The queen is able to call on her Vapour only once during her reign and even then only on one night of the year, known as the celestial equinox, when her god's constellation takes a certain position in relation to the other heavenly bodies.

This was the tale that Zharradan Marr heard from the wizard Hannicus. He pressed for more information and was told that the present Elf queen Ethilesse was reputed to have given birth to *three* Vapours!

Ethilesse was an exceptionally beautiful maiden, so during her divine communion she had been visited by three of the Elven gods: Euthillial, the god of languages; Ititia, god of reason; and Alliarien, the god of Elf magic. It was this last name that seized Zharradan's attention. For, as powerful as his magic was, that of the Elves was equally powerful. If he were to acquire the knowledge of Elven magic as well, he would be invincible! Zharradan's sharp mind was well aware of the possibilities and he thought deeply on the wizard's words.

But the ways of Elves are secretive and years passed before Zharradan Marr was able to make plans for finding the hidden village of Stittle Woad. His mines prospered and his power-base grew. Vallaska Roue had returned with new recruits for his forces. In a seedy inn in Zengis he had come across a burly Half-Troll named Thugruff. What started as a drunken brawl became a firm friendship, and Thugruff agreed to return with Vallaska Roue and join in service of Zharradan Marr. The necromancer took an instant liking to Thugruff, not least for his coarse sense of humour and his healthy streak of cruelty. He sent Thugruff into Knot Oak Wood to rebuild Hannicus's home as a hidden training ground, known as the 'Testing Grounds', for his troops.

Hannicus had little say in the matter. Marr was by now tiring of the wizard's ineptitude. In fact this was not all. Hannicus's control of security had been lax and, unknown to Zharradan, the odd party of Strongarms had succeeded in breaking into his dungeons and looting Marr's riches.

Though Marr had to wait two years for his arrival, Hannicus's replacement was far more suitable for the task. Vallaska Roue had returned from Port Blacksand with a sly grin on his face. He told of an encounter with a creature with exceptional qualities. Marr listened intently as he heard of Darramouss, a Half-Elf and one of the undead. According to Roue, he was a ruthless creature, who was totally without remorse and who took pride in torture and torment. As an officer in the army, he was known as one who would always welcome the order to kill the prisoners. When this order was given he would first torture them for his private pleasure, then kill them. Marr liked the sound of this creature and liked him even more when the tall figure walked in to introduce himself.

Darramouss was immediately given the job of master of the Yellowstone Mines, a position he excelled at. His first act was to end the system of paying the miners for their labours. From that day on they were his prisoners, and guards with bullwhips made sure that the miners were putting in their best efforts. When many of the miners died, he had Thugruff scour the countryside with his army to bring in more slaves. So successful was he that Zharradan Marr soon put him in charge of his whole underground operation, after making sure that the old fool Hannicus would offer no resistance.

DAGA WEASELTONGUE – THE INNOCENT TRAITOR

Thugruff's army grew and prospered, and the area of his Testing Grounds became a place of fear where forest creatures dared not venture. Perhaps it was inevitable, however, that the curiosity of the Elves would eventually precipitate a meeting and this dubious honour befell a young Elf, Daga Weaseltongue, cousin of Erulia Falsehope. A couple of Marr's legionnaires were strolling through the woods when they came across Weaseltongue, training his serpent-headed Ophidiotaur. A friendship was struck and regular meetings followed. When Thugruff heard of this encounter, he sent word to Marr, who journeyed immediately to the Testing Grounds. Disguised as a

Rhino-Man, he likewise befriended the Elf, and cultivated the friendship.

When he felt he had the white-haired Elf's trust, Marr skilfully manipulated Weaseltongue (under a Control Creature spell) into stealing the Vapours from his own royal priests. The Vapours were stored in his dungeons until he could research their secrets. Of course, nothing could be learned about the Vapours, as nothing was known of them outside Stittle Woad. Thus Zharradan Marr resolved to locate the Elven village.

THE *GALLEYKEEP*

Marr knew that the village would never be found simply by using his legionnaires to search the Forest of Spiders. Elf magic would ensure that it remained invisible to outsiders. However, reports were reaching him of another possibility. From the east, a great ship had been sighted. Its pure white sails billowed deeply to catch the winds. Its strong wooden hull would be almost impossible to hole. And its size was formidable; it would easily hold a thousand troops. All who had set eyes on the ship believed it to be of divine origin. For it travelled not through the water, but through the air! Folk referred to it as the *Galleykeep*, but none knew from where it came.

This seeded an idea in Zharradan Marr's mind. He must capture this ship! Not only would it be a symbolic throne, worthy of a ruler of his stature, but it may even help him to find Stittle Woad. Perhaps he would never find the Elven village from the ground, but it may well be unprotected from the air. Quickly he recalled Vallaska Roue and the two of them set off for the Testing Grounds to discuss the plans to capture the *Galleykeep* with Thugruff.

The success of their plan was a tribute to their military skills. The *Galleykeep* fell after a short but bloody ambush in the sky by Marr's trained Tooki troops, and he was delighted with his new vessel. Within days he had set up his headquarters in the ship.

So this is now his home, and he has begun his search over the Forest of Spiders for the village of Stittle Woad. Those in the know are terrified at the thought of his success. Should he find Stittle Woad, and the secret of the Vapours, then his mastery of sorcery will be invincible. It is because of this fear that interested parties throughout western Allansia have made plans to prevent him succeeding in his quest. Parties of brave adventurers from Chalice, Silverton and Stonebridge have been sent on missions to capture the Vapours and return them to the Elves. But, since no one has ever seen the Vapours, none of the parties know what they are looking for! In Mirewater, Calla Bey is recruiting an army of Birdmen to besiege the *Galleykeep* (but with little success, as the Birdmen fear the ship). From Salamonis, Elves are being persuaded to head north for the Forest of Spiders in order that word may reach Stittle Woad in time. But the forest Elves are suspicious even of their own kind and this expedition may never succeed.

Perhaps it is destiny that Zharradan Marr should rule these regions of Allansia. Only time will tell . . .

This is the background to *Creature of Havoc*. Much of what you have read will be of little help to you and some of the information may even lead you astray. As you will find when you start your adventure, you have only the faintest awareness of your surroundings and your actions will be ruled by instincts – the instincts of the creature you are. But gradually you will develop more control over your destiny. As the adventure progresses you will be asking yourself the questions that all must ask in life: *Who am I? Where do I come from? Why am I here?*

The answers you find to these questions will depend on which paths you chose as the *Creature of Havoc.*

YOUR ADVENTURE AWAITS!

MAY YOUR STAMINA NEVER FAIL!

NOW TURN OVER...

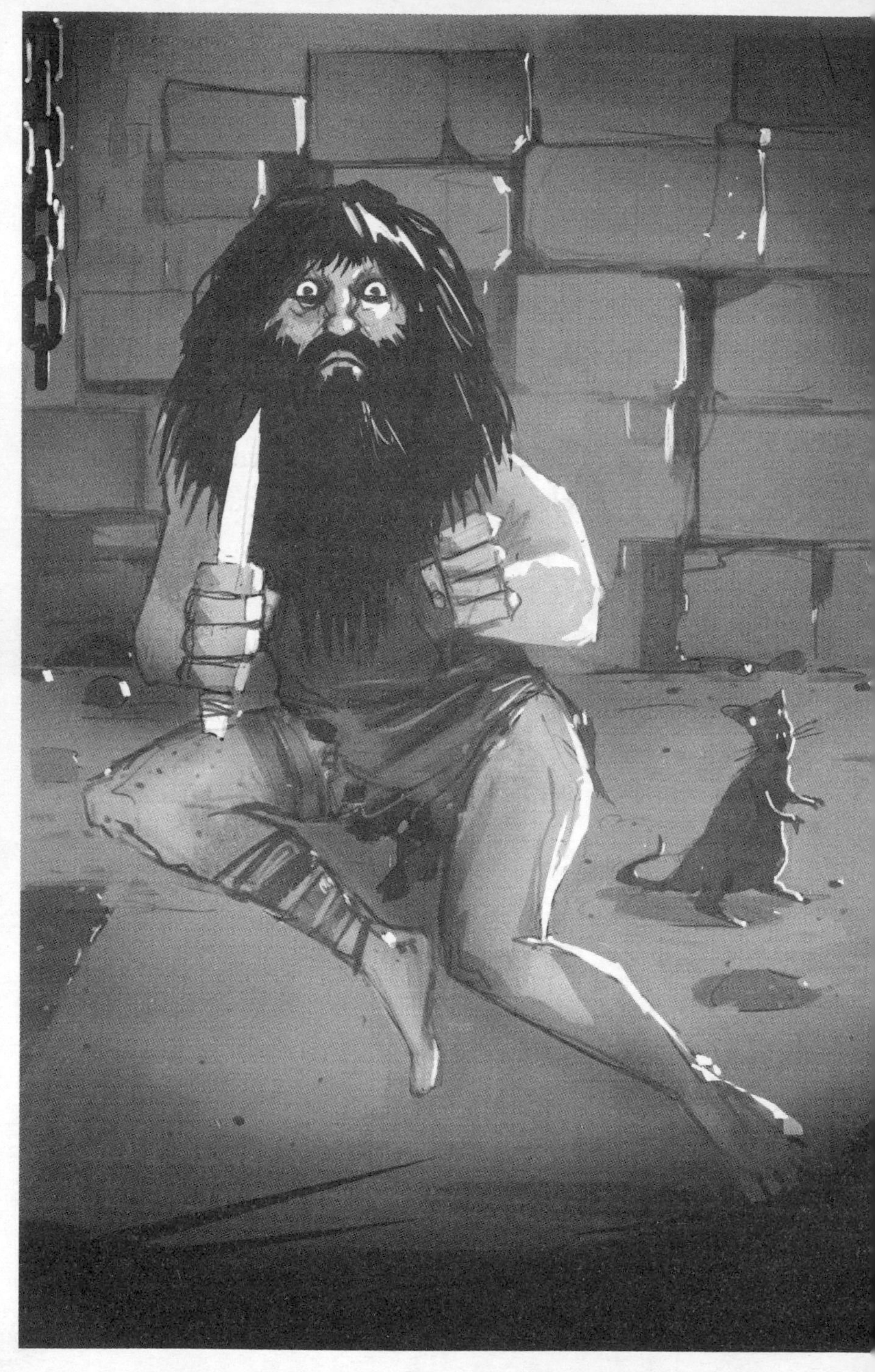

A look of terror streaks across the creature's face

1

The pain is unbearable! Summoning up all your energy, you open your eyes – first one, then the other. They narrow to slits as they adjust themselves to the strain of trying to see once more, then relax as they make out familiar shapes in the dim light: a dirt floor, rocky walls . . . Then the pain takes over. Your head rocks. Your eyes submit and close tightly in an agonized grimace. Instinctively you raise your hands to cup your face, and a low moan mingles with the rasping sound as your rough fingers rub the scaly skin above your eyes. After some time the pain begins to ease. You open your eyes once more and peer out from between your gnarled fingers. You seem to be at the dead end of a passageway. Your surroundings are barely visible, but a dull glow is coming from the northern extent of the passageway, which stretches before you. A sound is also coming from this direction – of irregular breathing. Something alive is up there! You heave your great bulky body to its feet. Along your back, the spines bristle. Swinging your heavy head slowly from side to side, your progress is decided: northwards is the only option open to you. Muscles strain and succeed in raising a lumbering foot, which thuds loudly down on the ground in front of you. You repeat the action, first with one foot, then the other. After four steps the motion has become automatic. You are moving more quickly and more quietly up the passage. When you reach

the end, your eyes are drawn to a huddled shape lying on the ground in front of you.

The small figure lies on its side, facing away from you. It is shrouded in a dirty brown cape tied around its neck and it lies in a puddle of thick red liquid. Its body rises and falls irregularly with each breath. Some unidentified feeling swells within you. Is it anger? Hate? Fear? Curiosity? Hunger? Or even sympathy? You bend down towards the little creature, uttering a meaningless grunt as you do so.

The sound rouses the figure, which rolls slowly over to face you. The creature's dirty face is light-skinned, though barely visible under the thick hair which shades its closed eyes and almost totally obscures its mouth. From its chin the hair rolls abundantly down its chest in a grey, unruly mass. Underneath the body, and now exposed by the creature's movement, is a sharp, shiny shaft and this catches your attention.

As you stand there staring, the creature's eyes flick open! They focus on your bulky shape and a look of terror streaks across the creature's face. In spite of its pain, it fumbles for and grasps the shiny shaft, holding its pointed end out towards you and baring its teeth.

The wounded Dwarf you have found is evidently in need of help. Will you:

Show him you mean no harm? Turn to **93**
Try to talk to him? Turn to **364**
Bring your foot down heavily on his neck? Turn to **185**

2

You sit down between the three Hobbits, licking your lips as you remember the tender taste of their flesh. Grabbing the nearest one, you sink your teeth ravenously into its meaty rump and let out a soft, low growl of contentment. For a short while you feast messily on the hapless creatures. Each Hobbit was carrying a small pouch of those flat, round, shiny pieces of metal and you may take these with you if you wish. They are, in fact, Gold Pieces and if you decided to take them, you are now carrying 12 with you. You may restore your *STAMINA* to its *Initial* level for the tasty meal and may add a *LUCK* point for your victory.

You must now leave the chamber. Do you wish to continue east along a passage opposite the one you entered by? If so, turn to **153**. If you wish to retrace your steps to the junction and take the northerly passageway, turn to **311**.

3

He eyes you suspiciously. 'Is that so? Well, no doubt he gave you the *gesture* too. Come on, then. Let's have it!' What will your gesture be?

The sign of a cross? Turn to **387**
The sign of a circle? Turn to **22**
You make no gesture? Turn to **437**

4

You summon up your strength and launch into battle, frantically trying to slash at the vines with your claws. But the tunnel is thick and the vines are difficult to cut (this is reflected in their high *SKILL* score). Resolve your battle with the tunnel of Gluevines:

GLUEVINES	*SKILL 10*	*STAMINA 13*

If you escape from the tangled mass of vegetation, turn to **36**.

5

Thinking quickly, you snatch the bird from the branch! It flutters in your hands, but a sharp squeeze silences it. The Ophidiotaur hears the rustling and turns to see what is happening. You step slowly from the undergrowth, holding out the bird towards it, as an offering. At first the creature is startled by your arrival, but your slow approach seems to reassure it. You hold the bird closer and its tongue darts out to snatch the food from you. You calm it down for a short time, then swing yourself up on to its back. It shrugs and snorts for a moment or two, but its protests are few and you realize that you now have a steed! After allowing the Ophidiotaur to drink from the river, you grasp its neck with your wide fingers and dig your heels into its haunches.

Without warning, the creature turns and gallops off into the undergrowth! Its strong legs take you faster and faster through the woods. Branches catch your legs and arms, while you are hugging the Ophidiotaur's neck tightly for balance and to protect your head. The journey continues for a seemingly endless time, until you are so sore from riding that you wish the beast would throw you off. But finally you arrive at a clearing where the creature pulls up and stops. With great relief you step down from its back and survey the area, while your steed gallops back into the woods. Turn to **366**.

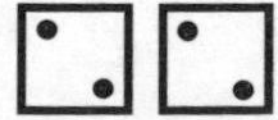

6

The door opens and you find yourself in a corridor which heads south for a few paces and then turns to the west. Your claws extend themselves, ready for a sudden encounter. You follow the passageway around the corner. Eventually you reach a point where the passage turns back southwards. But something on the rocky floor in front of you has attracted your attention. In the elbow of the bend is a large black circle which seems to shimmer in the blue light. Perhaps it is a pool of liquid? Or maybe some dark metallic substance? As you are considering this, you hear a noise behind you, which may have been a quiet footstep. Is someone following you? You turn round but can see nothing. Now you must decide what to do. Will you investigate the shape on the floor (turn to **445**), or will you try to avoid the circle by walking round it (turn to **30**)?

7

With the lifeless Blood Orcs lying at your feet, your attentions now turn to the human in the dirty robes. He is staggering about in fear for his life, his eyes tilted slightly towards the ceiling. ‘Hbvfem fr cy epn obabljndim bn a whpf vfre ypvubrf. Jfiypvub rfefr jf nde thfhel fbda mf efr pmothjsi plbcf. Jf iypv ubr fe fpfethf ne lfbvfe mfebf. Ypvu brf estrb ng f lyesjl fnt. Whpobr f eypv. Dpo ypvuvnd fr s tbnd amf. My eg pdo jn trvdfr. J fiy pvrupl bna jsit pod pob wbyaw jth jmf e thfne dpoj ti qvjc kl y. Pt hfrwj sf ebfe pf fow jthi ypv.' Jf iypv uc bnav ndfr stb ndath fehv mbnatvr nut por fffrf n cfetw po hvn drfd. 'Spo whbtajs ij ti tpobf. Jsinpto myomj sfrye fnp vgh. Shpw och br jty. Gj vfem feg pld o bnda f ffde mf. Prol fb vfem febf.' What do you wish to do with this creature? Will you ignore him and feast on the meat of the Blood Orcs (turn to **420**)? Will you slay him quickly to stop his noise (turn to **25**)? Or will you simply leave the room (turn to **138**)?

8

When he sees your Ring of Truth, he shifts nervously: 'Oop! Ahh . . . What am I saying? Of course; you said Stittle *Woad*, didn't you? Underground indeed! Silly me: the village is high in the tree-tops. Although I fear you will never find it and you are wasting your time looking. Our village is the home of the Vapours and while they remain safely in the village, sorcery disguises it to all but welcome eyes.' He now wishes to go, and you watch him disappear into the woods in the direction you came from. You may now leave the clearing by turning to **414**.

9

In a fit of rage you rush across the room and swing your fist, with claws open, at another head. Again the claws rip the head from its perch and send it flying out of the light and out of sight. And again you hear no sound to indicate it landing anywhere. This time your eyes are fixed on the vacant space illuminated by the light. Sure enough, the head floats through the air and comes to rest in its original position, the claw wounds showing up clearly on the side of its face. You hit it again. The same thing happens. But this time you feel the wave of pain coming on again. The pain grows inside you with an intensity much greater than before. You slump howling to the ground until it eventually subsides. Lose 6 *STAMINA* points. If you are still alive, you decide to leave the room quickly. Turn to **79**.

10

You leave the path and make your way through the undergrowth, following the sounds of his cries. But although you can hear him, you cannot see him anywhere! Your frustration builds up and you thrash about in the foliage. An unnatural click beneath your foot should have been a warning, but in your rage, it is a warning which you choose to ignore. An instant later, the trap has sprung and you are hoisted into the air by your ankle, and dangle helplessly from the tree-top! And there, hanging a short distance away, is the old Rhino-Man!

Your attempts to free yourself are all to no avail. Birds are beginning to circle round you, and you are feeling decidedly weak. But in the distant sky, a tiny shape comes into view. As it draws near, you realize it is not a bird. It is much too large to be any living creature and its size eventually frightens off the birds circling above you. The old Rhino-Man has seen it too. 'The *Galleykeep*!' he moans. You watch as billowing sails bring the vessel closer and closer, until it eventually stops above you. A pole is lowered over the side. It grabs the rope from which you are hanging and hoists you on to the deck. You are too tired and weak to resist as rough hands shove your neck through the nearby guillotine. This foraging expedition has been most successful. The crew will be provided with a hearty meal tonight . . .

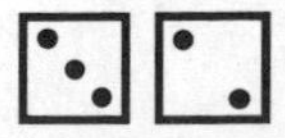

11

'Thank you,' she smiles, depositing the coins deep in the folds of her clothing. 'Now we may see what fate has in store for you. I will shuffle the Pack of Fate and you must tell me when to stop.' She picks up the cards and begins to shuffle them slowly, staring deep into your eyes as she does so. You grunt when you want her to stop. She then starts turning cards over.

The first card is black, with the symbol of a question mark delicately drawn in its centre. 'Ah, the mystery card.' Rosina smiles. 'All is not as it seems. There are many things about you, your past and your destiny that are unclear, even to you.' She turns over another card. Again it is black, but this one has a small yellow sun symbol in the centre. 'Hmm, yes . . . Light in the darkness.' She is becoming engrossed in the cards. 'This is good. Your destiny may be attained. But fate will not be kind to you. It may not be easy.' The next card shows a young pregnant woman in a coffin, and the next shows a cloak and wand. 'A mother deceased! And the mystic arts! Then surely must your birth have been one not of nature but of sorcery, I must concentrate . . .' She turns over another card and this one shows a man lying on a cloud, pointing into the distance. The next shows a man with two heads, looking in different directions. 'The geas! A mission to be fulfilled. You have been sent. But

I also see confusion. I must look further.'

She leaves the cards and moves her crystal ball into the centre of the table. As she concentrates on it, the glass begins to turn cloudy. An inner light shines from the ball and lights up Rosina's eyes. 'Sisters . . .!' she speaks. 'Sisters of Dree! So it is *you* who have set this task! But this creature knows not of Sculliweed or of the dangers of . . . I see. But I may shorten the search. My aid shall help fulfil its destiny.' The light in the glass fades and she turns to you. 'You have been set an unfair task,' she says. 'For the blue-stemmed Sculliweed grows only in the Swamps of the Toadmen on the southern shores of the Deedlewater. But even one such as you may not survive alone in these swamps. Without help you will surely die. I can offer you some help. Take the rope that hangs over there: it may prove useful. And may fortune sit astride your shoulders!' You take the coil of rope, sling it around your neck and over your shoulder and turn back to Rosina. But she has left the room. You may add 2 *LUCK* points for the information. You leave her hut and pause to consider what she has told you, then set off back towards the crossroads. Turn to **386**.

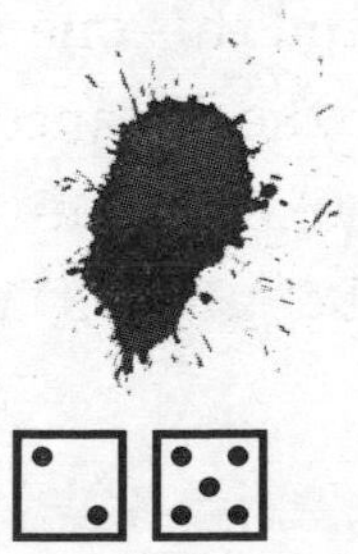

You swing round just in time to avoid the sharp blade of an axe

12

You follow the trail until you reach the top of a hill. The trail winds down into a valley. You pick your way cautiously down and reach the bottom safely. But as you pause to rest for a moment, you are startled by a rustling in the bushes behind you. You swing round just in time to avoid the sharp blade of an axe, which misses your face by inches! You growl deep down in your throat and turn to face the tall Woodcutter who has attacked. Resolve this combat:

WOODCUTTER	*SKILL 8*	*STAMINA 9*

If you defeat him, turn to **17**.

13

As the last adventurer falls to the ground and silence once more fills the passageway, you pause to rest from the exertion. You squat on your haunches and look at the two battered humans in front of you. You may now choose either to feast on the bodies to regain some of your lost strength (turn to **223**), search the bodies for anything that might be interesting (turn to **187**), or poke through the sack that the first adventurer laid to one side (turn to **147**).

14

You storm ahead up the passageway towards the Dark Elf, roaring loudly and with claws ready to strike. But the Elf does not budge. He merely notches another arrow and looses it towards you. This time the arrow sinks deep into your stomach and you clutch at the wound. Lose 3 *STAMINA* points. Tears of pain flood your eyes, but you will not hold back. Again you advance, and again the Elf notches his arrow. But this time the bowman's aim is true. The arrow is fired higher, at your face. Before you have time to react, his shaft has pierced your eye and lodged in your brain. Mercifully, your death is instantaneous.

15

All is silent as you enter. The room is large, with a high ceiling, and a musty smell permeates the air. There are four doors leading from the room, one in each wall. A long table stands in the middle of the room and on it is a short stick with a metal head lying next to some small spikes. A couple of planks of wood are resting against the table. This is evidently a workroom of some sort. In one corner of the room you find the products of the work carried on here. Two tall and thin wooden boxes, almost as tall as you are, are leaning against the wall. They are standing next to a hole in the wall, just above floor-level, which is wide enough to fit one of the boxes through. You puzzle over this for some time. What do you want to do:

Have a look inside the boxes? Turn to **217**
Investigate the hole in the wall? Turn to **319**
Ignore what you see? Turn to **436**

16

The spell begins to take effect. Your body feels as if each of its joints is being bent in a wrong direction! You drop to the floor and writhe about, wailing pitifully, but there is no escape from the agony that the necromancer is inflicting on you. Invisible knives are being plunged into your chest and each is being made to scrape slowly against the bones of your ribs. You hold up your hand for mercy and Marr releases the spell. Gasping in horror, in awe of the wizard's power, you take the knapsack and slowly hold it out towards him. He snatches it from you. Turn to **74**.

17

You can see ahead that a river runs through the valley, and you make your way to its banks. As you get closer to the water, you notice that the vegetation is changing. The lush green colour of the trees and bushes higher up the valley is replaced by a darker olive colour and the plants down here are decidedly less healthy. Spindly branches reach out at unnatural angles as if pleading for mercy. On the ground, many of the roots of the contorted trees are exposed and have been eaten away. The surrounding bushes are often leafless, and the effect is rather eerie. A faint smell hangs in the air.

You continue down towards the river. The closer you get, the stronger the smell becomes, until eventually it is overpowering. The stench seems to come from the river itself, and when you arrive at its banks, you can see why. Indescribable filth and excrement is being carried along by the foul waters. But as the only path runs along the banks, you will have to choose. Will you follow the river upstream (turn to **427**) or downstream (turn to **423**), or will you leave the path and make your way through the undergrowth (turn to **57**)?

18

You turn to leave the river-bank. But something is not quite right. You came along a trail, but that trail has now disappeared! Where you had expected it to be is now overgrown with tall rushes and the only trail leading away from the bank is one to your left. Bewildered, you follow it until you reach a clearing. Turn to **315**.

19

You turn from the door and plod once more through the cold slime. By the time you reach the passageway to the east, the cold has worked its way through even your thick, scaly skin. You must lose 1 *STAMINA* point for your freezing feet and turn to **84**.

20

You find yourself at a dead end: there is no way through. You will have to retrace your steps. Turn to **279**.

21

Although you are racked with the pains of hunger, your mind has made an intelligent deduction. Your hunger started when you threw the red robe about your shoulders. If you take the robe off, you should rid yourself of this curse. You grab the collar resolutely. But try as you may, you cannot pull it from your shoulders. Some powerful bewitchment is preventing your arm from flinging the robe to the floor! Incredulous, you struggle with yourself for some time, but finally give in to the mysterious force, which is much more powerful than your own will. Your hunger is now all-consuming. Turn to **109**.

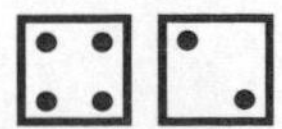

22

'A *circle*, eh?' he mutters. 'All right, then, in you come.' Amazed at your success, you enter the guardroom. It is a dirty place, with clothes and food strewn around and an unpleasant smell – a mixture of stale sweat and rancid ale – hanging in the air. When you are in the centre of the room, you turn to the guard. *Crack!* Had you turned an instant earlier you may have been quick enough to avoid the heavy blow which has landed on your head. You fall to your knees in a state of near-unconsciousness and you must lose 4 *STAMINA* points. Meanwhile the guard is advancing towards you with a heavy club in his hand. Turn to **98** to fight him.

23

You uncoil the rope from around your shoulder and search for something to lasso. But there is nothing around that would seem solid enough to let you pull yourself out. The bulrushes are certainly not strong enough to bear your weight. You have now sunk to your waist and unless you spy something soon, you will not be able to throw the rope! Frantically you search for something as you slip deeper and deeper into the mud. Then, hidden behind the rushes and reeds, you catch a glimpse of a tree-stump. It is not tall, but it looks sturdy enough. But how can you rope it? You fling the rope towards it – and something miraculous happens.

As the rope leaves your hands, it unfurls as if it had a will of its own. You watch it twist around itself in the air, forming a knot at one end. Then, as it falls, it snakes between the reeds, and drops with its knot wedged firmly in the shoulder of a branch. The rest of the rope trails out towards you and you test it eagerly, then haul yourself from what would otherwise have been a muddy grave. Filthy but safe, you stand on firm ground, marvelling at the enchanted rope.

But unknown to you, you are not the only one marvelling at the rope's powers. Two large, glistening eyes blink slowly in astonishment as the rope coils itself up, now that its work is done. While you are considering which of the two ways onwards to follow, a thin, webbed hand steals out, grabs the rope and snatches it back into the reeds. Your rope is gone! You search round for any sign of it, but can find none. You will have to continue without it. If you follow the trail to the north, turn to **267**. If you make your way to the north-east, turn to **114**.

24

You leave the path and clamber up over the rocks to get a look at the nearest hole. It is just out of your reach, and you must hoist yourself up to be able to peer into it. As your head comes up to the level of the hole and the glow splashes across your eyes, the cause of the light reveals itself – and gives you such a fright that you lose your grip and tumble down to the path. For you came face to face with a huge head, with grilled-patterned eyes and clattering mandibles. This Giant Hornet launches itself from its home and swoops down on you, its poisonous sting aimed straight at your chest! Turn to **332**.

25

Irritated by the human's constant rantings, you step across the room towards him. He does not react at all to your approach and it is an easy matter for you to swipe him with a clawed fist. Your blow sends him flying back across the room where he smacks his head against the wall and lands in a lifeless heap on the floor. You may now either feast on the bodies (turn to **289**) or leave the room (turn to **138**).

26

You wade slowly into the pond and relax in its cool, refreshing water. When you emerge from the water, you feel much better and may add 2 *STAMINA* points. But when you look down at yourself, you are astonished to see that your scales are no longer their usual dark browny-green colour, but are covered in a glistening layer of milky liquid which is drying to leave a silvery sheen. Although you try to brush it off, it will not smear – much to your annoyance! But in fact this silvery layer is a coating of a magical material that will act as thin armour. While you are covered in the silvery layer, you may add 1 to your *SKILL* score. But it will be washed off if you bathe in clear water. Now turn to **52** to continue.

27

The other three creatures back away from you as you turn from the dying Elf to face them. They scatter into the crowd. Turn to **348**.

28

If you picked up a crystal club during your adventure, you will have been given a reference number to turn to should you wish to use it. Do not turn to this number now, but instead add it to the number of this reference. Turn to the reference corresponding to this total.

29

The handle turns freely and you open the door. The room inside is lit by a single candle and your eyes adjust themselves to the dimness. The walls appear to be covered in a single continuous tapestry which depicts all sorts of scenes of death and carnage. Battles are being fought; creatures are feasting on other creatures; torture scenes are so vivid that you can almost feel the pain. You follow the tapestry, engrossed in its detail – so engrossed that you have not noticed the sinister figure seated in the shadows across the room. When it speaks, the shock of its deep voice makes you gasp!

'Who is this? Who *dares* disturb the rest of the Master of Hellfire?' You peer into the shadow to try to make out the figure, but you cannot see much more than the outline of a large figure, which heaves as it takes short breaths. As each breath leaves the creature, a gurgling sound comes from its throat. This noise is getting louder; the creature is rising from its seat! It stands up slowly and its silhouette becomes much larger than you imagined. Will you run from the room (turn to **113**) or face it defiantly (turn to **143**)?

30

You step over to the right and give the circle a wide berth. Halfway round, your ears prick up. Another footstep! With claws at the ready, you turn to face your pursuer. But again there is no one there! The quick turn in a narrow space causes you to stumble momentarily. You quickly regain your balance – but not quickly enough . . .

For as you put your foot out to steady yourself, you stepped on the edge of the black circle. Quick as a flash, the circle spread itself out and engulfed your foot! And now you realize the danger of the Black-mouth Floortrap. As you tumble into the black hole, you find yourself falling over and over through a dark void, until you lose consciousness. The real horror in store will, thankfully, never be known to you . . .

31

Without hesitating to consider your actions, you spring at the skeleton creature. Seeing you advance, it grabs two surgeon's knives from the desk and faces you. Resolve your battle:

QUIMMEL BONE	*SKILL 8*	*STAMINA 7*

If you defeat the physician, turn to **359**.

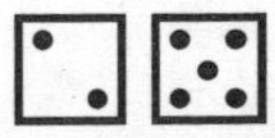

32

Inside the shack, sacks of grain and nuts lie on the floor, and strips of dried meat hang over the counter; loaves of bread and other foods are also to be found. Behind the counter, a puny villager is cowering behind a sack of weedroots. When you enter, he tries to hide from you, but you have seen him. If you have any coins, you may buy some provisions. If not, you may try to steal some, or you can leave. If you wish to buy provisions, you may spend 1 Gold Piece (turn to **131**) or 2 Gold Pieces (turn to **146**). If you want to try stealing, turn to **410**. If you leave and head west out of the village, turn to **274**.

33

You leave the room along a dusty corridor. A strange bluish light comes from glowstones set in the ceiling to light your way. With every step you take, a glowstone ahead of you lights up and one behind you fades to darkness; it is almost as if your progress were being monitored by some unseen entity. As you wait for your eyes to adjust to the light, you pause to consider the strange events in the previous room. You retract your claws and rub your rough, scaly belly thoughtfully. You can make no sense of what has happened. Eventually you set off once more and after a few paces you come to a junction. A passageway runs off to the north. You may take this (turn to **311**), or you may continue in an easterly direction (turn to **390**).

34

Once more the Shadow Stalker raises its knife and plunges it down into your shadow. Again you try to leap aside, but this time its blow grazes your chest. Lose 2 more *STAMINA* points. You try anticipating where the creature will be and slashing it with your claws, but your blow cuts through thin air. The Shadow Stalker does not even try to avoid you. Again you slash ineffectually, and this time the creature plunges its knife into your shadow's back. The pain shoots through your body; lose 3 *STAMINA* points. Now you must decide what to do. Will you try to escape by leaving the room (turn to **242**), or will you stop your attack and try to make peace with the Shadow Stalker (turn to **135**)?

35

The old woman can hardly walk and you leave her behind as you head for the market. She wails pitifully as you ignore her pleas, but you have no wish to get involved with her. The sound of the market soon drowns out her cries. You wander round the barrows and begin to head for the street performers, when a fat man comes over to you. He approaches you cautiously and whispers to you: 'Pssst. Say, handsome! I got a little . . . er . . . *proposition* for you. Want to hear about it? Come round here.' He leads you round a corner to a secluded alley.

'Hey, I could *use* someone with your strength in my business,' he says enthusiastically. 'It's not easy to go collecting all these cursing ingredients. I figure you and me could make a fine team. Well?' He claps his hand on your shoulder as you both turn round the corner into the alley. Waiting in the alley are two unkempt, burly men, who are holding a net. As you turn the corner, they fling it over you and pull you to the ground! You struggle to break out of the net, but the more you struggle, the tighter it seems to wind around you. Eventually you can struggle no more and you lie back exhausted. 'Phew!' puffs the fat man. 'A real fighter! Too bad we can't use this one, eh, boys? But I think I know an old sorcerer in Chalice who will pay handsomely for this fellow's internals. Right, Slitter, do your stuff. But make sure your knife don't do no damage inside. Remember it's got glands in its neck and they no doubt will fetch a fair price . . .'

36

The struggle has been monumental and you lie down on the ground exhausted. The wrecked tunnel has collapsed and you stare at it, gasping to regain your breath. The sound of your own breathing drowns out the sound of the small creatures approaching . . .

Chattering excitedly to one another, a small band of Forest Imps has arrived at their trap to take home the day's meal. Unaware that you have already destroyed the trap, the tiny, spindly creatures enter the far end of the tunnel easily. You do not even hear them until their shrieks of anger, on discovering that their trap has been ruined, break through the sound of your heavy breathing. Twelve skinny pairs of legs carry the noisy, green-skinned Imps scurrying along towards you. When they discover you, they halt, wary of your immense strength. But you are too tired to survive a fight against twelve armed Imps. And you have no chance when their spears have been dipped into a fast-acting poison from the deadly Stingroot plant . . .

37

The descent is long and steep, but eventually you reach the foot of the staircase, where you find a deadly cluster of iron spikes waiting to greet creatures less fortunate than you in maintaining their balance. However, beyond the spikes, there appears to be no way onwards. You have reached a dead end. You step up to examine it more closely. As you are doing so, a shiver passes over you and you feel an overwhelming desire to sneeze! No matter what you do, you cannot avoid the sneeze and it eventually erupts with force enough to shake the very walls around you! You open your eyes and rub your nose with a scaly hand. Your surroundings have changed! No longer are you at the foot of a staircase with a dead end before you, but instead you are standing at a spot where the dead end is to the *west*! Where are you? You wander eastwards along the passage until you arrive at a junction. If you wish to walk north, turn to **443**. If you want to go east, turn to **50**.

38

Eventually the guard returns, panting, 'It seems you were right.' He shrugs. 'There's no sign of him anywhere. Mind you, I can't let you through here. No one's allowed through without Darramouss's permission. At least, not unless . . . er . . . certain . . . ahem . . . *special arrangements* are made, if you understand my meaning.' He looks at the pendant hanging round your neck. 'That's a handsome little piece,' he says. 'Now I'm sure special arrangements could be made if you were to leave this behind. Just our – shall we say – *bond* to make sure you return. And mine to keep if you don't!' If you wish to give him your pendant, he will let you through his guardroom, but you may never again find secret passages without it. Make your choice. If you will pay his price, turn to **442**. If this price is too high, the only way you are going to get through is by attacking him (turn to **73**).

39

No sooner have you dealt the final death-blow than another Chaos Warrior appears at the archway. Resolve your combat with the creature:

CHAOS WARRIOR	*SKILL 9*	*STAMINA 7*

If you defeat the Warrior, turn to **397**.

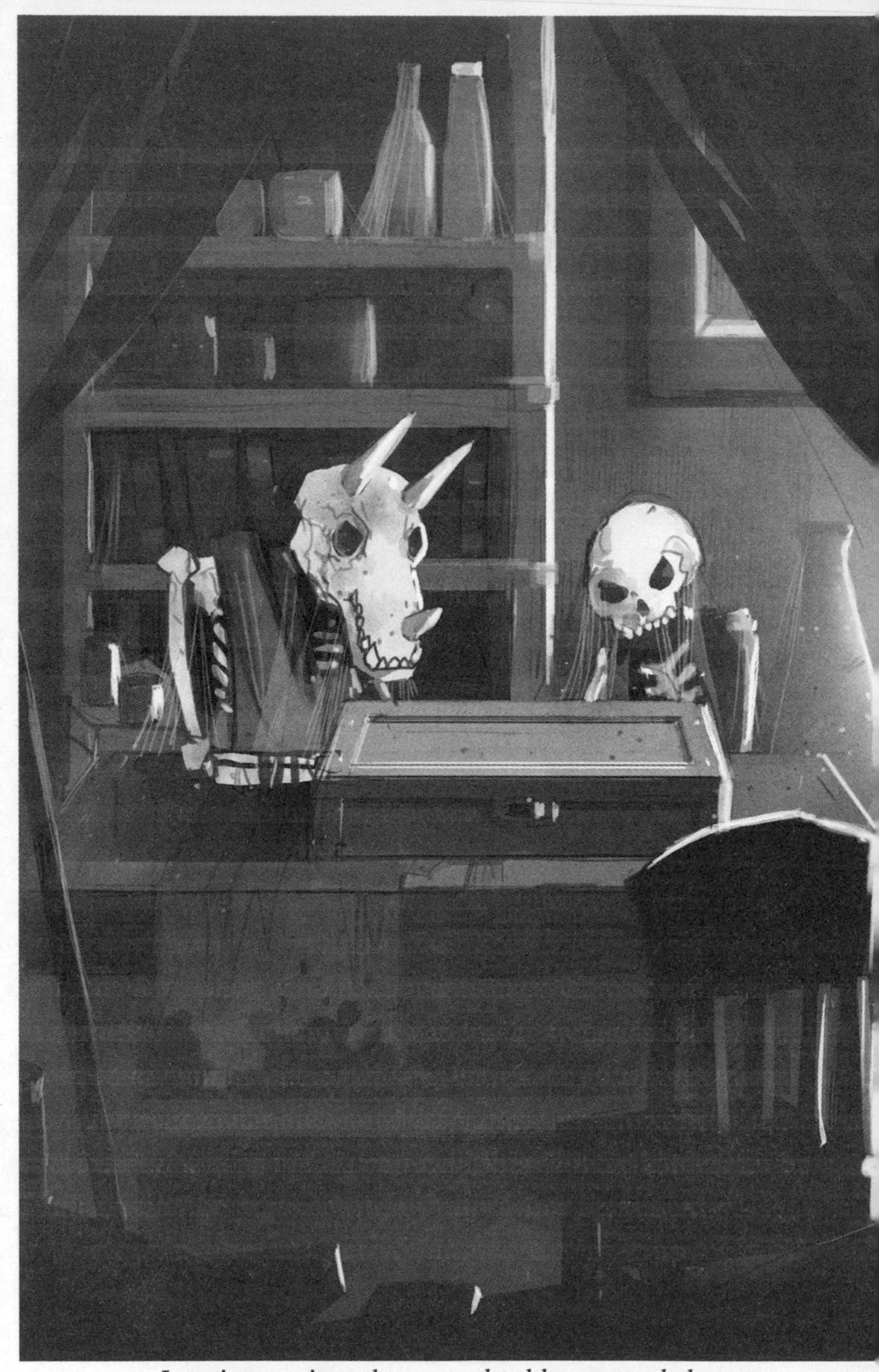

Leaning against the central table are to skeletons

40

As you are about to turn to leave the dead end, the pendant around your neck suddenly starts to vibrate! Remembering what happened last time this occurred, you hold the talisman out towards the rock-face. A low humming comes from the charm and its vibrating becomes more pronounced. Eventually, the blue stone set in its centre begins to glow and a narrow beam of blue light illuminates a small catch in the rock. You release the catch and the rocky door rumbles aside to reveal a small room ahead in the rock. In the room is a long wooden box on a sturdy table. Around the room are a variety of objects – plates, candlesticks and many other artefacts arranged on shelves and smaller tables. Leaning against the central table are two skeletons. One looks human, but the other looks decidedly non-human, having the jaws of some sort of creature of Chaos. A musty smell comes from the room; it no doubt has not been visited for some time. Will you venture inside (turn to **296**), or will you ignore the room and leave the area (turn to **279**)?

41

You leave the cavern and head along the passage which leads to the north. Again the route twists and turns, but you progress without incident. Eventually you reach the foot of a flight of stairs carved out of the rock and leading up into darkness. You climb the stairs and reach a junction where you may head either north (turn to **136**) or east (turn to **156**).

42

The excitement is too much. Your blood boils with the fire of battle and the promise of feasting on the juicy bodies of the three Hobbits. You cannot control yourself and you launch yourself into the chamber, claws poised to strike. As you rush towards them, the Hobbits shriek in terror and draw their shortswords to defend themselves. Resolve the battle:

	SKILL	*STAMINA*
First HOBBIT	*6*	*6*
Second HOBBIT	*5*	*6*
Third HOBBIT	*6*	*7*

The Hobbits will all attack at the same time. If you defeat them all, turn to **2**.

43

The idea of serving as a guard on the *Galleykeep* attracts you. Sailing through the air on missions of mayhem and destruction; helping your glorious leader defeat his enemies; a life of purpose and excitement instead of one of aimless wanderings. Your mind is made up. You will make a formidable guard for Zharradan Marr; your loyalty will be assured by the generous doses of Droneweed fed to you daily in your Hobbit broth . . .

44

You ignore the words of the foul witches and you may continue straight away. Will you return to the stones and investigate them (turn to **198**)? Will you continue past the stones into the wood (turn to **261**)? Or will you investigate the building you are in (turn to **253**)?

45

You leave the Chubbley tree and continue along the trail. A little further on you pause on top of a hillock and survey the area. In the distance to your right you can see a great forest, and straight ahead a river cuts through the landscape like a gaping wound. To the left, the green colour of the grassy countryside fades to sandy brown as the bleak Windward Plain stretches west as far as you can see. You head on and, shortly after you have left the hillock, another trail joins yours from the left. Turn to **134**.

46

Your hope fades as *another* Chaos Warrior raises his weapon and advances to do battle:

CHAOS WARRIOR	*SKILL 8*	*STAMINA 8*

If you win this battle, turn to **39**.

47

With shining white eyes, the Weather Mage turns towards you. He holds his hands in front of his eyes, and his long fingernails obscure them from you. When his hands finally lower; a small dark cloud hovers in the air before him. You are fascinated by this display and can do nothing but watch as the tiny cloud drifts across the room, and stops in mid-air, a short distance from you. A shrill whistling starts as the cloud begins spinning. Faster and faster it spins until its underside drops slowly to the ground, and the tornado drifts towards you. Too late you realize its deadly purpose. When the tornado touches you, even your great strength cannot prevent your being sucked inside and instantly crushed to death by the Weather Mage's creation.

48

Ignoring the weaker-looking of the two humans, you face the figure in clinking armour. He holds his ground, his sword poised ready to strike. Resolve your combat with the Knight in plate-armour:

ARMOURED KNIGHT *SKILL 8* *STAMINA 9*

If you defeat him, turn to **392**.

49

The passage leads east. A short distance ahead, you arrive at a rocky bridge across a deep chasm. Far below you can hear the sloshing of a slow-moving river and you step up to the edge of the bridge to get a better look. A disgusting smell is coming up from the river, and as this hits your nostrils, you stagger a few paces backwards. But this is the only way on. The bridge is narrow and wet from the moisture in the air: no doubt it is slippery too. Nevertheless, you have no choice. You hold your breath and step on to the bridge. But halfway across, you lose your footing on the slippery bridge. *Test your Luck.* If you are Lucky, turn to **457**. If you are Unlucky, turn to **60**.

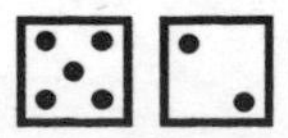

50

The passage continues east and you pass under two carved archways before you finally find yourself in a small, circular room with no apparent way onwards. While you are considering what to do, you feel a slight shift in the ground beneath your feet. Almost as if you had pressed some invisible switch, your surroundings have now changed! Frantically, you look round to find the tunnel by which you entered, but it has disappeared. There is now no way out of the room. A rumbling noise from beneath the floor is followed by a fierce roaring. But this is not the roaring of a creature! Smoke seeps from the walls and you begin to sweat as the temperature increases. The room is becoming an oven in which *you* are beginning to roast! As the temperature becomes unbearable, you search round for any means of escape. Are you wearing a pair of yellow metal bracelets? If so, turn to **202**. If not, turn to **339**.

51

You leave the room along a passageway which runs west, your thoughts still dwelling on the mysterious smoke creature. After a short time, you find that the passage is bending this way and that through the rocky earth. But your progress is aided by the strange blue glowstones which are set into the roof of the passage. As you progress, glowstones ahead of you light up and bathe the area in an eerie blue light. When you look behind, you can see that they magically turn themselves off. Suddenly a distant echo reaches your ears and you stop dead in your tracks. Again you hear the sound – and it is coming closer! Footsteps and muffled voices are heading towards you. You are fortunate in having the advantage that your own footsteps are virtually silent, so you continue ahead, ready for a fight with anything that may come along. You approach a bend . . .

A shrill scream pierces the air and for an instant you are not sure whether it came from your own throat or that of the terrified adventurer with whom you suddenly found yourself nose to nose, when you turned the bend! But you recover quickly and slash furiously at the hapless human, who is still trying to compose himself after his fright. You catch him across the skimpy leather armour he wears on his chest, and send him crashing into the rocky wall where he loses his grip on the sword he is carrying. His two companions are close behind, so you must finish off the Strongarm without delay:

STRONGARM	*SKILL 7*	*STAMINA 8*

If you defeat the warrior, turn to **320**.

52

You leave the glistening pond and continue along the path. It winds through the trees until you eventually reach a fork, where you may continue either to the left or to the right. In the centre of the fork a pole has been fixed into the ground and, hanging from the pole by his wrists, is a sight which widens your eyes. Half-dead from exposure, but looking plump and tasty, is a Hobbit! Mouth watering, you rush up to the little creature. As he hears your footsteps, his eyes open slowly. 'No . . .' he moans, guessing that your intentions do not involve greeting him warmly. 'Please let me down and leave me be. I can tell you where both of these paths lead, and how to avoid the dangers along them . . .' You are hungry and the sight of this tasty morsel is an unexpected treat. Will you cut him down and make a meal of him (turn to **206**), or will you cut him down, listen to what he says about the paths ahead, and release him (turn to **70**)?

53

You crash off through the reeds in pursuit of the creature, though the going is difficult. You catch sight of it again and this time it seems to be hopping rather awkwardly through the reeds. Your foot slips and you sink up to your knee in muddy water, but this does not deter you. However, following the creature is quite difficult. You lose sight of it and must now follow by the sounds of it crashing through the reeds. You climb on to a bank and find yourself in a circular clearing. All is quiet; there are no signs of the creature. But then suddenly the reeds behind you part, and you spin around, just as the wide-mouthed Toadman you have been following springs at you. Turn to **68**.

54

You wait until the guard has disappeared round the corner and sneak into his room. It is dirty and untidy; old food moulders in corners; the bed is filthy, and dirty blankets are strewn about on the floor. And there is a smell hanging in the air which is a mixture of stale human sweat and rancid ale. On the far side of the room is a metal door. A barred viewing-hole is open and through the hole you can see stairs beyond, leading upwards. Suddenly a noise from behind startles you and you swing round just in time to see a huge wooden club descending on your forehead! The blow knocks you to your knees and you must lose 4 *STAMINA* points.

'Just as I thought!' growls the guard. 'Darramouss no more gave you permission to leave than he would have given permission to the black-eyed fool!' Your ruse has been discovered. His club is raised once more and you must defend yourself. Turn to **98**.

55

The road out of Coven leads you past a disused building. Grog stops. 'Wait here,' he says. 'I buried something in this building before I entered Coven . . . er . . . just some worthless family heirlooms. Sentimental value. Back in a flash.' He soon returns with a knapsack, which obviously contains something quite bulky – a box, perhaps. You are curious, but he makes no mention of the contents of his knapsack. 'Look, you're a strange creature,' he says as the two of you set off once more. 'Nothing to say, nowhere to go. Where do you come from? Are you just wandering about? Or are you on some sort of mission?' You nod enthusiastically. 'Ah, I see. But you can't talk?' You shake your head. 'Hmmm. But you can shake and nod your head. Well! We're in no real rush, are we? Let's make a game of it. I'll try to find out about your mission and you can tell me whether or not I'm getting close to the truth. Is it *something* you're looking for, rather than *someone*?' You nod. 'Do you know where it is?' You shake your head. And so the journey continues.

The trail sweeps round to the north until it eventually reaches a crossroads. Grog's face lights up. 'I know!' he exclaims. 'Rosina! She will help us! We must go west.' Will you follow his advice and go west (turn to **177**), or will you instead go east (turn to **203**) or continue north (turn to **130**)?

56

You climb through the hole in the wall and hold your breath as you step through the cloud of settling dust. The area is not much deeper and when you reach its end, you discover what the glittering is. From high in the ceiling, a powdery trickle of Elven Dust is falling through the air. It drops gracefully down from the ceiling, glittering as it falls, but by the time it reaches the ground it has disappeared! The magical dust is showering you as you stand looking up at it, though you can feel nothing. Elven Dust is a magical powder which is an essential ingredient in white Elven magic. Though its effects may remain a mystery to you in the immediate future, you may well wonder about the significance of your find. Someone has been trying to wall the Elven Dust in. Why? Eventually you decide to leave the recess and the chamber. Turn to **405**.

57

You make your way through the undergrowth. Your progress is very slow. Your bulky body is impeded by branches and vines, and the going is both difficult and tiring. And you are not certain which way you should go, when all directions look the same. You try various different directions until you find yourself passing a tree which you can remember passing just a short time before! You have been travelling in circles! Your anger builds up and you thunder through the foliage. An unnatural click beneath your foot should have been a warning. But in your rage, it is a warning which you choose to ignore. An instant later, the trap has sprung. Your foot has stepped into a rope noose attached to the supple stem of a sapling. The noose tightens around your ankle and with a whip-like action you are hoisted into the air, until you dangle helplessly from the tree-top! Turn to **175**.

58

'Stittle Woad is not far from here,' he starts. 'It is near the Rainbow Ponds. I would say it is two days' journey from here. Travel in an easterly direction, keeping the setting sun behind you. If you manage to find the vicinity of the village, do not look for it on the surface. It has remained hidden for so long because it is *under the ground*. More than this I may not tell.' He picks himself up and stretches painfully. After dusting off his robes, he bids you good day and sets off. You watch him disappear. Turn to **414**.

59

As well as the naval uniforms, you find civilian clothes and dress for special occasions. But there is nothing unusual or anything which could provide a clue as to Marr's whereabouts. Your frustration grows. Your heavy fist smashes into the wardrobe, splintering its timbers. The hanging clothes fall in a pile on the floor and from the back of the wardrobe, a round metal shield rolls forwards and drops to a wobbling spin on the floor. You stoop to get a look at it. Turn to **302**.

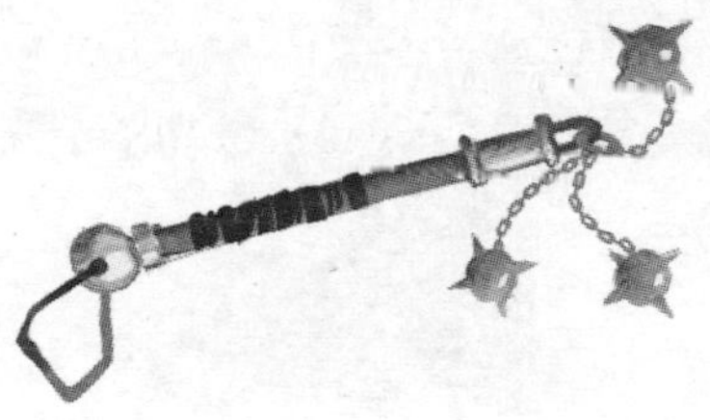

60

You try to regain your footing, but the bridge is too slippery. You lose your balance completely and tumble over the edge and down, down towards the stinking waters below. The current drags you down and your lungs fill with the putrid waters of the Bilge water. Your death is not pleasant . . .

61

You turn east and follow the passageway. You pass under a narrow archway and find yourself in an open room, which is well lit by torches fixed high on the walls. You look around for a way onwards, but the only passage leading from the room is the one you arrived along. The room is bare except for a small pile of what looks like black cloth lying against one of the walls. Do you want to investigate the room further (turn to **334**), or would you rather leave (turn to **444**)?

62

The creature is somewhat taken aback when you show that you understand his words. Although you are of similar sizes, you certainly *look* the more powerful of the two and it is probably for this reason that the

Rhino-Man invites you into his guardroom. 'Are you also one of Marr's creatures?' he growls. When you look puzzled, he snorts. 'If you don't know, then you must be looking for either the Yellowstone Mines or the Testing Grounds in Knot Oak Wood. Looking at the size of you, I'd reckon the Testing Grounds were more likely. Darramouss will know. He knows everything that happens in these parts. He'll set you right. But don't cross him. Even one of your size cannot hope to tangle with such a foul-tempered lifeless one. And if you make it to the Testing Grounds, oblige me by finding . . . oh, what was his symbol? They don't have names in the Testing Grounds – except for that foul-breathed weapon-master, Thugruff. Legionnaire twenty-nine, I think: a Rhino-Man like me. If he's still alive, he ought to know this: *Gat H'Oulie has escaped with the ring to the Forest of Spiders!* But of course, you cannot speak, can you? Here, I'll write it down for you.' He hands you the message. If you come across 'Legionnaire twenty-nine' later in your adventure, you may pass on the message by adding his number to the reference you are on at the time when you identify him.

You rise to leave the guardroom. The Rhino-Man gives you directions. 'Leave through the north door here. When you arrive at the T-junction, turn right and follow the passage.' You take his advice. Turn to **298**.

Standing before you is a tall, thin figure

63

Standing before you is a tall, thin figure. It is dark and humanoid in appearance, although you cannot make out much in the dim light. You can, however, clearly make out two large green eyes. The figure is shrouded in a brightly coloured cape and its hair is gathered on top of its head in a tight knot. It steps towards you and flings its cape back to reveal its left hand, which grips a short bow. Reaching over its back, it draws an arrow from a quiver, aims at you and shoots you in the shoulder! Lose 2 *STAMINA* points. You howl with pain and turn towards the bowman, baring your teeth. But he has yet another arrow poised to fire. This second arrow rips into your forearm with such force that it comes out the other side and clatters off the wall behind. Lose another 2 *STAMINA* points. Your fury is now uncontrollable. Will you unsheathe your claws and advance on your attacker? Or will you retreat from this deadly foe? Roll one die. If you roll 1–4, you are so enraged that you blunder ahead towards the Dark Elf bowman without a thought of the danger (turn to **14**). If you roll 5 or 6, fear for your life takes over from your anger and you retreat (turn to **260**). You may *Test your Luck* if you wish, but you must do so *before* you roll the die. If you are Lucky, you may choose your own option. If you are Unlucky, you must let your instincts decide and roll the die as normal.

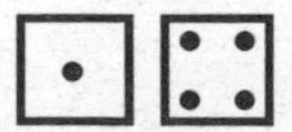

64

The broken bones on the floor seem to have belonged to a medium-sized creature. Many of them have marks as though they had been gnawed by some hungry beast with strong jaws. You bend down to look at them – and to see whether there may be any morsels of meat left – when a rustling noise from behind startles you. But before you are able to turn, you feel sharp teeth digging into your neck. The creature from the chair! Lose 2 *STAMINA* points. You must now resolve your battle with the hungry Blood Orc which stands before you:

BLOOD ORC	*SKILL 7*	*STAMINA 5*

If you defeat the creature, turn to **207**.

65

You manage to keep your balance all the way down the rock-face until you reach the hole. As you step into the hole, your feet once again touch solid ground. Your left foot bangs against something straight and solid. When you bend down to investigate, you find a long length of straight metal, about as wide as your hand, which runs deep into the hole. Another identical length runs alongside the first and the two are held a short distance apart by a series of blocks of wood. You decide to see where they lead, and you enter the tunnel. No glowstones light the way here, so you follow the tracks into darkness. A short distance ahead you reach a fork. Will you follow the tracks to the left (turn to **182**), or will you enter the tunnel on the right (turn to **424**)?

66

You fling open the door and rush into the room, snarling viciously, ready to take on the creatures you heard inside. But the scene within is not what you expect. Turn to **161**.

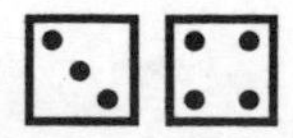

67

There are a number of crypts around, but you choose to enter one which is larger than the others. You slowly push the door open and it creaks on rusty hinges. The room inside is dark and empty except for the great stone tomb standing in the centre of the room. Your claws clatter along its surface as you walk around, studying it. But suddenly another sound catches your attention, the sound of slow shuffling feet, coming from outside the crypt. You open the door and just as quickly slam it shut again. Advancing towards you from the gravestones, with staring, lifeless faces, are a dozen living corpses. No doubt they are intent on ridding themselves of this intruder! Your eyes dart round the crypt for a hiding-place, but there is none. In desperation you grasp the lid of the tomb and heave it aside. It is empty! But something is happening on the floor of the tomb. Your removing the lid seems to have triggered a secret catch, and the base of the tomb has begun to rumble. It slowly slides aside to reveal a narrow staircase leading downwards. Do you wish to see where the staircase leads? If so, turn to **454**. If you would rather take your chance with the army of Zombies arriving at the door, turn to **321**.

68

He shoves you back into the centre of the clearing and your feet splash in the wet mud. Suddenly you stumble as your foot sinks deep. You try to step out, but it is no use; the more you tread with your feet, the deeper you sink . . . The mud reaches your chest, then your neck, then begins to fill your mouth and nose. The Toadman watches your final struggles and a smile spreads across his toothless mouth . . .

69

The desk is solidly constructed. The papers scattered around are written in a strange language which consists mainly of numbers and symbols. You leaf through the books and find many anatomical diagrams of a variety of types of creature. The drawers are full mainly of more papers, but one drawer is locked. Do you wish to ring the bell (turn to **236**) or examine the specimen jars (turn to **97**)?

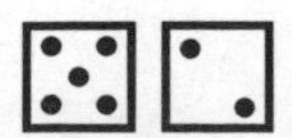

70

A wave of relief passes across the Hobbit's face as you reach up to bite through his ties. 'Oh, thank you, thank you,' he sobs. 'I will keep my side of the bargain and tell you what lies down both of these paths. The path to the left will lead you to a dead . . . Wait! What are you doing? No!' The little creature has noticed the mounting frenzy in your eyes as you try to subdue your natural instinct. You have been battling valiantly against an impulse to silence the little creature for good and devour him. But it is hopeless; you cannot fight your natural passion. A single blow sends the Hobbit crashing senselessly to the ground, and soon you have picked his carcass clean. Restore your *STAMINA* to its *Initial* level and choose whether to take the fork to the right (turn to **183**) or the path to the left (turn to **351**).

71

You try to keep your balance as you descend the narrow stairs, but they are damp and slippery. At one point you slip and totter perilously near the edge before regaining your balance and continuing down. But six steps later, you lose your balance once again, and this time you are not lucky enough to regain it. You plunge over the edge of the staircase and down, down into the filthy depths of the Bilgewater River below. The impact is enough to knock you senseless. And, unable to fight against the current, you are swept downstream to oblivion.

72

With one hand you swat the door. The force is great and your fist succeeds in cracking the wood. But the door does not open and your anger rises. A sound stirs within the room! You listen carefully and can hear heavy breathing coming from within, mixed with a shuffling sound, as if something were slowly moving around. A growl, deep and low, comes from your throat. Will you risk facing whatever is beyond the door? Or will you try the safer route, back past the Dwarf? Roll one die. If the result is **1**, turn to **419**. If you roll **2–6**, turn to **170**.

73

With a snarl you leap at the guard's throat and send him sprawling back into the room. You both land on the floor amid piles of old clothes and half-eaten meals. There is a foul smell in the air, a mixture of stale sweat and rancid ale. He manages to free himself from your grip and grab a club from a table. Turn to **98**.

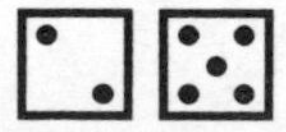

74

You hand the knapsack to Zharradan Marr. 'That's right!' he smiles. 'Now I shall keep my side of the bargain. You have sought me out and found me, overcoming all opposition. That shows resourcefulness and intelligence. You are a powerful creature, and you have had training in leadership, did you but know it. Do you enjoy the excitement of battle?' You nod. 'Then so be it. You shall become my Commander-in-Chief. Will you serve me?' The prospect of a life of conquest and adventure does indeed excite you. 'Very well, then,' says Marr. 'You shall start duties immediately. Your first task is to execute your predecessor, Vallaska Roue. Not only has he failed me in allowing you through to my private quarters, but he has so far failed to locate the Rainbow Pools. His usefulness is at an end. Once Roue is dead, you shall have command of the *Galleykeep*, under my orders!'

And thus your fate is decided. How you will fare as Commander of Zharradan Marr's forces will be decided by your own *skill*. Your leader is known for his ruthlessness. Perhaps you will be remembered as his greatest Commander; perhaps your fate will be that of your predecessor. Whatever the outcome, one thing is for certain; your aimless life will finally have a sense of purpose . . .

75

The passage heads straight for some time until you finally reach its end at a junction. You may turn either east or west here. If you wish to go east, turn to **326**. If you wish to go west, turn to **353**.

76

You arrive back at the tree and study it incredulously. There it is standing right in the middle of a path which you walked along only moments ago. Yet it seems to be as lifeless as a gallows' pole, and its roots are well buried in the ground. Are you imagining things? Unfortunately for you, you are not, as you realize the next instant when a branch catches you on the shoulder. You recoil in fright and look up to see the branches of the tree slowly shifting round, as if blowing in the wind, and bending towards you. *The tree is alive!* One of the branches catches your arm and wraps its tip round like a bullwhip! You flinch and snatch your arm away . . . and at that very moment, the creature's eyes flick open!

The Tree Spirit's icy glare freezes you to the spot. Your heart is pounding, but you are unable to move! Finally, you break its stare and manage to turn round and run. But only then do you realize the secret of Xenowood, as this mysterious part of the Forest of Spiders is known. *Another* Tree Spirit is blocking your way, and more are shifting slowly towards you. A huge circle of the creatures surrounds you! Turn to **434**.

77

You enter the passage. It twists and turns through the rock in a haphazard way until it finally opens out into a small cavern. You pause to get your bearings and search for the best way through. Leading off to the north is a wide passage which seems to be going somewhere. But to get to it you will have to cross the cavern, and crossing the cavern is not an inviting prospect. For in the cavern wall to your right are two caves, and in a neat pile outside the first cave is a mound of bones – some broken, some just chewed. But judging from the size of some of the bones, whatever was eating them was no mere Half-Orc. Will you head for the caves to attack whatever is inside (turn to **88**), or will you simply cross the cavern and see what happens (turn to **430**)?

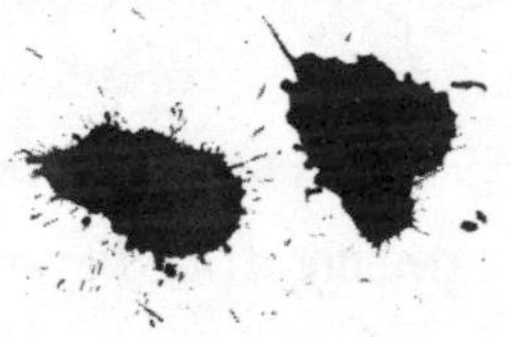

78

You watch each guard in turn and wait until they are preoccupied with whipping the miserable creatures, when you are able to move slowly across the vast chamber unnoticed. But as luck would have it, a small creature turns a corner round the rock and bumps straight into you! You both jump in surprise. But then your lips curl back and a delighted growl comes from your throat. Your tongue licks lustily round your mouth as you grab the unfortunate Hobbit that has walked straight into your clutches! Its screams are quickly silenced, but not before the guards are aware of your appearance in the mine. They surround you, brandishing their bullwhips, and you are trapped. The penalty for you is not death – though some would consider death more merciful. Killing you would be a wasted opportunity. You are much more useful spending the rest of your life toiling as a slave in the mines of Zharradan Marr.

79

You rush across to the secret entrance and find yourself bathed once more in the eerie green light. The instant you step into the passageway, the door slams shut behind you and this is much to your relief, as you were anxious to leave the mysterious room. The passage continues in a westerly direction until you arrive at a junction. A sign is tacked to the wall and an arrow on it points westwards. There is a message on the sign which reads: 'Yfllp wst pnfe mjnfs eth jsiwby.' The other passage leads to the south. A few paces down it is a small pile of bones – or rather a pile of small bones. They look like human bones, but from a creature much smaller than a human. You must now decide which way to continue. Will you head west (turn to **142**) or south (turn to **273**)?

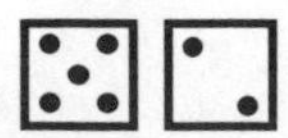

80

You step through the door and your claws clatter along the rocky walls as you feel your way. Staggering slowly along the passageway, you shake your head from side to side in an attempt to rid yourself of the affliction. You reach a bend in the passage where the wall turns to the right. Suddenly your foot steps forward on to nothing! Before you can stop yourself, you are falling uncontrollably down, down into what seems to be a deep pit. You prepare yourself for a heavy landing, but instead you continue to fall. Eventually the speed becomes too much for you. Consciousness fades and you never awaken. Your life has mercifully ended here before you were able to discover who – or *what* – lay in store for you at the bottom of the Blackmouth Floortrap . . .

81

The passage turns to the left and you follow it for some time until you feel that perhaps this corridor has no end! Eventually you see a particularly dark area straight ahead. Will you investigate, or would you rather turn round and go back? If you would rather go back, turn to **279**. If you want to investigate the area, turn to **20**.

82

You remain at the Testing Grounds, learning what you can about the ways of war. While you are being trained, you are well fed on Hobbit broth. Restore your *STAMINA* to its *Initial* level, increase your *Initial SKILL* by 2 points and increase your current *SKILL* to this level. But you have taken a dislike to the foul-breathed Half-Troll and you are already scheming how to catch him unawares. Finally, your opportunity comes one night when you spy him walking in the courtyard. You leave the castle and creep up on him. When the opportunity presents itself, you attack! Resolve this combat:

THUGRUFF	*SKILL 11*	*STAMINA 14*

If you manage to reduce him to a *STAMINA* of 4, turn to **305**.

83

Your situation is hopeless. With nothing to grasp to pull you from the mud, you cannot hope to do anything but struggle vainly as you sink deeper into your grave. The mud reaches your chest, then your neck, then begins to fill your mouth and nose. You take your last breath . . .

84

Though particularly rocky underfoot, the passage is far preferable to the cold, muddy slime. A short distance along the corridor, you come to a door which is firmly closed. Although its timbers do not look too strong, a quick shove from your elbow has no effect. From slight gaps both underneath the door and in the timber panels you can see a flashing light coming from within the room. The flashing is irregular and is accompanied by no sound. Will you smash the door to investigate (turn to **268**), or would you prefer to return to the main passageway and head north through the dark slime instead (turn to **232**)?

85

You turn round and pass through the arch. There are four others in the chamber. You choose another and peer into its gloomy depths. You can see nothing. You pluck up courage, step inside and feel around. It appears to be empty. Your hand touches a rocky wall at the back of the alcove. There is no point in investigating it further. The other alcoves are similar and you decide to leave the chamber. Turn to **405**.

86

When you have finally killed the little creature, you must turn your attention to the other two humans. While you have been battling their companion, they have been preparing to attack. The red-robed figure is facing you, pointing the little finger of each hand at you and mumbling. The shiny human has grabbed a sword – similar, you remember, to the Dwarf's, but larger – and is shouting to the other: 'Cpn tr plojt simjn dishbmbn! Jtim by abfeb blfe tp olf bda vsu tpothb taswj nf bfbr dacvr!' You cannot fight both at once. Which will you direct your attention towards? Roll one die. If you roll 1–4, you decide to take on the shining figure (turn to **48**). If you roll 5 or 6, you turn towards the man in the red robes (turn to **292**).

87

They chase after you, hurling their stones and abuse until you are well out of their field. Luckily, no stones hit you and you are soon out of range. You continue along the path, which winds towards a spreading forest, until you reach a sign which reads: 'Knot Oak Wood'. The path leads deep into the forest and you follow it. Turn to **244**.

There is a look of pure fury in its ghostly white eyes

88

You creep up to the first cave and peer inside. It is dark and you can see little. But the thing that strikes you immediately is the smell of rotten flesh! Whatever lives in here certainly has a large appetite for meat. You poke your head further into the cave and you can see a large furry ball heaving up and down in one corner. You step forward to catch the sleeping creature unawares. But your foot kicks a loose stone and sends it scuttling across the cave towards it. The creature shudders, awakens and gets up. By now you have already decided to attack and you are virtually on top of the creature as its face turns towards you.

There is a look of pure fury in its ghostly white eyes as the Devourer opens its mouth to defend itself. Two layers of jagged, bloodstained teeth part and sink into the scales of your arm. You howl and spring back out of its clutches (lose 2 *STAMINA* points for the bite). The creature is as tall as you and as bulky, but has a shaggy, furry body. You must resolve your fight with the creature:

DEVOURER	*SKILL 10*	*STAMINA 8*

If you defeat it, turn to **41**.

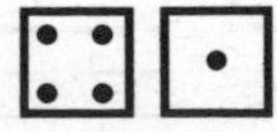

89

You rest for a few moments to catch your breath and then you survey the room. Your curiosity overcomes you, and you begin to investigate the seven bodies in the room. The pug-faced Orcs are dirty and smelly. You try a mouthful of flesh, but spit it out in disgust. Around their waists they carry small bags which, when ripped open, send a shower of small bones flying across the room. The two adventurers are not much more interesting. Similar pouches contain those round pieces of shiny metal which you came across before. They scatter on the floor and you ignore them. The pack on the back of the adventurer in the winged helmet is decorated and attracts your attention. One of the straps breaks as you rip it off his back and grope clumsily inside: you feel something solid. As you fumble angrily with the rucksack, a hard wooden casket drops to the ground and falls open! Inside is a clear smooth flask which contains swirling purple gas. Your curiosity is captured and your huge clawed hand tries to grasp the delicate flask. But this turns out to be hopeless. Eventually, you pick up the casket and drop it on the ground. As luck would have it, the flask jumps in its cradle and lands in such a way that the stopper flips out of the flask! The purple gas within swirls tempestuously and its vapours seep slowly from the neck of the flask. Turn to **382**.

90

You growl defiantly at the voice. The four lights flicker and extinguish. Almost immediately a background luminosity begins to light up the area and you can see where you are. The room you are in is large and appears to be quite important, judging by the rich drapes and gilt-framed paintings which hang on the walls. The scenes depicted in the paintings seem to be of Hell itself. The four faces you saw are elaborate carvings in a soft clay-like material. Standing before you is a tall, gruesome creature dressed in a flowing black cape. Two red eyes shine out from the depths of its hood. Darramouss turns to speak to you:

'You are a recent arrival in these dungeons,' he says. 'You are a fine specimen and are a credit to your creator, Zharradan Marr. Yes, this is so. You have been *created* by Marr and created for a purpose. Zharradan Marr and his physician, Quimmel Bone, are obsessed with marrangha – the re-formation of life. They continually experiment with the effects of potions and spells on creatures. Some they merely transform from one type into another. Others they *create* from preserved organs. Their experiments are not always successful, but when one does succeed, it is sent to me here for observation before its future is finally decided. A future has been decided for you, though I know not what it is. This is of no concern to me. But your immediate duty *is* my concern.

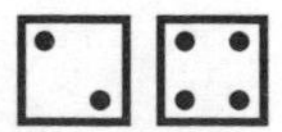

You must be put to work in the Yellowstone Mines. But I will offer you one other alternative. If you do not wish to work in the mines until Marr calls for you, you may choose another future for yourself: *Death*!'

His final word turns into a chilling laugh which resounds around the room. You set your teeth and glare at the creature. You will not be ordered what to do! 'I take it, then, that you choose my second alternative!' he says, opening a book on the desk. He begins to read something from it aloud. Will you step over and grab him by his neck (turn to **402**), wait to see what happens next (turn to **286**), or try to escape down the secret passage in the west wall (turn to **384**)?

91

There are 3 Gold Pieces lying on the ground next to the creature's body. You may take these with you. If you want to eat the creature, take it with you out of the village and eat it at your leisure for 4 *STAMINA* points of nourishment. Leave the village of Coven by turning to **107**.

92

You continue along the trail. By now it is getting quite dark and a full moon is rising in the sky. You decide to sleep for the night beneath a spreading tree at the side of the road. You soon drift off to sleep.

You are tormented that night with a vivid dream. The three witch-women have returned. Each has hold of one of your limbs and is pulling it. The women possess tremendous strength and you feel as if you are being torn apart by the foul creatures. One of them seems to be trying to keep you from the other two, who are cackling gleefully: 'Ours! The creature shall be ours! To Dree for marrangha it must go!' The other is pulling your arm. 'No!' she screams. 'It shall not be! You shall have the creature only if it fails to bring us the Sculliweed!' Finally the three release their grip. 'The root! The root!' they chant. 'Give us the root!'

You wake up in a cold sweat. The tree is being blown by wind. A howling sound whistles through the branches and another sound mixes with it: *Whoooo! Whooo! Psssh! Rhooo! Rhooot! Pssssh! Root! Root! The root! The root!* The sound fills your ears and you spin round to see the grinning faces of the three Women of Dree! They are asking for the root. Do you have any plants with you? If so, you will have noted down a number. Add the number to this reference and turn to the new reference. If you do not have any plants with you, turn to **222**.

93

You reach down with your hand to help him to his feet. But as you move, the little creature strikes and his sword cuts into your forearm. Luckily the tough scales prevent it from doing any real harm, but you must still lose 2 *STAMINA* points. Considering your size in comparison to his, his action was understandable!

Now, instead of reaching for his arm, your hand opens and grips the Dwarf's neck. You struggle to control your actions, but to no avail. Your sharp talons dig into the unfortunate creature's flesh. His eyes bulge and he tries to scream. Frantically, he hits you again with the sword, but the blow lacks power. Deduct 1 more *STAMINA* point. Then his body goes limp.

Your tremendous strength put the poor creature out of its misery, but the incident has left you feeling very strange. Although you wished to help the Dwarf, you have helped him only to an early grave. Will you put these thoughts out of your mind and leave the area (turn to **248**), will you try to hide the body (turn to **218**), or will you examine the body (turn to **399**)?

94

You creep up behind one of the trucks and join a team of creatures who are pushing it. Suddenly a guard with a bullwhip taps you on the shoulder. You suspect trouble and tense yourself for battle. But the guard has not spotted you as an impostor. He is simply motioning for you to leave the truck you are pushing and move over to another one which has to be pushed in a different direction. You shuffle over to the truck. A rather emaciated Troll is your only partner. You and the Troll, coaxed by a guard who is clearly waiting for an excuse to use his bullwhip, push the truck through the cavern, along a tunnel, past a side tunnel to the left and towards an opening. Light enters the tunnel through the opening.

But just as you reach the opening, the long-suffering Troll collapses; the effort has been too much for him. The guard seizes his opportunity and his bullwhip flashes! Although this has no effect on the unconscious Troll, the sting of the whip certainly has an effect on you. Your fury turns to pain and fear, and one thought is prominent in your mind. *You must keep pushing the truck!* You shove it with such force that it launches itself through the opening and out into mid-air! For an instant you recognize the ledge and the steps down which you entered the mines. But only for an instant, since your momentum has carried you after the truck! You look down at the filthy Bilge water below. In a few seconds, you will be entering its depths at a speed which will ensure your death on impact . . .

95

Just a short distance south of the building and the graveyard lies the peasant village of Coven, whose inhabitants live in constant fear of the evil that surrounds them – the growing power of Zharradan Marr and his ruthless henchmen and the devilry of Dree, haven of witchcraft. Its buildings are basic and the main route into the village is dusty and bumpy. There is nothing to suggest anything but poverty. As you follow the trail, villagers are going about their daily business ahead of you. But when they see you, they rush quickly away and hide in their wooden shacks. Eyes watch you from within the hovels, but no one dares venture into the street. Some of the huts have signs above them. One reads 'Provisions' and another reads 'Medicine-Man'. Will you see what you can get in the way of provisions (turn to **32**), visit the medicine-man (turn to **211**), or will you leave Coven along a street leading west (turn to **274**)?

96

In the distance ahead you can see the bleak wastes of Windward Plain. But before the plain, you reach a junction where another trail crosses your own. You may continue west (turn to **177**), or you may turn north (turn to **130**) or south (turn to **330**).

97

The jars contain the eyeballs, brains, hearts and limbs of all sorts of animals. A jar half full of yellow liquid has in it a red lump of flesh the size of your finger and is labelled: 'Firebreath organ – Hellhound'. Another jar contains an organ which is smaller and green in colour. This one is labelled: 'Invisibility organ – Snattacat'. Suddenly your concentration is broken. 'Do you find my specimens . . . *interesting*?' says a strange voice, talking in a series of clicks. You turn round in the direction of the voice, towards the desk. 'No doubt you have come here for some medical advice,' says the skeletal figure sitting behind it, teeth chattering excitedly. The hanging skeleton has disappeared – or rather is now sitting at the desk. 'I am Quimmel Bone, physician and surgeon on the *Galleykeep*. Now, what do you want in here?' Will you spring over to attack him (turn to **31**), or will you pretend you have some ailment which you would like him to treat (turn to **297**)?

98

Resolve your combat with the dark-skinned guard:

GUARD	*SKILL 9*	*STAMINA 10*

If you defeat him, turn to **349**.

99

Angry and frustrated, you snatch the rope and jerk it towards yourself. It offers little resistance, although the faint *click* you hear would have warned an astute human adventurer. It was caused by the hair-trigger springing on the deadly trap which has now taken you by surprise. The trigger has released razor-edged spears from the two side walls. Even your tough scaly skin cannot defend you against them, and your body is riddled with a dozen spears.

As quickly as they appeared, the spears slide neatly out of your lifeless body and disappear back into the walls. You slump to the ground. Eventually your blood will dry and your flesh will decompose like that of the previous victims of the Dark Elves' grim Deathspear Trap.

100

The rolls of parchment are meaningless to you. You step up to the desk and grab one which is open. But as you touch it, a loud noise startles you. You wheel round and your eyes widen as you see a hideous beast taking shape in the corner, materializing out of thin air! It is taller and bulkier than you, and its rough skin looks to be made, not out of living flesh, but out of the rock itself! Its huge fists are covered in irregular bumps and its eyes glare at you in fury from its wide-mouthed face. The Rock Demon you are facing takes a step towards you and you must quickly decide what to do. The creature looks much more powerful than you are. Will you battle the Demon (turn to **327**), or will you escape from the room? If you choose to escape, you may head either for the door in the east wall (turn to **365**) or the door in the south wall, through which you entered (turn to **450**).

101

The door cracks under the force of your blow. A hole appears and you rip the timbers away until it is large enough for you to pass through. Torches are mounted on the wall of the room inside and there are two doors, one to the east and one to the west. There is no furniture to speak of, but some remains – perhaps of a table and chair – litter the floor among a thin covering of dirty straw. The wood has been broken in what appears to have been a furious battle, the result of which lies before you.

In the centre of the room is a familiar sight. Casting your mind back to the battle you have just won, you recognize the figure of an armoured Knight lying face down in the straw. His face is hidden under an elegant helmet decorated with wings coming from above each ear. A dark-bladed sword has entered his body through a gap in his armour between his arm and shoulder. Lying next to the Knight are three other figures. One is similar in stature, but wears a tough leather tunic and helmet. A bloody stain around his belly indicates how this adventurer came to grief. The other two figures are not so familiar. They are shorter than the others, and are dressed in armour of scaly brown hide. They have gnarled, pug-nosed faces with vicious teeth set in their lower jaws. All four bodies are long dead.

You step forward to get a better look. Suddenly you hear a chomping sound coming from somewhere in the room – in fact several places – but you cannot see anything which might make such a noise. Your eyes pass over the adventurer in leather armour and you suddenly freeze: while you are watching, *a chunk of flesh disappears from his thigh!* You watch incredulously for a few moments more. Not only does more flesh disappear from the adventurer's leg, but you also notice the body of one of the pug-nosed creatures twitch as its forearm suddenly loses a fleshy lump! This scene is worrying and you must decide what to do next. Roll one die. If you roll 1, 2 or 3, you decide to investigate the bodies further (turn to **234**). If you roll 4, 5 or 6, you head quickly for the door to the east (turn to **168**).

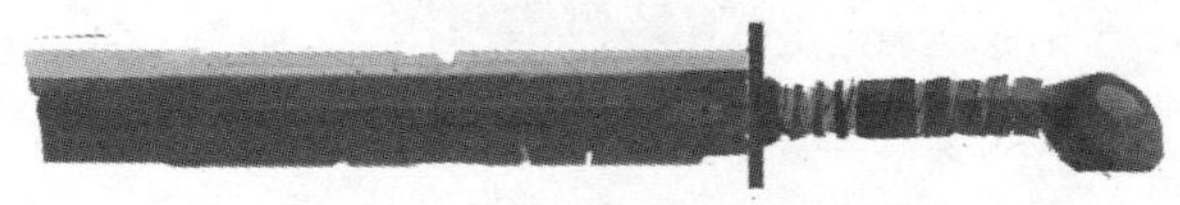

102

You quicken your pace away from the strange, misshapen tree, glancing over your shoulder as you run. But you run straight into something solid. You lose consciousness momentarily and drop to the ground, to be awakened seconds later by a tickling sensation around your head and shoulders. Another tree, as dead as the first, stands in the centre of the path and you ran straight into it! When you discover the source of the tickling, you recoil in horror. As if being blown by some unholy wind, the tree's branches are wafting towards you, gradually drooping lower and lower. The tips are now around your face and neck and they are trying to get a grip! You cannot understand how the scrawny tree, with its long-dead branches, can have such powers and you instinctively roll out of its reaches. At that moment its eyes flick open . . .

The Tree Spirit's knotted, hollow eyes pierce your mind and hold you powerless before it. Under its will you take a step nearer to it, then another. Your foot kicks a rock and you wince in pain, and break free of the creature's gaze! You turn to run from the Tree Spirit, but only then do you realize the hopeless situation you are in. More of the creatures have closed around you in a circle. Each way you look, your escape-route is blocked. Turn to **434**.

103

The Elves become especially agitated and all four turn on you. One of them is more courageous than the rest and tells you to 'Sniff for filth in an Orc's latrine!' (mind your own business). This is fighting talk and to ignore this insult would be a sign of weakness. The Elf is ready to do battle:

ELF	*SKILL 7*	*STAMINA 6*

If you would rather not fight the Elf, turn to **243**. If you do accept the challenge and defeat the Elf, turn to **27**.

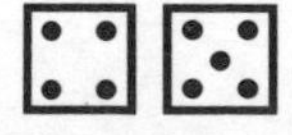

104

You glance from arch to arch, trying to decide whether to investigate them. The stillness is unnerving. Whatever happened to the voices you heard? As if in answer to your question, a sound drifts out from one of the alcoves: 'Pvf rehfrf. Cpm fep vfrehfr fe jfiypvu wb nta tpolf brnapfog rf bta rj chfs ejn ithfs fe pbrts. Dpoy pvu nptov ndf rstb nd ath fehvm bnatpn gvf? Pf rhb psa thfneypvus pf bkat hfetrpl lolbn g vbgf. C'rgga gvonusoog mg pa'sthwag ig thaan'g. Va n'oigg? What about this? Is that better? Ah, yes. I can tell you understand me. Look, I can help you. Maybe you would like me to direct you to a tasty morsel? Two fat Hobbits? Or shall I tell you about he who knows all your secrets? I speak, of course, of Zharradan Marr. Come, talk to me.'

You are stunned to silence by the voice speaking to you in your own tongue. It is inviting you towards one of the arches. Will you enter and speak to the being within? Or are you suspicious of this strange voice? If you enter the arch and talk to the owner of the voice, turn to **323**. If you wish to leave, turn to **405**.

105

You ignore the creature and turn your attention once more back to the tapestry which hangs on the walls. Then a hand – a cold, clammy hand with bony fingers – lands on your shoulder! You spin round and stare into the face of a long-dead Zombie, whose decaying flesh is being eaten away by grubs. The figure on the floor has risen to avenge your attack! Your gaze has been captured by the creature's eyes, which are far from dead. The flames you saw are burning even brighter now. Suddenly, two streams of fire streak from its eyes and burn into your own! You scream in agony at the pain from your blinded eyes, and a slow smile spreads across the creature's face of death. It has only just begun its attack. Your death will be slow and painful.

106

This plant has mysterious properties. You may or may not get the opportunity to find out what it can be used for. If asked to present this plant to someone later in the adventure, remember the number forty-nine. Now you may leave the river-bank by turning to **18**.

107

You continue along the trail which leads out from Coven. It winds past a disused building, now mostly rubble, and sweeps round in a northerly direction. Eventually you come to a crossroads where you may turn either west (turn to **177**) or east (turn to **203**), or continue northwards (turn to **130**).

108

You must stoop to enter this tunnel and you inch forward, feeling the walls ahead with your hands. The ground underfoot is becoming wet and each footstep comes down with a splash. Then you lose your footing and slip down a muddy slide, until eventually you land up to your chest in what feels to be a pool of thick mud. You try in vain to drag yourself from the pool.

The movement is almost imperceptible at first. But without doubt, something smooth and slimy is working its way up your body. And as more of the mud seems to join in the flow, you realize that this creature is very large! Finally the muddy surface breaks and a jelly-like blob is crawling up your chest and neck, drawing the mud behind it. You try to slash it with your claws to keep it away from your face, but your hands pass through the creature as if they were passing through the mud itself. It reaches your mouth and nose and flows deep down your throat and up your nostrils. You cough and splutter, trying desperately to take gulps of air, but it is hopeless. The Mud Slime whose lair you have fallen into cannot be defeated with your bare hands. It kills its prey by suffocation. When your breath runs out and you slide deep down into the mud pool, it will digest your body at its leisure.

109

You sit down once more next to the Orc's carcass and begin snapping off the bones to clean every sliver of flesh from them. But there is little meat left on the body. What you do manage to eat does something to abate your hunger and your attention turns back to the door. No matter how you try, however, there appears to be no way through it.

Hours turn into days, which you spend alone, frustrated and starving, in the room. On the third day, a young Dark Elf arrives at the door and pushes it open. Relieved to have found a way out of the room, you spring up from the seat towards the door. But you so frighten the Elf that he flees from the room in terror, slamming the door shut behind him! No, you think. That is not the way to escape. When the next creature arrives, you must remain motionless until you can seize your opportunity to attack. Unfortunately for you, however, you are becoming weaker and weaker through lack of food. Your skin is being stretched across your skull and your eyes are bulging. When another creature arrives in the room, you will doubtless be too weak to put up a decent fight . . .

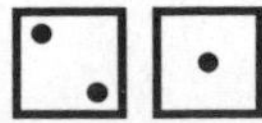

110

You have chosen a crystal club. It is not valuable but, to your way of thinking, it is a beautiful trophy. However, it is quite brittle. If at some time in the future you wish to use it in a battle, turn to reference **333** to find out what happens. But you must remember the number of the reference you are on at the time you choose to use the club, so you may return there afterwards. Now leave the chamber and turn to **257** to continue your journey.

111

The room you walk into is large but cluttered with innumerable items of a biological nature. Bookshelves line one wall to your right, while the wall opposite this is brimming with specimen jars. Straight ahead is a large porthole in the wall, letting ample light into the room, and there is a desk beneath the porthole. A bell rests on the desk among the papers and books, next to a long quill. To one side of the desk a human skeleton is hanging on a hook; to the other is a selection of anatomical charts pinned to the wall. There is a door to the right. Will you examine the desk (turn to **69**)? Will you ring the bell on the desk (turn to **236**)? Or will you examine the specimens in the specimen jars, (turn to **97**)?

112

Alas, this choice will do you no good. Having never come across keys or locks before, you have no way of knowing what a key would look like or what you should do with it! In any case, your large, clumsy fingers could never manage to insert a small key and turn it. Unless you wish to try battering the door down (turn to **128**), you have reached the end of your journey.

113

You rush to the door and grab the handle. 'Simple creature,' says the figure in its gurgling voice. 'You have the audacity to disturb my rest and believe you can simply run away from my wrath? You will pay the penalty. You will learn the real meaning of suffering!' The handle freezes in your hand. It will not budge! Turn to **143**.

114

You follow the trail until you reach another clearing. Turn to **315**.

115

Before you finally leave the adventurers, you may decide to feed on them. If you do, you gain 4 *STAMINA* points. Then you continue. All is silent as you walk carefully along the passage. Eventually, your ears pick up the sound of running water, and the air becomes moist and cool. The sensation would be quite refreshing if it were not for an unpleasant smell, which gets stronger as the sound of the water becomes louder. Soon you find yourself on a ledge in the face of a rocky cliff. Looking out, you can see you are high over a vast cavern through which a river flows. Leading down from your ledge into the centre of the cavern is a flight of rough-cut stairs. This precarious staircase spans the river and is the only way onwards, but the thought of descending the stairs is not one which fills you with enthusiasm. The narrow steps have been made for human-sized feet and your large pads will make your descent awkward. The smell, which was unpleasant before, is now horrendous and seems to be coming from the river itself. Its waters are murky brown and the smell of excrement and decay is overpowering. Nevertheless, your only way on is downwards, so down you must go. *Test your Luck*. If you are Lucky, turn to **166**. If you are Unlucky, turn to **71**.

116

The door leads to a passage which takes you west until you

reach a T-junction where you decide to turn north. Turn to **144**.

117

You hold up the Ring of Truth. When he sees it, the white-haired Elf begins to shift uneasily. 'Look, er . . .' he stammers, 'I made a mistake. Pah! My memory! Getting worse, it is. I have been banished from Stittle Woad for – well, it's a silly thing really – for talking to a friend. I suppose he did happen to be one of Zharradan Marr's legionnaires, but he was a friend to me. At least I *thought* he was until he abused my friendship. And when I invited him to my village . . .' He is becoming quite distressed and does not want to tell you any more. He makes his way off into the woods. Turn to **414**.

118

'A fine display,' says Thugruff, nodding. 'You will be a valuable addition to the legions. Come with me and I'll see you get some food. If I remember right, Hobbits are a favourite of your kind, no? Or maybe you'd prefer to meet some of the other legionnaires. Make this place your home. But watch out for the Rhino-Men. Thick as Zombie blood, they are. And dangerous as Dragon breath!' What do you want to do? If you want to eat, turn to **216**. If you would prefer to mingle with the others, turn to **157**.

119

'*What!*' screams the witch with glazed eyes. 'We asked for Sculliweed, not for the Fishbait Flower! We cannot prepare our Potions of Fortune with Fishbait!' Turn to **222**.

120

You set off quietly through the undergrowth and give the creature a wide berth. It stops and cranes its scrawny neck around as you rustle through some bushes, but then resumes its drinking when it can see nothing. Further downstream you rejoin the river and follow it onwards. Turn to **388**.

121

The necromancer continues: 'I have been developing marrangha for many years now. Previously, my successes have been limited to vermin – rats to Jib-Jibs, mice to Graunies, and the like. You and your colleagues were my first successes with higher animals. Never before had I managed to transmute a *human*. And into such a fine creature, as you will doubtless agree.' You are shocked into a stunned silence. *A human!* And what of these *colleagues* that Marr is speaking of?

'My experiments, at least the ones which survive, are carefully studied and then preserved in the dungeon beneath the village of Coven. All my creations are sent there so that we can assess their abilities. You and your crew were transported there.' *Your crew?* What does he mean? Thoughts are racing through your mind. Some are vague and others are being sparked off as your memory is jolted by his words. Your eyes dart round the room, at the desk, the bed, the wardrobe. It is all starting to come back! Marr smiles slyly.

'I see it is coming back to you now,' he continues. 'You recognize this room. A little dusty now, and a little untidy, but it is as you left it.' Your head is spinning. Everything around you is now so familiar. 'I regret that your officers have not fared so well. Remember Ligge, the first mate? He took the form of a Blood Orc and was placed in charge of the blind fool, Hannicus. And Burgon the cook? You ran into him soon enough. The fat man was transformed into a Hobbit. He joined up with a Shaman and a Strongarm. I think you will remember running into them.' By now you are in a state of utter confusion as your past comes back to you. And after all this time you are back in your own private quarters! Turn to **199**.

The three old women are dressed in tattered rags

122

You follow the passage eastwards, peering ahead as the glowstones flick on to light your way. Eventually you arrive at two doors and you listen for any clues as to what may be beyond. No noise comes from behind the door in the north wall. But there are definite sounds coming from behind the door in the east wall. A heavy breathing is unmistakable and is interrupted by loud snorts. This sounds ominous. If you wish to try the door in the north wall, turn to **154**. If instead you decide to charge the door in the east wall, turn to **263**.

123

You walk towards the old building, still in awe of your new surroundings. As you approach, you can hear voices inside. They are faint at first, but the closer you get, the clearer their words become. 'Tonight is the night, sisters of Romeena!' cackles one of the voices. 'When will it come?' shrieks another, gleefully. 'Quiet!' snaps a third. 'Its presence is close! I can feel it!' You step up to the door of the building and shove it aside. Screams come from the three women within. But not screams of terror; these are more like screams of excitement!

The three old women are dressed in tattered rags. Each has long white hair and a stubbly chin, and rubs her wrinkled hands together in anticipation. They are

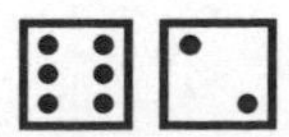

human-like, but smaller. These three ugly witches are the Women of Dree. 'Come in, come in, friend,' beckons one, who is blind. 'We have been waiting for you.' 'Yes!' says another, whose mouth is toothless and black. 'We are the Women of Dree. We are to help you fulfil your destiny!' The third one steps forward and speaks with a voice which hisses like a serpent: 'Yesss, missserable creature – sss! We know *what* you are and *who* you are – sss – though you do not. The godsss have chosen usss to be instrumental – sss – in your dessstiny. We cannot control your action – sss – for you mussst make the final choice. But we can ssshape your dessstiny through our knowledge – sss – and we will watch your progressss!' 'Yes!' adds the blind woman. 'Have you not wondered why one such as you is able to take such steps of wisdom as would befit none less than a scholar?' The three hags turn to one another and chuckle like naughty children. Finally they turn to you.

'But before we tell of your destiny,' starts the black-mouthed witch, 'there is something you must do for us. Sleep tonight and awaken fresh on the morrow. Then set off on a search for us. Bring us what we need for our potions. Bring us Sculliweed root! For this we will tell you what you must know. We will join you on the night of the full moon.' With those words, the women once more begin their cackling, which is beginning to annoy you. You step forward but, before you can reach them, they have faded to nothing! As silence spreads through the building, leaving only the night sounds outside, you reflect on their words. Will you take up their quest? Or would you rather ignore them and make your own way in life? If you wish to undertake their quest, turn to **324**. If you want another destiny, turn to **44**.

124

Rhino-Men are rather dull, bumbling creatures, not known for sharpness of wit. Orcs, on the other hand are more quick-thinking and cannot resist the opportunity to torment. Thus the argument turns into a brawl, as one of the Orcs pushes the Rhino-Man to the limits of his temper. But before any damage has been done, Thugruff appears with armed guards to break up the fight. The two groups are separated. Thugruff takes you aside and into the castle for some food. Turn to **216**.

125

'This is Rosina's cottage,' announces Grog. 'She'll be able to help. But you'll need some money to pay her with, so here's 2 Gold Pieces. Go inside. I'll wait here.' You take the coins and then you must decide what to do. Return to **177** to make your choice.

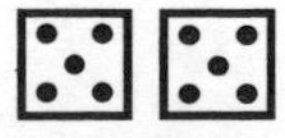

126

You leave the ruins and continue along the path, heading further into the wood. The path becomes quite overgrown and it is evidently not used much. You reach a point where the overgrowth is so thick that the path continues through a sort of tunnel. Vines and creepers droop from the overhanging bush. If you were half your size, you would be able to nip through it quite easily. But you will have to crawl along it. Do you wish to get down on your knees and follow the path (turn to **343**), or will you leave the path and make your way through the wood (turn to **57**)?

127

You creep forward until you are quite close to the creature. As you stand there motionless, patiently waiting for the right moment, a bird flutters down to land on a bush in front of you. You must now decide how you will approach the Ophidiotaur that you have encountered. Roll two dice. If the number rolled equals or exceeds your *SKILL*, turn to **238**. If the number is lower than your *SKILL*, turn to **5**.

128

You charge into the door. It clangs loudly, but does not budge. This only angers you even further and you try again. But once more the door shows no sign of weakening. You, on the other hand, have hurt your arm and must lose 1 *STAMINA* point. If you wish to keep trying, turn to **150**. Otherwise you may look for a key (turn to **112**).

129

The door has no handle. You try shoving against it. At first, the door will not budge, but then you hear a small *click* and your next push is successful. You step into the room and close the door behind you. Again you hear the *click* as the door swings to. The room has a porthole, but curtains have been pulled across it, so the room is dark. In the centre of the room is a large stately chair with ornate carvings on its legs and on its high back. A silent figure is sitting on the chair, wrapped in an elaborate red cape. Its eyes are closed and it is motionless. In one corner of the room is a pile of scattered bones. What will you do:

Investigate the figure on the chair?	Turn to **452**
Search through the pile of bones?	Turn to **64**
Turn round and leave the room?	Turn to **347**

130

You follow the trail northwards. By now it is becoming quite dark. The setting sun gives way to a bright moon which is almost full. Eventually you decide to rest for the night, and you settle down to sleep behind a large boulder. The night passes peacefully and you may gain 4 *STAMINA* points for the rest. The next morning you continue northwards until you reach a fork in the path. A signpost stands by the side of the road. The way to the south is signposted to 'Dree**'. To the north-west, the signpost reads 'Coven' and to the north-east it reads 'Bu Fon Fen'. Will you follow the trail to the north-west (turn to **190**) or the north-east (turn to **134**)?

131

The shopkeeper is amazed when you offer him the gold coin. He shuffles diligently around the shop, gathering together for you a generous collection of provisions. You receive two strips of dried wildcat meat, a bag full of Jimweed root from the sack on the counter, a skin of mulled wine and a fresh loaf of corn bread. You then leave his shop, and sit down outside to eat. Add 4 *STAMINA* points for the meal and continue out of the village by turning to **374**.

132

Had you been a little more observant, you would have noticed how the footprints all avoided the centre of the clearing. As you step towards your chosen trail, your foot sinks deep into mud. This happens too quickly for you to pull yourself back and, to your horror, you find yourself sinking deep into the muddy swamp! There is nothing around for you to grab hold of. If you have a length of rope, turn to **23**. If not, turn to **83**.

133

Marr's eyes open wide. 'But you may not refuse!' His anger is mounting. 'For I am your creator! You may not defy me. Do you not think that, if my power is sufficient to create you, it is also sufficient to punish you? Very well. I give you a glimpse of the living Hell I may make you suffer.' His eyes roll backwards and he mumbles a few incomprehensible words, pointing his hands out of the mirror at you. You wait apprehensively to see what happens. Did you bathe in the magical Elven Dust? If so, turn to **417**. If not, turn to **16**.

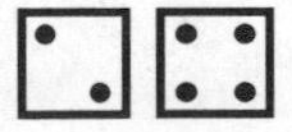

Eventually you arrive at the outskirts of a gloomy village

134

The trail eventually merges with another. You follow it over hills and a rickety wooden bridge which spans a fast-flowing river. Eventually you arrive at the outskirts of a gloomy village. No one seems to take much notice as you arrive. It strikes you that *all* the humans seem to be aged women. They are a dirty lot, wrapped in tattered shawls, and they spit and scratch as they talk to one another, ignoring the scenes of chaos around them. For the other inhabitants are a cacophony of strange creatures – hunchbacked, misshapen, mutilated, wretched things that grub about in the dusty gutters looking for scraps of food. Some hop, some hobble, some cannot move at all and are dying in the street. One legless creature pulls itself towards you by its hands and grabs your ankle. Its bleeding fingers are inflamed and septic and you quickly kick it away. An ugly old crone comes from her hut and flings a bucket of stinking sewage into the street. Immediately, the contents are being devoured ferociously by a dozen of the accursed creatures.

The sight repulses you. Looking around, you notice also that the place seems to be unnaturally dingy. The prevailing colour is black; all homes and clothes – and even the creatures – are black. Dust hangs heavy in the air, and is continually being stirred up by the filthy creatures which live and die in the gutter. It is with some reluctance that the sun shines at all in the cursed village of Dree.

But your anonymity is comforting. You continue towards the centre of town, where many of the old women are milling around a street market. By the side of the market, performers are showing off their acts. You head towards them, but before you reach the market, you hear a woman's voice calling to you from behind. Will you stop to see what she wants? If so turn to **210**. If you want to continue towards the market, turn to **35**.

135

You withdraw your claws and hold your hands out in a sort of gesture of submission. The creature's knife rises once more ... and stabs downwards! This time the blow lands in the centre of your shadow's chest and you collapse in a heap on the floor. The evil spirit has no comprehension of truce. It knows only that it must bring death to any living thing it encounters. For this is the way of the Shadow Stalker.

136

The passage heads north for no more than a few paces before meandering off in a north-easterly direction. Undisturbed layers of dust and dirt on the floor indicate that this corridor is little used. Eventually, the passage straightens and heads east. You soon come to a junction where you may either continue east (turn to **373**) or turn to the north (turn to **404**).

137

Bewildered by your experience, you wander off north along a main passageway. You soon reach a junction where you must decide whether to continue north (turn to **144**) or turn east (turn to **204**).

138

You turn south outside the door and head down to the next door. There is no other way onwards. You open the door. Turn to **15**.

139

You follow the path carefully, watching the way ahead. It seems to lead straight into the heart of the forest and the foliage gets denser as you continue. You come across a building in ruins, apparently a house in days long gone. The doorway remains, however, and a coat of arms decorates its rotting timbers. The coat of arms depicts two symbols: a mailed fist and a morning star. Do you want to search through the ruins (turn to **400**), or will you ignore them and continue along the path (turn to **126**)?

140

You remember the words of the blind wizard Hannicus and you hold up the silver ring before Darramouss. 'What is it? What sort of a gesture is . . . *the Ring of Holy Blessing*! Where did you get that? Give it to me! *This instant!*' His sunken eyes narrow and his gaze becomes fierce and pierces deep into your eyes. For a moment you feel him entering your will and your hand extends the ring towards him! His hand reaches out to take it from you . . .

But suddenly you manage to break out of your trance. You step over to the wall and crush the ring's large bulbous stone against it. The creature behind the desk shrieks as the stone shatters and a sweet-smelling gas fills the air. Darramouss steps back against the north wall and thumps a panel in the wall with his hand. Almost immediately, the wall draws aside and reveals a secret passageway! He takes a step towards the passage, but it is too late. The perfumed aroma has entered his body. Darramouss drops to his knees, clutching his throat. He topples over backwards and sprawls lifeless before you. You have killed the foul creature! You may now choose your next direction, through one of two secret passageways. Will you head to the west (turn to **79**) or the north (turn to **184**)?

141

'*Ssssooo!*' hisses one of the witches, holding her hands high. 'The creature sssucceedsss!' 'Sculliweed root!' exclaims another. 'Then indeed we are to be instruments of your destiny! Give us the root. Then we may tell you what you must know.' You handover the plants to the witches.

'So be it,' starts the black-mouthed witch. 'The test has been passed. We must tell this creature of its past, its present and of its future. You are a creature of Zharradan Marr, this you know. You are his creature as he is ours. But now you must destroy our unholy son, for he seeks to alter the very balance of nature. Evil must not triumph over all; Chaos cannot reign supreme. For the balance is vital. We cannot get near Zharradan, for he knows that we would prevent his plans. But his vanity is great. *You* are his creation. He will not turn you from his door. And when you meet him, you must destroy him. When you do this you will save the balance. And your own truth will be revealed. We may not tell you more lest your thirst for knowledge be quenched and you abandon your destiny.'

The sightless witch continues: 'We do not know how you may meet Zharradan. But we can offer you one more ally. In Knot Oak Wood you must meet the white-haired Elf, Daga Weaseltongue. He can tell you how to enter the

Galleykeep, for he has been there himself. But beware his words! Weaseltongue speaks untruths as if they were truths. Should his sentence begin with a vowel, then it is truth. Otherwise trust not his words. But this Ring of Truth may help you. Make sure you show it to him.' They place a shiny jewelled ring on your finger. Should you meet Weaseltongue, he may offer you some information. You may gain more reliable information by revealing the witches' ring and deducting 50 from the reference you are on at the time, for you are able to see through his lies.

The witches continue: 'We know not where in Knot Oak Wood he is, but we know this. The Ophidiotaur is his ally. He will lead you to Weaseltongue. And we can lead you to the Ophidiotaur. Just sleep when we have left. This is all we can say. Now we must leave you. But your gift to us will be used to produce a Potion of Luck. We shall try to bestow its powers on you from afar. Farewell.'

With these words, the wind picks up once more and a gale whistles through the tree. The images of the witches fade in the wind and calm settles around you. A faint breeze blows across your brow and it seems to soothe you. You lie down once more on the ground beneath the tree and drift off to sleep. You may increase your *LUCK* score to its *Initial* level, as this encounter has indeed been fortunate.

When you awaken, you do not recognize your new surroundings. You are no longer under a solitary tree in a barren landscape. Instead you are in a rich forest! Birds twitter high above in the branches of the many trees which shade you from the sun. You look around and find that you are lying beside a flowing river, whose cool waters are gently spraying your face. You feel invigorated and you may restore your *STAMINA* to its *Initial* level. Turn to **423**.

142

A foul smell wafts along the passage and seems to get stronger as you continue. The air becomes cool and moist and you eventually hear the splashings of flowing water. The glowstones light up the way ahead and you can see that the passage turns into a narrow arch of rock stretching across a wide chasm. A murky river runs through the chasm and it is this river that is responsible for the stink which fills the area. The bridge is so narrow that, for a creature of your bulk, the crossing will be extremely hazardous. But there is no other way onwards. You step on to the near side of the bridge. *Test your Luck.* If you are Lucky, turn to **221**. If you are Unlucky, turn to **193**.

143

Your anger grows as the figure steps forward. The candle throws a flicker of light across its face and you can see that an expression of fury knits the creature's brow. You can also see flames burning in each of the creature's eyes, but perhaps these are only reflections of the candle flame. Nevertheless, your own eyes are held fast by the creature's stare. A hand reaches out and steely fingers close around your neck! You begin to choke, and are unable to do anything while you are transfixed by the creature's burning eyes. Finally you break its gaze and force its hand from your neck. You must resolve your battle with the creature:

MASTER OF HELLFIRE *SKILL 14* *STAMINA 14*

If you manage to reduce it to a *STAMINA* of 2 or less, turn to **266**.

144

The passage twists and turns until it leads you into a wide cavern. You pause to survey the way ahead. There are no creatures to be seen and all is still except for a dull humming which is forming an almost unnoticeable background noise. The wall to the left is riddled with large holes like a huge honeycomb and many of the holes are lit with a yellow glow. In the centre of the cavern, a few steps off the path, is what seems to be a small pool of shimmering liquid. Do you want to pass through this chamber as quickly as possible (turn to **239**)? Do you want to investigate the light coming from the holes (turn to **24**)? Or will you have a look at the pool of shimmering liquid (turn to **180**)?

145

The Toadman feints at you with his trident and you leap into action. Resolve your battle with the creature:

TOADMAN	*SKILL 9*	*STAMINA 9*

If you defeat him, turn to **287**.

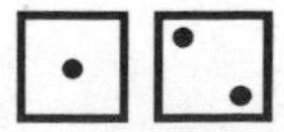

146

You follow the nervous shopkeeper round and corner him. His terrified expression turns to one of astonishment when you hold out the gold coins. When he sees that you have come to eat his wares, not him, he rushes off round his shop to serve you. He gathers together for you a generous collection of provisions. First of all he gives you three small bags of Abundance Nuts. You also receive two strips of dried wildcat meat, a bag full of Jimweed root from the sack on the counter, a skin of mulled wine and a fresh loaf of corn bread. You leave his shop and sit down outside to eat. You eat everything but the Abundance Nuts, as the shopkeeper recommended that you take them with you for later in your journey. Add 4 *STAMINA* points for the meal. You may eat a bag of Abundance Nuts at any time during the rest of your adventure except when in battle. Each bag will restore 4 *STAMINA* points when eaten. You can now continue out of the village by turning to **374**.

147

There is something solid inside the sack. You fumble with the cloth, but cannot seem to find a way inside.

Eventually you become frustrated, pick the sack up and shake it.

A small wooden casket drops out. As it lands on the ground, the catch flips open. Inside is a flask and the bump has loosened the stopper. You watch as a green liquid inside bubbles and boils, turning to a green gas which slowly seeps from the neck of the flask and drifts upwards in the air before you. You are mesmerized by the swirling mists which gradually become recognizable as a face! It is thin, with angular features and is decidedly human. Eventually its eyes open and stare into yours. 'Jih bvf ebffne bwbk fnf defrp mom yoslvm bfr! Whpocbllsa p not hfevb ppv rupfot pngv fs. T hf chfbvfnl yebp dj fseh bvfe tbkfneth fjri pp sjt jpns. M yo gjf tijsig rb ntfd. Fpro bfttf repro fpr owp rsfem ye rfl fbsfe bfs tpws opno ypvuth fevnd frstbnd jng iyp vu dfsjrf. May you use your gift wisely.' Having said these words, the green gas swirls once more and the face disappears. As if sucked by force, it disappears once more into the flask. Once it is inside, the flask and the casket begin to fade. Moments later they have disappeared! But your unintentional encounter with the Vapour of Tongues has been fortunate. The spirit has bestowed on you its gift of language. From now on you will understand most languages as spoken or written. You may translate coded speech by turning to reference **283**, where you will find the secret of the code.

148

You decide to follow the passage east, to your right. Your first steps are slow, as you take in the encounter with the Dwarf. After a few paces, the corridor turns north. You approach a stout wooden door and must make a decision. Will you smash the door from its hinges and continue? Or will you give up on this route and return to the Dwarf's corpse? Roll one die. If the result is 1 or 2, turn to **419**. If the roll is 3–6, turn to **72**.

149

You quicken your pace along the passage, away from the stink of the stream. Suddenly, your foot steps forward into *nothing* and you are falling downwards through the air! Your bulky body picks up speed quickly, but luckily the fall is not a lengthy one. You land in a heap at the bottom of the pitfall you have walked straight into. If it were not for your bulk, you might have landed unharmed on the straw-strewn floor. But you groan as you nurse your right leg. Blood is seeping from between the scales and you have twisted your knee badly. You must deduct 3 *STAMINA* points for the fall. Now turn to **257**.

150

You try beating the door with your fists. It has been specially made to withstand batterings of this sort and all you succeed in doing is injuring your hands. Lose 1 *STAMINA* point. If you wish to continue trying to break down the door, turn to **398**. Otherwise you will have to search for the key (turn to **112**).

151

Angrily you slash at the fortune-teller. Resolve your battle with Rosina of Dree:

ROSINA OF DREE	*SKILL 8*	*STAMINA 7*

If you defeat her, turn to **264**.

152

You step forward and swing your fist hard into the glass. The sound of the impact echoes round the room. But, rather than the shattering sound you were expecting, the noise is a deep rumbling, as the mirror vibrates. 'Fool!' screams Zharradan Marr. 'Did you really think the portal between my world and yours would be so easy to destroy? Why, if that were so, I would be at the mercy of a simple accident – or even rough weather!' He is right: it would indeed have been foolish of him to be left so vulnerable. 'My mirror cannot be harmed; you waste your time and mine. I can see you have no desire to join me. But our futures are intertwined. If you will not consider yourself my friend, then you must become my enemy!' The image of Marr fades from the reflection and your own begins to reappear. You react quickly in frustration, and prepare to try another blow, but this time with all your might. Turn to **302**.

153

The easterly passage leads you down a slight incline and along a narrow route which is cold and wet underfoot. The glowstones light your way once more. You soon find yourself sloshing and splashing along the corridor, and you look down to find that your feet are walking, not through ordinary mud, but through a thick, jelly-like substance which appears to be dark blue in colour. The passage bends sharply round to the north, and you plod onwards. Your progress may be unpleasant, but you feel no ill effects from the slime. Eventually, you reach a junction. Ahead, straight up the corridor, the slime changes to an even darker shade of blue. To the right, a single step upwards leads to a dry passageway heading east. If you wish to continue heading north, turn to **232**. If you step out of the slime and head east, turn to **84**.

154

The door is locked. It may be possible to break it down, but you could damage your shoulder, as the timbers are heavy. If you wish to try breaking the door, turn to **396**. If instead you would prefer to try the door in the east wall, turn to **263**.

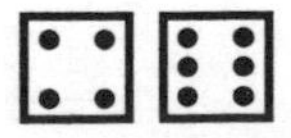

155

You approach the orb. Its perch is only slightly above your head and you reach up to take it in your hands. But as your fingers close around it, you suddenly leap away! Although its appearance gives no warning, it feels red hot to the touch! Lose 1 *STAMINA* point for the burns. Then a shape begins to form in the crystal. Moments later, a shrivelled, death-like human face within the orb opens its eyes and glares at you. Its mouth begins to speak and an eerie voice booms out along the corridor: 'Fp plj shicrfb tvrf. Djdiypv uthjn k iypvucpvl duthj fvfe thfep rbop fodbrr bmp vss? Np n fem byat pvch umy us bcr fd ecr ystb la fpr oj tij simy ify fseb nd afb rs. Bn damy awf bppns obsa ypvus hbl lasff.' What will you do now? Do you wish to wait and see what the face in the orb does next (turn to **428**), or will you leave it and either take the other branch of this passage (turn to **81**) or return to the crossroads and go west (turn to **213**) or east (turn to **50**)?

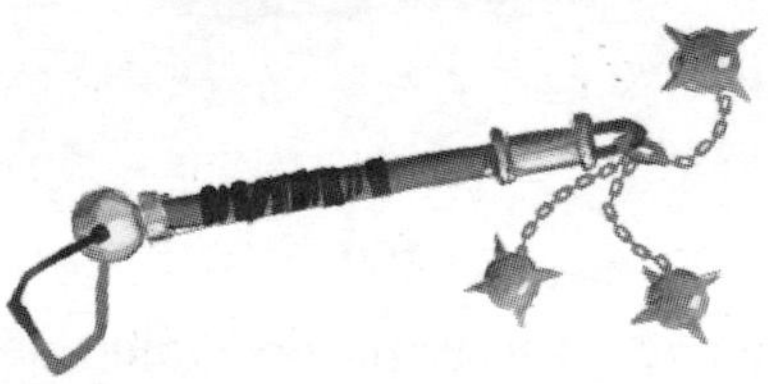

156

You follow the passage to the east and you find yourself wandering down a long, straight passage. After some time, you arrive at a crossroads and you must choose which way to turn. As you are considering your choice, you are startled when all the glowstones you are relying on to light your way go out simultaneously! You are now stranded in the pitch-blackness! Which way will you go:

North? Turn to **354**
South? Turn to **212**
Straight on? Turn to **310**

157

You leave Thugruff and move around the courtyard, mixing with the others. They are an unruly lot, spoiling for a fight. Each wears the studded black leather tunic which is the *Galleykeep* uniform. Each also wears a medallion around his neck with his number on. You decide to mix with some of the groups to try to learn what you can about the place. Will you mix with a group of Orcs and Rhino-Men squabbling in the corner of the courtyard (turn to **377**), or a group of Goblins and Elves in the centre of the courtyard (turn to **284**)?

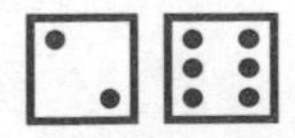

158

The door opens into a large room, which is not the dark, dingy room you were expecting. It is well lit by sunlight streaming in through a large porthole in the far wall. Bookshelves line the walls, along with charts of the heavens. A desk in front of the porthole is laden down with books, charts and strange devices, and other bulky pieces of scientific apparatus stand on the floor. There are two side doors leading from the room and one is opening to let someone in.

'That's right. Come in, come in. Don't bother to knock. My room is your room. Bah! I'll not return to this cursed ship ever again. When we reach Dree, I shall leave and ride to Blacksand. You won't catch me on one of these damned cloud-ships again, that's for sure.' He is an old man with long greying hair. He mutters away to himself, wrapped up in his own thoughts. Finally he turns towards you and looks over the top of his half-moon eyeglasses. 'Yes? Well, come on! Lost your tongue, have you? Or are you just so stupid that you can't remember what you came for. If that Vallaska Roue wants another storm to appear, just so he can strike another poor Ophidiotaur with a bolt of lightning, tell him not to waste my time, and . . .' He has noticed your look of bewilderment. 'Look, you great brute, are you in the right place? Did you intend to visit me, Nimbicus? When people visit a Weather Mage, they normally want something. So?

Ye gods! This creature's got the mind of a Jib-Jib. *Fearsome out of sight; feeble in the light.* Look. If you want something, speak to me. If not, get out!' He is getting impatient. Do you want to leave the room? If so, turn to **459**. If you want to search round his room, turn to **303**. Otherwise you may attack him (turn to **254**).

159

You allow him to take the ring and he steps back towards the wall. You have found the conversation interesting, but now you are anxious to move on. Turn to **138**.

160

As the creature dies, you sink your teeth into its arm to taste its juicy flesh. But then you remember the other two adventurers. The red-robed figure is facing you, pointing the little finger of each hand at you and mumbling. The shiny human has grabbed a sword – similar, you remember, to the Dwarf's, but larger – and is shouting to the other: 'Cpn tr plojt simjn dishbmbn! Jtim by abfeb blfe tp olf bda vsu tpothb taswj nf bfbr dacvr!' You cannot fight both at once. Which will you direct your attention to? *Test your Luck.* If you are Lucky, turn to **292**. If you are Unlucky, turn to **48**.

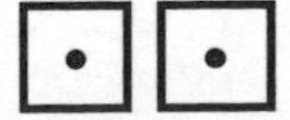

161

The room is roughly circular, with doors in the north, south and west walls. Around the walls, in between the doors, are dark arches – a total of six – which are large enough for you to enter. But from your position it is impossible to know how deep they are. The voices which you heard earlier have stopped, as if your entrance has surprised whoever – or whatever – was talking. There is no sign of any living creature in the room. You step into the centre and you are startled when the door slams shut behind you! You must now decide what to do. Will you leave the room through one of the doors (turn to **405**) or stay to investigate the room further (turn to **104**)?

162

A cloud drifts overhead and blots out the moon. In pitch-blackness, the going is difficult for you. You grope your way along, trying to be as cautious as possible. Suddenly you step into an unseen ditch! You lurch forwards and your head cracks against a low branch. Consciousness fades, and you slump into the ditch. When you open your eyes once more, it is light! You rub your sore head (you must lose 2 *STAMINA* points for the injury) and pick yourself up. You continue your journey through the wood. Turn to **244**.

163

Had you been a little more observant, you would have noticed how all the footprints avoided the centre of the clearing. As you step across towards your chosen trail, your foot sinks deep into mud. This happens too quickly for you to pull yourself back and, to your horror, you find yourself sinking deep into the muddy swamp! There is nothing around for you to grab hold of. If you have a length of rope, turn to **23**. If not, turn to **83**.

164

You creep cautiously and somewhat clumsily around the outside wall, keeping well out of the way of the black circle. It continues to shimmer mysteriously as you edge round it, but nothing happens. When you have passed it, the passageway narrows again to a moderate size and heads due east. You follow it until you reach another bend, this time to the north. But this passageway is quite short and ends at a wooden door. When you listen at the door, you can hear voices – either two or three different ones. The conversation rises and falls in pitch as if the creatures (or humans) were locked into a long discussion. This is your only way onwards. Will you try the door and attempt to creep slowly into the room (turn to **276**), or will you attempt to surprise whatever is inside by charging into the room with claws drawn (turn to **66**)?

165

Roll one die. If you roll 1–3, you decide to head north into the wide cave entrance ahead of you (turn to **408**). If you roll 4–6, you take the narrower cave entrance which leads west (turn to **344**).

166

The descent is dangerous and several times you lose your footing and stumble on the slippery steps. But your luck holds out and you finally arrive at the foot of the staircase. The stench of the river is especially foul to your sensitive nostrils and your eyes search desperately for a way out of the cavern. You discover two openings in the rock-face ahead of you. One leads to the west and the other to the north. Will you continue north (turn to **358**) or turn west (turn to **77**)?

167

Whiteleaf beams with pride at the chance to tell of his adventures. 'My family is well respected in our village,' he starts. 'My mother – rest her soul – was a lady-in-waiting to our Queen Ethilesse, while my father served in the Royal Guard. I earn my living tending our aviaries, for we of Ethelle Amaene are great bird-lovers. Our birds are trained to work for us, gathering food for our cooking-pots and herbs for our potions. Anyone who is trained in the art of bird-caring can communicate with the birds, whose wisdom is great. They know the solutions to most of our problems and want to help us. They carry me about in the woods and, any minute now, I expect Cheree and Chitta will arrive to take me back to patch up my wounds.' He looks anxiously into the skies. Birds fly about above the trees, but none come down into the clearing. After waiting for a few moments, he decides to leave and sets off in the direction you arrived from, with a wave and another expression of thanks. Turn to **414**.

168

You make your way cautiously towards the door, horrified by the sight of the bodies slowly disappearing. As you step across one of the pug-nosed creatures, your foot catches something in the air. A screeching noise from somewhere is followed by a yelp of pain from you, as sharp teeth clamp on to your foot! Lose 2 *STAMINA* points. The shock causes you to tumble over and this frees your foot. But as you lift yourself up, something is happening in the room. Three shapes are materializing in front of you. Turn to **447**.

The huge Clawbeast, whose peace you have disturbed, slashes at you with its deadly talons!

169

Pretending not to understand, you stare at him wide-eyed. 'Stupid creature!' he says scornfully. 'You'll not be much use outside if you don't speak the language. Got lost, did you? Turn round and go back the way you came, serpent-face. And if it's a journey you fancy, jump into the Bilge water and see where it takes you!' The guard laughs and turns back to his room. The only way you are going to get past him is by attacking. Turn to **73**.

170

Fury builds up within you! You step back and with a loud roar you charge into the door. The hinges crack and are ripped off as the door crashes inwards. There is no furniture or decoration in the cave that greets your eyes. There is a seat carved out of the stone, but the room is clearly the dwelling of a captive or slave. Your eyes then switch to the room's inhabitant – and your reaction is swift! The huge Clawbeast, whose peace you have disturbed, slashes at you with its deadly talons! You lurch back and avoid the creature's onslaught. But this attack serves only to fuel your rage. Your own sharp claws slide out and you turn to the Clawbeast. Resolve this combat:

CLAWBEAST	*SKILL 9*	*STAMINA 14*

If you defeat the creature, turn to **389**.

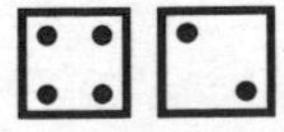

171

Your hands comb the walls for signs of an entrance or any other way onwards, but in vain. You are in a dead end. You will have to return to the crossroads and take either the passage to the north (turn to **354**) or the passage to the south (turn to **212**).

172

The northward passage is short and ends at a stout wooden door. If you wish to force the door open, turn to **15**. If you would prefer to return to the main passage and follow it west, turn to **149**.

173

'*Fool!*' cackles the blind witch. 'Do you think we cannot tell the difference between Sculliweed and Purity Plant? What use is Purity Plant to us? We must prepare our Potions of Fortune, not cleansing balms.' Turn to **222**.

174

You ignore the old Rhino-Man's cries and continue northwards, following the trail through the wood. After many hours you reach a clearing. Turn to **366**.

175

Your attempts at freeing yourself are all to no avail. Night comes, followed by the morning sunrise. Birds are beginning to circle round you and you are feeling decidedly weak. But in the distant sky, a tiny shape comes into view. As it comes closer, you realize it is not a bird. It is much too large to be any living creature and its size eventually frightens off the birds circling above you. When it comes close enough for you to see, you can make out its shape clearly, although it is something with which you are not familiar. A huge vessel, with billowing sails above it, is heading towards you! You watch as it gets closer and closer, and eventually stops over you. A pole is lowered over the side. It grabs the rope from which you are hanging and hoists you on to the deck. You are too tired and weak to resist as rough hands shove your neck through the nearby guillotine. This foraging expedition has been most successful. The crew of the *Galleykeep* will have a hearty meal tonight ...

176

If you simply rest by the pond, turn to **453**. If you drink from it, turn to **391**. If you would prefer to bathe in it, turn to **26**.

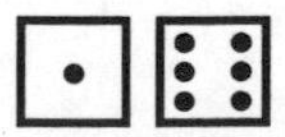

177

The trail leads to a small copse growing on a solitary hillock which is the only noticeable feature of the otherwise flat countryside. When you reach the hillock, you can see a face of bare rock. Set in this rock are a number of small cave entrances facing the trail. In the centre of these, backed up to the rock-face, is a hut, and smoke drifts lazily from its chimney. Someone is at home. Looking out westwards beyond the hillock, the ground is flat for as far as you can see. Your eyes scan the inhospitable wastes of the Windward Plain. Nothing about its bleakness looks inviting. You turn your attentions once more to the hut. Will you enter through the front door (turn to **252**), or will you try one of the caves set in the rock-face (turn to **340**)?

178

You turn from the dead skeleton. But this is a mistake. For as soon as your eyes have left the undead creature, its bones knit quickly together. It grabs the knives and springs on your back! You must continue your fight with the physician:

QUIMMEL BONE	*SKILL 8*	*STAMINA 7*

If you defeat it, turn to **407**.

179

You can find no clues as to how to get further along the passageway. Angry and frustrated, you stamp your foot on the ground and smack the rocky wall with your fist. This was not a wise thing to do. The rock overhead was loose but delicately balanced, and now the roof and walls come crashing in on top of you. You have indeed come to a dead end in the dungeons of Zharradan Marr.

180

You leave the path and walk towards the shimmering liquid, treading carefully across the rough boulders. As you get close, you see something that causes you to stop, blink and look again. Out of the corner of your eye, you are *sure* you saw the liquid suddenly rise in the air, then fall almost immediately to become smooth once more. But this happened without any sound. You take another careful step forward and, as you are now next to the 'pool', you realize to your horror the mistake you have made . . .

This is no pool at all. The shimmering surface is in fact the gloss on the wings of a Giant Hornet, which is feeding in a crevice. As you look down on the creature, it turns its large, ugly head up at you, mandibles clicking hungrily. With a flutter of its wings, it takes to the air and hovers ready to attack! Aiming its sting at your chest, it plummets towards you. Turn to **332**.

Any pauses in the work are rewarded by painful slashes from these whips

181

This plant has mysterious properties. You may or may not get the opportunity to find out what it can be used for. If asked to present this plant to someone later in the adventure, remember the number eighty-one. Now you may leave the river-bank by turning to **18**.

182

After following the tunnel for some time, you begin to hear clinking noises and voices from somewhere ahead. You round a corner and enter a large chamber lit by the flickering light of many torches, where creatures of all sizes and shapes are swinging implements at the rock-face. Their hard work is watched by several large, heavily armoured guards, who brandish long bullwhips, and any pauses in the work are rewarded by painful slashes from these whips. The creatures at work seem to be digging out the rock-face and loading it into trucks. The trucks are then pushed along the tracks you have found by other minions. Will you try to creep through the chamber, keeping out of sight of the guards (turn to **78**)? Or will you step behind one of the trucks and see where it is to be pushed to (turn to **94**)?

183

The path winds tortuously through the forest and you follow it up hill and down dale. Although you pass many types of birds and other small animals, there seems to be nothing menacing about the wood and you are soon feeling quite carefree – until you notice that the wood has been changing very subtly. The general colour of the forest is imperceptibly changing from rich browns and greens to duller shades of the same colours. You are entering the Forest of Spiders.

When you first notice this, you think little of it. But now the atmosphere of the wood is changing too. The chirping of songbirds is replaced by the cawing of crows; previously there were brightly coloured butterflies flitting from flower to flower, but now only black and brown buzzing insects are to be seen. Your steps slow to a more cautious pace. Your eyes dart from tree to tree as if you were expecting something to spring out at any moment. But there is nothing. Then a noise behind you catches your attention and you twist round to a startling sight. Standing directly in the middle of the path behind you is a tall tree! Its gnarled branches are dead and twisted; its trunk is stout and knotted. *But you are certain that it was not there when you passed along that part of the path!* Will you go back to investigate the tree (turn to **76**), or will you quicken your pace away from it (turn to **102**)?

184

You are glad to be out of the room and away from the vile creature. You take long strides and follow the passage north. It turns to the west and your nose twitches at the foul smell of sewage. A strong wooden bridge takes you across the stinking Bilge water. You are forced to hold your breath as you cross, but on the other side you quickly leave the filthy river and the passageway turns once more to the north. You arrive at a heavy door carved out of the rock which blocks the way onwards. As you are considering what to do, the door opens.

A burly, dark-skinned human stands in the doorway. His face is badly scarred and one of his eyes is half-closed. His lips curl back in a sneer which shows his few, dirty teeth. 'Well?' he asks. 'What is it? Has Parramouss sent you? Have you permission to leave Marr's dungeons? Come on! Where's your tongue?' Will you nod to let him know you have been allowed to leave by Darramouss (turn to **3**), will you play stupid and see what he does next (turn to **169**), or will you grab him in your claws and do battle (turn to **73**)?

185

The little creature screams in horror as you raise your foot over its head. 'Lfbv femfeb lpnf,' it squeals, as it swings the sharp sword in its hand towards your leg. But the blow is weak and glances off your tough scales; you feel nothing. A second later you are looking down with mixed feelings at the lifeless form of the Dwarf. Will you examine the body (turn to **399**), will you attempt to hide the body down the passageway you have just come from (turn to **218**), or will you quickly leave the area (turn to **248**)?

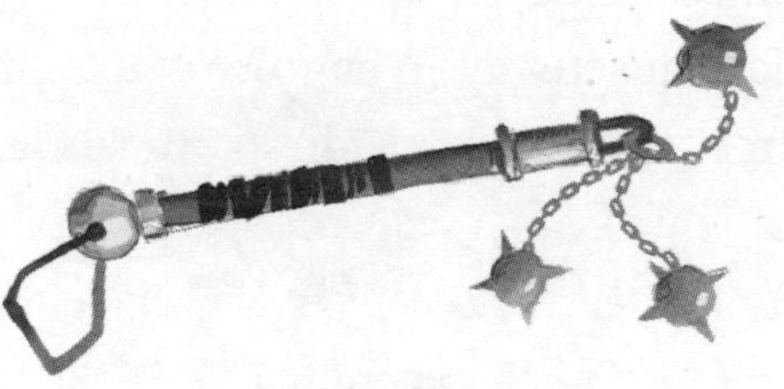

186

You cannot resist the temptation to find out what is bound inside the sack. You squat down next to the squirming figure and prod it with your hand. It squeals pitifully and its hopeless attempts to wriggle free become frantic. Suddenly the creature's smell hits your nostrils. This smell has a curious effect on you. You are spoiling for battle. But alongside this, your mouth is watering; you have the compelling desire to sink your teeth into a large chunk of flesh to satisfy your appetite. Thus your craving is both hunger and rage, and your passion is uncontrollable!

Your talons slide from your fingertips and you slash furiously at the ropes binding the sack. They fray and snap, and out falls a battered and bloodied little human-like creature. It is clean-shaven, with brown hair on its head, its hands and even on its feet, which are not covered with footwear. The creature's weary head rolls around towards you and its eyes gaze into yours as if to plead for pity. But when it realizes what you are, a look of stark horror spreads across its face! It screams in anguish and fights desperately to break free. But it is no use. You have the little fellow securely in your grip. Your fangs sink first of all into its neck to quell the struggles. Then you feast greedily on its soft body. You may restore your *STAMINA* to its *Initial* value. When you are finished with the Hobbit, you look up along the passageway. You are startled to discover that you are being watched! In the darkness down the passage is a mysterious figure. Turn to **63**.

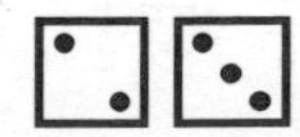

187

The second adventurer carried, around his waist, a short wooden shaft with a two-edged metal plate on the end. You pick up this axe and turn it over in your hands inquisitively. Grasping the shaft awkwardly, you raise it over your head and bring it down on a rock by your side. The rock shatters. But unfortunately the shaft also breaks and the metal head goes skidding along the corridor away from you. As if in response, a glowstone suddenly lights in the passageway ahead! A tiny face pokes round the bend and surveys the scene. You see the face only for a moment, but the effect is immediate. Turn to **403**.

188

The old man fusses about with his jars of potions. He is nervous in your presence and his hands shake, rattling the bottles. 'I-I think th-this will do it!' he stammers, pouring the contents of two bottles into a saucer. 'C-c-come here and put your head over this saucer.' You are suspicious, but you do as he says. When your head is in position, he grinds a little powder into the liquid with his fingers. The effect is startling and you draw your face back as the liquid vaporizes as thick brown smoke. You cannot help but inhale the smoke, and you cough and splutter, rubbing your watering eyes. But the medicine-man has not deceived you. His herbal medicine is able to remove curses and the effects of any curse you may have had cast upon you is now neutralized. Still coughing and rubbing your eyes, you leave the shack and head out of town. Turn to **374**.

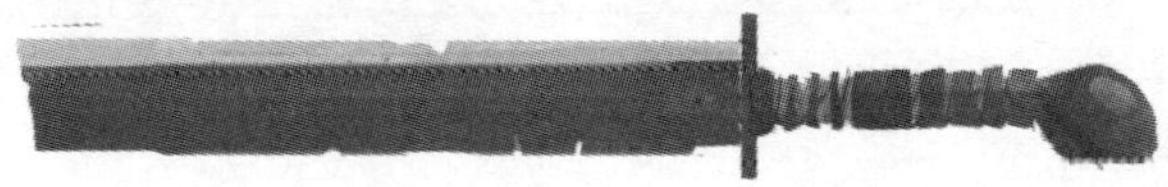

189

You leave the clearing and stomp off through the undergrowth. Birds twitter excitedly as you crash through the woods and you turn your head up to watch them. Far in the distance you see a black shape, hovering in the sky. It is too large to be a bird and has none of the familiar shapes of a flying creature. The *Galleykeep*! You remember Weaseltongue's words. But how will you ever be able to find a hidden trap among all the trees? *Test your Luck*. If you are Lucky, turn to **341**. If you are Unlucky, turn to **376**.

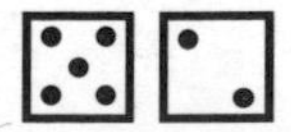

190

As you follow the trail, the vegetation changes. The flat grassland begins to be replaced by taller reeds. The going underfoot becomes muddier, until eventually you reach an area where bulrushes tower over your head. Will you continue into the rushes (turn to **307**), or will you head back to the junction and take the north-east trail instead (turn to **134**)?

191

You press on northwards, following the trail through the wood. If you are hungry, you may try to catch some food by turning to **368**. If you are not hungry, turn to **229**.

192

Once more you pick up the parchment and stare at it. The writing is not neat, but you can just about make out the following message:

'Bjp grbp hyapfoz o mbrrap bgfen jnf tyet hrff: . . . th vsu cbmf embr rat pobbbn dpn othfephy sjcbla wprld obnd atbk fe rffvgfe jnihj sipwn. Ba strb ngfenfth frwprldowhjc hip ccvp jfsen pospbc fej nit hfew prldo wfe mpr tblsa knpw. Ba wprl dopf ojllvsjpn oj niw hjchiw hfr fehfe bpp fb rse tpo bfe hfej sanpt. Bnda bawp rldo jni whj chith psfesf brc hjngifpr ohjmi wpv ldujnstfb daf jndit hfmsf lvfs. Hfeh bsab vt upn fewfbkn fss ejnihj sin fwew prld obndat hbt ajsibac ry stbla clvbuw hjch imbyab fev sfde tpodfs trp yofprfv fret hfegbtfwb yabf t wffne pvruw pr ldobndahjs.' Jfi btas pmf etjm fejn ithfe fvt vrf eypv ubfl jfvf eypv uhbvf elpcb tf det hf efnt rbnc fet pombrrsan fth frwpr ld odfdvct uth fep bg fe nvmbfrebbpv fef rpmoth ferfffrfn cfe ypvubrf epnobt ath fetj mf eb ndatv rnut poth jsi rf ffr fncf. Jfiypv ub r fecp rrf ctey pv uwjl lim f ftet hf enf crpm bncfr. Fproh b vjng it hfegp pdo fpr tvnfe tp ofjn dithjsip br chmfnt eypvumb ya rfstp rfeypvru lvckus cp rfetp ojt sij njtjbl al fvfl.

After you have studied it for some time, you leave the room. Will you leave through the door in the east wall (turn to **365**) or the door in the south wall (turn to **450**)?

The creature suddenly sits bolt upright and two streams of fire from its eyes burn into your own!

193

In the centre of the bridge, you glance down. The sight of the filthy water down below is unnerving and for an instant you lose your balance on the slippery bridge! Your fate is to plunge head first down into the disgusting Bilgewater below, never to emerge alive, unless your *SKILL* is great. Roll two dice. If you roll a number greater than or equal to your *SKILL* score, your adventure ends here, plunging down into the foul river below. If you roll a number less than your *SKILL*, then you regain your footing (turn to **221**).

194

You bend down to grasp the creature's body, which lies face down on the floor in front of you. You turn it over, unaware of the deadly surprise in store. For as the light falls on the creature's face, you see that the creature you fought has disappeared! In its place is the grotesque head of a long-dead Zombie, whose rotten flesh is being eaten by crawling grubs. Its fiery eyes are still alight and they once more capture your gaze. As you stare transfixed, the creature suddenly sits bolt upright and two streams of fire from its eyes burn into your own! You scream in agony at the pain, and a slow smile spreads across the creature's face of death. It has only just begun its attack. Your death will be slow and painful.

195

You growl impatiently at the medicine-man, but he is adding ingredients to his herbal broth and continues to ignore you. Finally you will wait no more. You step up to him and swipe at the boiling broth. Most of the liquid splashes up into the face of the medicine-man, who screams in agony and clutches his eyes. He falls to the floor, sobbing and moaning. When he eventually looks up, his sightless eyes search aimlessly around the room. He is totally blind and is in no fit state to help you. You may leave him and the village by turning to **374**. Or, if you prefer, you may put him out of his misery (turn to **456**).

196

She shuffles off into the house for your Potion of Healing. You take a sniff of the yellowy liquid and gag. It smells disgusting! 'Come now, it will do you good,' coaxes the hag. 'Drink it all up. And all your problems will vanish.' You take a deep breath and swallow the contents of the bowl. It washes down your throat, leaving a bitter taste in your mouth. You cough a few times, but soon it has settled. You turn to go.

'There really is no need for you to go so quickly,' chuckles the old crone. 'You may as well get to like it here.' You are puzzled by her words. 'For you will not be leaving for some time. After all, now that Shanga cannot serve me, and I cannot keep up this home without a slave, can you blame me?' You are still not sure what she is talking about, but you notice you are feeling warm – and even *happy* – inside. The old witch now seems to be not so much a dirty hag but more a kindly soul and her words are like music to your ears. 'There are many chores that you will busy yourself with,' she continues. 'And you will be fed well. Look – Shanga can be your first meal. You will be happy spending the rest of your life in Dree.' And every day you will receive *another* tasty bowlful of my special Potion of Obedience.'

197

When strapped to your arm, this plate will make a useful shield in battle. While using this shield, you may add 1 point to your *SKILL*. In addition, any more metallic discs of gold and silver may be carried in the pouch on the back. Finally, the spike on the front will allow you to break down doors more easily. If you are told to lose 1 *STAMINA* point when attempting to break down a door, you may ignore this penalty (if the damage is more severe, then even your shield will not help you). Now leave the chamber and turn to **257** to continue your journey.

198

Hooo-oo-oo. A bird's cry pierces the night air as you step through the mysterious stones, looking for anything unusual. You pause by a tall, smooth, black stone and study the writing on it. 'Here lies Sogarth Foulblade, smitten in the Sculliweed plague, leaving good wife Millinia and sons Chard and Seth. May Chlorissian take his soul.' Not far from this is an ornate stone covered in small carvings of winged creatures and fierce-looking gargoyles. Its inscription is in smaller print and you must step right up to read it: 'The ground is cursed where I, Donag Haddurag, lie. Let not man or beast dare set foot on my grave, lest he feel my wrath and the ground open up to disembowel his miserable body. Donag Haddurag, necromancer of Coven.'

You look to the ground and see your own foot planted squarely on the centre of his grave! Will you wait to see whether or not the threat is an idle boast (turn to **411**), or turn and find somewhere to hide (turn to **67**)?

199

Marr's eyes open wider and he leans forward. His head protrudes from the mirror as if it were a pool of water, held on to the wall by magic. 'Now I can help you, *but you must give me the Half-Orc's knapsack*!' What can he want with Grog's knapsack? It contains only a few of the creature's possessions and a box ... Of course! The box! You now remember that you have seen similar boxes twice before. Once just before you found you were developing control of your destiny and again just before you started to be able to understand the languages of other creatures. Perhaps this box is what he is after. Marr holds his hand out and it too emerges from the mirror into the room.

'Vallaska Roue has failed me,' he says. 'For the *Galleykeep* has not enabled us to find the Elf village. There was only one way to test the powers of the Vapours: to use them on a living creature. I care little for the "power of reason" or the "power of languages", as these are *skills* I already have. It was much more profitable to allow you to use these Vapours. But the Vapour of Life is mine. Give it to me!'

Will you give him the box as he wishes? If so, turn to **74**. If you refuse, turn to **133**.

200

The old man offers to help if you will lead him out of the dungeon. 'My name, if you wish to know it, is Hannicus. I know much of what goes on here,' he starts, 'for I was the keeper of these dungeons before Zharradan Marr decided that an undead would be more ruthless than an ageing wizard and gave that damned Darramouss – curse his soul – my position. The only reward for thirty-six years' service was my black-eye curse and a future as a plaything to be held captive at Darramouss's pleasure.' All this is interesting to you and you allow him to continue. 'I can lead you straight to the undead keeper if you will lead me – if you see what I mean. We must travel east until we reach the lair of the Chattermatter. But ignore his prattle, for he seeks only to feed on your flesh. North then we must travel to reach Darramouss. I can help you slay him, with this!' From inside his robes, he pulls a silver ring which has a large bulbous stone set in it. He walks over to you and gropes for your hand, finding it eventually. 'Look, this ring will fit any finger – even yours. There! When you meet Darramouss, smash the stone into the wall. It will break and release a deadly gas – deadly, that is, to the undead Half-Elf. It will not harm humans and will no doubt have no effect on you.' Add 2 *LUCK* points for this information. You look at the ring on your finger admiringly. The human is asking for it back. Will you give it to him? If so, turn to **159**. If not, turn to **360**.

201

The door in the south wall opens to reveal a short, narrow corridor. But as you are considering whether or not to step through the door, a creaking sound comes from behind you. You swing round to see the door in the east wall slowly opening. Glowstones in the passage outside flick on to light up your way. You cannot resist this invitation, and you leave through the east door. Turn to **49**.

202

The heat is becoming unbearable. Your thick scales serve only to make matters worse and you drag yourself round the walls, searching desperately for a way out of the furnace. You pound on the rock, hoping to find a loose stone, but there is none. However, at one point you bash the two bracelets together. The ringing sound becomes unnaturally loud and, as it does so, the roarings of the furnace subside. The vibrations on your wrists increase and eventually all is calm and the temperature has been restored to normal. An opening appears in the west wall and you can leave. You arrive at a familiar crossroads, but this time you choose a different direction. Will you turn right (turn to **443**) or continue westwards (turn to **213**)?

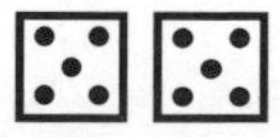

203

You follow the trail east for some time, until a familiar shape looms on the horizon. The building in which you met the Women of Dree! You realize that you have retraced your journey, so you decide to return to the crossroads. Lose 1 *STAMINA* point for the wasted journey. At the junction, will you turn north (turn to **130**) or continue west (turn to **177**)?

204

The passage runs straight ahead until you reach a solid wooden door. It is locked and looks much too sturdy for you to break down. But in the centre of the door is a huge metal plate with a heavy ball pivoted above it. Will you use the ball to hit the plate to attract the attention of whoever is inside (turn to **435**), or will you return to the junction and take the passage to the north (turn to **144**)?

205

Roaring like an enraged Demon, you rush into the open chamber, ready to take on whatever is inside. Terrified shrieks come from the small party of adventurers huddling round a makeshift campfire in the centre of the area. Three figures are warming themselves by the fire. One wears shiny clothes that clink as he moves. Another is dressed in red and also grows long dark hair from his chin. The third is a tiny creature with polished hide on his chest. He has no hair on his chin, but has plenty on his feet, which he has been holding up to warm at the fire. Your eyes fix on the smallest of the three. Your breathing gets heavier and a feeling of pure hatred grips you. Without hesitating, you stomp across and grab the miserable Hobbit with your claws. The other two are caught off balance and are slow to react. The Hobbit has no weapon and should be an easy victim:

HOBBIT	*SKILL 5*	*STAMINA 6*

If you defeat the creature in three straight Attack Rounds, turn to **160**. If it takes longer than three rounds, turn to **86**.

206

You ignore the pleas of the miserable little creature. After chewing through the rope to cut him down, you put him out of his misery and feast ravenously on his tasty flesh. Restore your *STAMINA* to its *Initial* level. You must then decide which way to turn at the fork. Will you go left (turn to **351**) or right (turn to **183**)?

207

You slump to the ground, exhausted from the fight. During the battle, the creature's red robe fell to the floor and this now catches your attention. You pick it up, admiring its richness and its feel. You stand up, swing it over your shoulders and proudly take a few steps, watching how it flows with your movements. You sit down again, happy with your new possession. But then a strange feeling comes over you. A pain in your stomach is followed by an overwhelming hunger. You must eat something! The dead Blood Orc lying at your feet suddenly looks delicious and you eat heartily. For the time being your appetite has been satisfied. Add 4 *STAMINA* points.

You are now ready to leave the room. You step up to the door and attempt to open it. But there is no handle. Your claws dig into the wood and you pull hard, but to no avail. The door is closed tightly and is being held by some catch. You cannot open it. You try charging the door, but it is much too strong for you ever to smash down. But your frustration soon turns to a quite different feeling as another wave of hunger spreads through you. Will you step over to the Orc's bones to suck them clean (turn to **109**), or will you instead attempt to remove the red robe (turn to **21**)?

208

Once more the glowstones light your way as you tramp

along the passage. The walls begin to glisten and from ahead you can hear the splashings of an underground river. As you approach, a strong smell begins to waft towards you. The disgusting smell, which comes from the river itself, causes you to stop for a moment to catch your breath. After a few more paces, you reach a rocky bridge. Steep chasm walls stretch down to the bubbling river below and you look over the edge to get some idea of the distance. The bridge is narrow, and wet from thc moisture in the air; no doubt it is slippery, too. Do you want to risk crossing the bridge (turn to **265**), or will you turn back and take the easterly passage (turn to **122**)?

209

You may, if you wish, regain your strength by waiting for a few moments in the room before continuing. You can pass the time by feasting on either of the dead creatures. Which looks the tastiest: the Manic Beast (turn to **231**) or the human carcass (turn to **249**)? Or will you ignore the food and simply leave the room (turn to **293**)?

210

You stop and wait as the old hag hobbles up to you. 'Praise be to Nanagga that you stopped, strange creature,' she croaks, panting from the effort of catching up with you. 'My rainwater barrel has fallen from its perch and I cannot lift it on my own. If you will lift it for me I will reward you well. My speciality is potions and I wager a dose of Healing Potion would not go amiss, eh? Well?' Will you help the woman out as she wants? If so, turn to **224**. If you would rather not, turn to **35**.

211

Strange smells of boiling herbs reach your nostrils as you enter the shack. Inside, the room is cluttered and disorganized and the pungent smell of the boiling herbs is particularly offensive to you. Standing over the pot of herbs is an old, white-haired man holding a ladle in one hand and an open book in the other. He wears a long, black robe and is concentrating intently on his potion. You stare at him for a few moments. He does not even notice you until you accidentally kick a large, round vegetable and send it scuttling across the floor. The man throws back his long hair and glances up at you. He seems to look *through* you; you are not sure whether he is seeing you or not. He waves you over to a chair to wait until he has finished. Will you wait as he wishes (turn to **316**), or do you refuse to wait (turn to **195**)?

212

You grope your way along the passage for several paces and find that it comes abruptly to a dead end. You may either search the walls for any signs of a way through (turn to **245**), or you may return to the crossroads and choose the north passage (turn to **354**) or the easterly one (turn to **310**).

213

You reach a dead end. The light is dim and it is difficult to see, so you grope around for a possible way onwards. There is none to be found. You turn round and return to the crossroads. Will you now continue north (turn to **443**) or east (turn to **50**)?

214

Your struggles against the sticky Gluevines are hopeless. The more you try to free yourself, the more entangled you become. But in your hand you carry the bottle of green liquid taken from the skeletal hand. The glass stopper has popped out in your struggles with the vine and you decide to take a sip. The liquid tastes sweet and you pour the remaining drops into your mouth. Miraculously, this seems to have the desired effect! One by one the vines release you!

The green liquid you found was, however, *not* specially formulated to repel Gluevines. The Gluevine tunnel was constructed by Forest Imps as a trap. Gluevines are very useful for traps of this sort as they have the ability to tell whether or not the prey they catch is fit for consumption. Any animal not fit for consumption is not entangled or – as in your case – released. For if you were to be eaten by the Forest Imps, you would doubtless poison them as they eat. The liquid you have drunk is in fact a slow-acting poison, the effects of which you are only now able to feel. You clutch your stomach and double over. Minutes later, you die an agonizing death.

215

'You can go after that thing, whatever it was, if you like,' says Grog, looking quite worried. 'But I'd just like to get out of here safely.' Return to **267** and make your next choice.

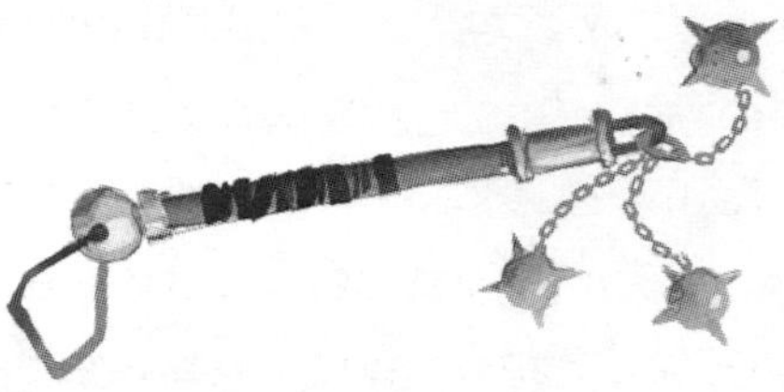

216

Thugruff takes you into a room where you both sit down at a table. A short while later someone arrives with a large bowl full of meaty broth and places it before you on the table. You catch the smell from the broth. Hobbit! Ravenously you grab the bowl and pour its contents into your mouth. The broth is hot and burns your throat, but you may add 5 *STAMINA* points for the meal. Thugruff tells you about his legions. Half of his forces are now with Zharradan Marr in a great floating ship known as the *Galleykeep*. It is cruising over the Forest of Spiders searching for the Rainbow Ponds, for the village of Stittle Woad is near the Rainbow Ponds. If you are lucky, he promises, you may even get to join Marr on the *Galleykeep*. Meanwhile you are deciding what you will do next. Thugruff takes you outside and offers to give you some instruction in weapon technique. Do you want to take him up on his offer (turn to **271**), or will you make plans to leave the Testing Grounds (turn to **455**)?

A bulky creature with a hairy face, razor-sharp teeth and wild eyes

217

You step over to the two boxes and shake one of them. Something soft and heavy bumps about inside. This arouses your curiosity and you search for a means of opening the box. But none is apparent. In your frustration, you tip the box over and it crashes to the ground. Your attention focuses on the wider end as a splitting sound from within the box gets louder. Suddenly a crack appears in the wood! Then another! Finally, the front of the box smashes apart and your eyes widen as they catch sight of the hideous thing within . . .

A human shape appears – or rather, something resembling a human corpse. But it is not dead, as its thin lips are slowly curling back to reveal sharp teeth and a forked tongue. In an instant, the creature suddenly sits bolt upright and turns its head towards you! Its eyes flick open.

'Whpodj st v rbsut hfer fs tep fothfec vrs fwjtchfs. Fpvl ucrfbt vrfey pvudbb blf ew jthi whb tayp vudp on pt ovn df rst bnd. Npn femb yajntf rffrfew jthi pv rupfbc fesbv fefpr ozh b rrbdbn ambrra th fe mbstfr. Yp vu mvstubf etb vghtutpo rfspfc te thfe slff pepfoth fev ndfbda bn day pvum vstub fem bdfe tpo ffflet hfewr bth apfo thf ecvrsfw jt chfs.'

The creature's eyes fix on to your own. They glow white and you find you cannot break from the gaze. When its eyes finally close, you feel strangely lightheaded. As if in

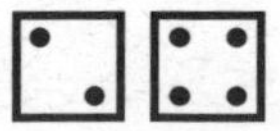

a trance, you step away from the corner and head towards the door in the east wall. You open it, step through and it closes behind you. Only then do your thoughts return to normal. But you are far from normal. You have been cursed and, until you are able to find someone who can remove the curse, your *Initial SKILL* has been reduced by 2 points and your *Initial STAMINA* by 5. If your current *SKILL* and *STAMINA* points exceed these limits, you must reduce them as necessary. Now you may continue by turning to **436**.

218

You plan to drag the body down the short passageway to the south. You bend down to grip the lifeless figure. But instead of responding to your wishes, you find that your body has other ideas of its own. Turn to **399**.

219

You hold up your Ring of Truth before him and his tone changes. He shifts nervously from side to side. 'Er, perhaps I have not remembered things quite accurately,' he stammers. 'It is not true that the *Galleykeep* comes to ground near here. It hardly ever comes to ground, for then it is too vulnerable. There are only two ways that I know of to get on board the *Galleykeep*. Every day, the ship goes gathering food for the crew. I have seen their catapult traps, which are scattered all around these woods. If you get yourself caught in a trap, you will be hoisted on board. All over the forest, they are.

Alternatively you can search for Thugruffs Testing Grounds and have yourself recruited into the crew.'

Weaseltongue backs away from you across the clearing. 'Ermm, I ... ah ... suspect,' he stammers, 'that you wish to *find* Zharradan Marr and you wish me to help. That I cannot ...' His face makes a grimace as he glances at the ring 'Of course. I must tell you what I know. For the Ring of Truth was forged by Elven smiths. If meet Zharradan you must, you will find him on the *Galleykeep* in a room with a certain symbol on the door. I know not this symbol, but I do have a clue as to its nature, contained in the words of this rhyme:

'When fire meets ice, who ends the fight?
Who stands between the two?
His symbol keeps them both apart,
Not red, nor white, but blue.

'I know no more that will help you,' he adds hastily. 'And now I must be going!' He holds up his hand as a parting gesture and turns into the woods. You watch him go. Ahead, the path continues to the north, but you can see through the trees that it splits, one path heading to the east and the other to the west. Do you want to head north and then turn either to the east (turn to **272**) or to the west (turn to **139**), or would you rather ignore the path and set off through the undergrowth (turn to **189**)?

220

You are suspicious of this mysterious figure. You back out of the arch and poke your head into the one next to it. This one is also dark. But from somewhere in the darkness you can see a faint glittering, as if tiny raindrops are sparkling as they fall. You cautiously step in to investigate. You reach a pile of rubble lying on the ground. Stones are scattered about as if from a wall which has recently collapsed. You could easily cross the rubble and make for the twinkling lights. While you are considering whether or not to do so, a crash is followed by a shower of dust as a rock falls from the ceiling! Will you climb through regardless, to investigate the glittering lights (turn to **56**), or will you leave this alcove and try another (turn to **85**)?

221

You cautiously make your way across to the far side of the bridge where, with a great sigh of relief, you step on to safe ground again. You rest for a few moments and then turn west to continue. But your eye catches sight of footprints which seem to head not towards the bridge, but to the edge of the ledge you are now standing on. Looking more closely, you can see that, just over the edge, a series of rocks protrude from the side of the chasm as rough stairs. They lead down to a hole in the cliff. If you wish to climb down the steps, the going will be perilous, as they are narrow and there is nothing to hold on to. Otherwise, the westward passage leads you on for a few paces to a strong wooden door with iron fastenings. Will you attempt to force your way through the door (turn to **425**), or would you like to investigate the steps leading down to the hole in the side of the chasm (turn to **313**)?

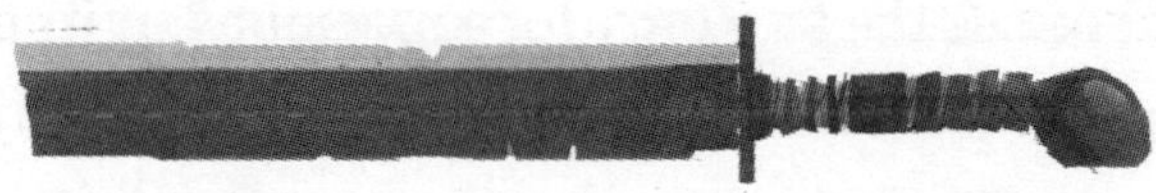

222

'Failed!' cries one of the witches from between black teeth. The creature has failed! It has no root! *Hyaaahhhh hee heeyah!* Its future is ordained. Let us be gone. The creature deserves no higher destiny.' The wind sweeps through the branches of the tree with the force of a gale. But as quickly as it rose up, it dies and soon all is still. The Women of Dree are gone! Unsure of what has happened to you, you settle down once more and drift off to sleep.

When you awake the next morning, the disturbance in the night is but a faint memory of a bad dream. As the rising sun warms the air, you set off. Add 4 *STAMINA* points for the rest and follow the path heading north-east, signposted towards 'Bu Fon Fen'. Turn to **134**.

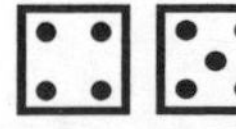

223

The bodies are a little scrawny, but still provide welcome food. You may gain 4 *STAMINA* points for your meal. While you were eating, you also poked through the bodies of the adventurers, but found nothing of particular importance. Suddenly, a glowstone lights in the passageway ahead of you! A tiny face pokes round the bend and surveys the scene. You see the face only for a moment, but its effect is immediate. Turn to **403**.

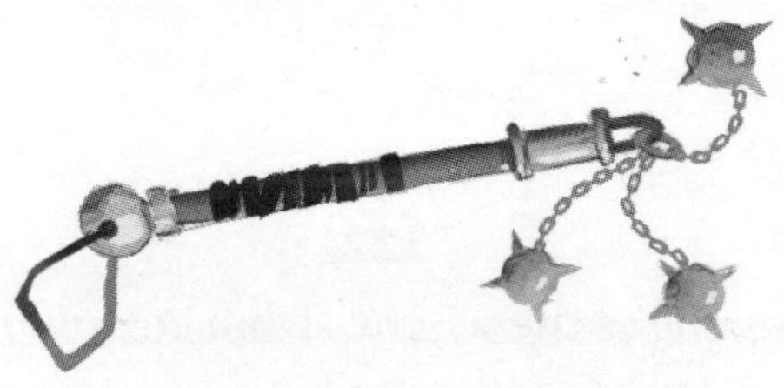

224

You follow her round the back of a dirty hovel. The stale smell of human sweat wafts from the rundown shack and round the back you nearly tread on a wild-haired semi-human creature which is lame and cannot move. The wretched thing jabbers at you in meaningless whelps, but you ignore it and concentrate on the woman's plight. She shows you an overturned barrel which has evidently fallen from a platform behind the house. ''Twas the wind last night,' she moans. The barrel fell with a terrible crash! 'Twas full; and it landed on poor Shanga here who was tied up beneath it. Can you put it back for me?' You grasp the barrel around the middle and climb the frame carefully. When you have replaced the barrel, you step down, ready for your reward. 'Let me see . . .' she muses. 'Promised you Healing Potion, is that not so? But would you prefer a Potion of *Fortune*? Perhaps you would. Well?' Which would you prefer? The Potion of Healing (turn to **196**) or the Potion of Fortune (turn to **294**)?

225

Your curiosity aroused, you step up to the device and study it. It does not seem to be a weapon of any kind. There is a polished, clear glass at each end. You place your eye up to the narrowest end and peer through. To your amazement you can see the trees in the forest far below as clearly as if you could reach out and touch them! Birds – and the occasional noisy Treehoppper – flit about between the branches and spring for cover as the *Galleykeep*'s shadow passes over them. In a small clearing you can see a thin, white-haired figure stepping into a pond of pink water, but again, as the ship's shadow comes into view, the figure darts off for cover in the woods. You are fascinated with your discovery and you spend time scanning the tree-tops with the device. Turn to **302**.

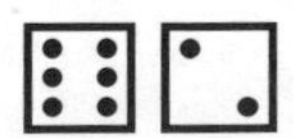

226

Undead creatures do not die. After the battle, their battered remains slink back into the graves from which they came and the stones shift back into position. Perhaps you have won this battle, or perhaps they are simply regenerating within their graves. Either way you decide not to wait to find out. Will you take the path to the east into the wood? If so, turn to **261**. If you wish to try looking around the rest of the graveyard for anything unusual, turn to **67**.

227

You follow the passage back to the junction and turn left in the direction indicated by the arrow. Turn to **142**.

228

You lie back and relax while the physician pours the potion into your mouth. You become drowsy and eventually drift off into a peaceful sleep. Almost immediately, you start to have a disturbing dream, in which you are lying down and being attacked by knives wielded by a skeletal hand. You struggle to escape, but your movements are slow and ineffective. Again and again the knives are driven into your chest and abdomen.

The shock makes you wake up immediately. You are unable to move at all. All you can do is watch as a specimen jar is held over your chest and a bony hand drops an organ into it. The organ is beating and the *thub-thub, thub-thub* noise fills your ears. Your last perception of life is watching your own heart slowly stop beating.

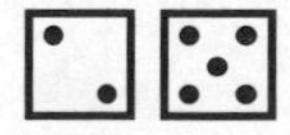

The grounds are milling with creatures

229

The trail eventually takes you to a pair of large metal gates. Through the bars of the gates you can see a large fortified building, but there are no signs of life. You are looking for some sort of clue as to what place this is when . . . *pop*! Suddenly a creature has appeared out of thin air and is opening the gate for you! In size, he is taller than a Hobbit but smaller than a human. He is thin and dark, with a withered face. Although he does not glance up at you, he is talking away: 'Come in. I hope you have not been kept waiting. Oh dear, I shall be in trouble if you have been waiting long. Let me take you to Thugruff. Fine day, isn't it? Follow me. Er, do you have any smoking-weed? No, of course not. Here we are . . .' You follow the twittering little creature round the back of the building into an open courtyard.

As you turn the corner, you stop in your tracks. The grounds are milling with creatures: Goblins, humans, Orcs, Elves, the odd Rhino-Man, Lizard Men and many others, talking, exercising and practising with weapons. In the centre of things, a huge, burly Half-Troll in a black tunic is moving between the groups and barking orders. Your guide pushes through the crowds and grabs the Half-Troll's tunic. 'Thugruff! A visitor!' He grunts and turns to you. 'A visitor, eh? Hrmmph. Were you kept waiting at the gate?' he asks, aiming a fiery glance at the little creature.

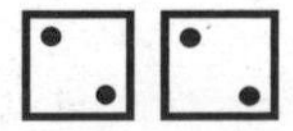

You shake your head. 'So you've come to join us have you?' he continues. 'Marr's legions could do with the sort of strength I can see in those arms. Let's see what you can do. Eleven! Over here!' Each of the legionnaires wears a medallion around his neck with his own number on. A lightly armoured human wearing number eleven comes over carrying a sword in one hand and a mace in the other. 'All right, Eleven,' chuckles Thugruff, who evidently despises the man. 'Let's see how you fare against our friend here.' Eleven looks at you and gulps. A circle forms around you and you must fight:

ELEVEN	*SKILL 7*	*STAMINA 9*

When either of you is reduced to a *STAMINA* score of 2, turn to **352**.

230

Your vengeance on the Clawbeast is not yet complete. You must satisfy your lust for the spoils of victory! You kneel by its side and feast on the flesh of your victim. You may add 2 *STAMINA* points for the meal; then turn to **165**.

231

The Manic Beast's meat is a little bitter for your liking but it provides a satisfying meal. You may add 4 *STAMINA* points. Now turn to **293**.

232

Your first step into the dark-coloured slime makes you shiver. It is considerably colder than the lighter-coloured variety. You quicken your pace and continue northwards. The dull light of the glowstones lets you see that your chilly ordeal will soon be over. A few paces ahead, a step takes you out of the strange slime and on to dry ground. You step up eagerly and peer ahead into the bluish gloom for some clue as to where you are heading. You can just make out an arched doorway ahead, and you soon reach a solid door of thick timbers and sturdy metal fastenings. You can hear irregular heavy breathing coming from something behind the door. The breathing is punctuated by occasional resonant snorts, and the overall impression is of danger! Something *large* is behind the door! Will you charge the door, prepared for anything within (turn to **263**)? Or will you ignore this room and head back down the passage to take the easterly way you found earlier (turn to **19**)?

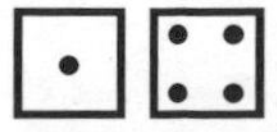

233

While you are groping around the end of the passageway, you suddenly notice a slight humming coming from your pendant! It is vibrating and, as you move towards one particular spot, the vibration becomes stronger. You grasp the talisman and watch as the blue stone begins to glow. Finally, a beam of blue light shoots from the pendant and lights up an area of rocky wall. You feel around the area and your hand comes to rest on a small hidden catch. When you flick the catch, the dead end before you comes to life! Smoke hisses from the crevices around the wall, forcing you to step away from it. When the smoke clears, a gap has appeared in the rock-face; an eerie green light lights up a narrow passage beyond. Will you step through and explore the secret passage? If so turn to **369**. Or would you rather return to the crossroads and take either the way to the north (turn to **443**) or the way to the east (turn to **50**)?

234

You approach the smaller of the two pug-nosed creatures and prod it with your foot. Its lifeless body shrugs and lies still. But a similar prod on the leather-armoured adventurer's leg produces a startlingly different result. A shrill screeching sound shocks you to attention! As if this were some kind of signal, something starts to happen in the room. Three shapes begin to materialize in front of you. Turn to **447**.

235

In the heat of the battle, you have forgotten all about the little Half-Orc, who has disappeared. Then your attention is captured by his familiar figure making its way through the reeds behind the Toadmen. Grog is creeping round the back of the circle. You glance around. No one has noticed him! From the corner of your eye you watch as he takes off his knapsack and lays it on the ground by the trail, then steps stealthily through the reeds towards the Toadman leader. When the time is right, he takes a flying leap! As fate would have it, one of the Toadmen notices the Half-Orc at that very moment, and his trident flies through the air and sinks into Grog's neck in mid-flight. The Half-Orc dies instantly.

But the trident does not prevent his body from continuing through the air to collide with the Toadman leader, who tumbles into the Sinkpit in the centre of the clearing! When this happens, the Toadmen forget all about you and rush about, trying to prevent their leader from sinking. You take advantage of the situation and creep round the outside of the clearing. You pick up the poor Half-Orc's knapsack and make off along the trail.

A short while later you are leaving the marshes. When you are well away from danger, you become a little curious about what Grog carried in his knapsack. There is certainly

something solid in there. You pull back the top and reach inside. Your fingers touch a wooden box and you pull it from the bag. It is closed with a delicate clasp which your awkward fingers cannot open. But apart from the box, Grog also carried a small vial of Potion of Fortune. If you wish, you may drink this and it will restore your *LUCK* to its *Initial* level. Then you may proceed by turning to **92**.

236

You ring the bell on the desk and scan the room suspiciously, waiting for something to happen. Nothing does. You watch both doors carefully. Again you try ringing the bell, but again there is no response. Your attention begins to wander towards the specimen shelves and the bookcase and you step over to the latter to look at the books. The largest volume is entitled *Practical*

Anatomy of the Creatures of North-western Allansia by Doctor Quimmel Bone. The book next to it is by the same author and is entitled *Transmutation Theory – Fact or Fantasy?*

A voice comes from behind you: 'Most definitely *fact* . . .' The voice startles you and you spin round to face the desk. 'I see you are interested in my works,' says the skeletal figure sitting behind it, teeth clattering excitedly. The hanging skeleton has disappeared – or rather is now sitting at the desk. 'I am Quimmel Bone, physician and surgeon on the *Galleykeep*. Now, what do you want in here?' Will you spring over to attack him (turn to **31**), or will you indicate to him you have some ailment which you would like him to treat (turn to **297**)?

237

As you shuffle around the wall of the cavern, you suddenly notice a strange sensation coming from your neck. The pendant you picked up is beginning to vibrate slightly and is giving out a faint hum! But when you continue around the wall, the vibration fades until the pendant is once more still. You puzzle over this for a few moments and step back to where you were before. Again, the vibrations and humming come from the pendant and you pause to look at what is happening. The dull blue stone set in its centre is beginning to glow and you watch in amazement

as its colour changes from blue to a living red, as though a fire were burning inside it! An instant later, a single beam of red light shoots from the stone to a point on the wall in front of you. Following its direction, you can see what seems to be a piece of rock hanging in mid-air! As if ordered by the pendant, you grasp the rock and pull. It is not hanging in mid-air, but is attached to a rope and your tug is answered by a rumble in the rock in front of you. A doorway is opening!

The pendant you have found is in fact a magic talisman which has a special power. It is able to detect hidden doorways. In future, it will warn you of the presence of secret doors, but you will have to watch for the warning signs! If you reach a reference which begins: 'You find yourself . . .' then you may look for a secret passage using the talisman's help. Add 20 to the reference you are on at the time and turn to this new reference. If a secret door is present, the new reference will make sense and the talisman will show you its secret (if the new reference makes no sense, then there is no secret door). If you are able to, you may add 1 *LUCK* point for finding the secret door.

You may now either enter the secret door you have just found (turn to **458**) or return to **257** to continue on your way.

238

You creep as close as possible to the Ophidiotaur and finally spring out of the foliage at it! The startled creature is caught unawares. It splashes in the water and kicks high with its hind legs. But its fright is momentary. The creature rapidly composes itself and turns towards you, tail swinging and tongue darting in and out of its wide open mouth, in which two dangerous-looking fangs are poised to strike. It is ready for battle and you must resolve your combat:

OPHIDIOTAUR *SKILL 9* *STAMINA 8*

The creature has a stinging tail which it lashes at you. Each time the Ophidiotaur rolls a double when attacking, its tail stings you for 2 *STAMINA* points of damage (irrespective of whether it wins or loses that Attack Round), unless you *Test for Luck* and are Lucky (you may choose whether or not you wish to *Test for Luck*). If you defeat the creature, turn to **416**.

239

You take the path carefully through the cavern so as to avoid any danger. The path leads out through a narrow archway into a passage which you follow east until you reach a junction where a side passage leads southwards. Turn to **298**.

240

Desperately you wrest yourself free from the Bugs and you race off northwards up the passageway. As you step away from them, you feel a sharp slice into your ribs. Dark blood seeps out from the wound and you must lose 2 *STAMINA* points. But you are now out of range and, as you turn a corner to the east, out of sight as well. You turn south, then west. But as you turn the next corner, your heart sinks. Another of the creatures is arriving for its meal! To get past, you will have to defeat the Bug:

CARRION BUG	*SKILL 7*	*STAMINA 6*

If you defeat it, turn to **227**.

241

As soon as you enter the room, two Blood Orcs – warty creatures with powerful jaws and piercing front teeth – get up from a table and grab their swords. A voice is coming from behind them and you look up to see an elderly human with dirty robes and a long white beard groping the air in front of him and calling out: 'Whpojs ijt. Whb tajs i hbp pfnjng. W hbta hb sad jstvr bf devs. Plf bsfe gpdor fl fbsf ethjs iblb cka fyfec vrsf.' You must resolve your fight with the Blood Orcs, who are now upon you. They both attack together:

	SKILL	*STAMINA*
First BLOOD ORC	*7*	*7*
Second BLOOD ORC	*8*	*7*

If you defeat them, turn to **7**.

242

In a state of panic, you lumber towards the door as quickly as you are able. The Shadow Stalker, however, is quicker and its knife finds your back as you flee. Lose 3 *STAMINA* points. When you reach the archway, your two shadows separate. The Shadow Stalker becomes faint as the light fades. In the light of the glowstones you hardly cast a shadow at all and this seems to worry the creature. It slips back along the wall into the room and settles on the floor. You blink and look again. The creature now looks like a pile of black cloth! You turn and leave the room, still not certain of what has happened. Eventually you reach the junction and continue westwards. Turn to **309**.

243

The four creatures taunt you as you back away from the Elf. Though you feel anger building up inside, you manage to contain it and walk away. Your 'cowardice' is not without its consequences. Lose 1 *SKILL* point for as long as you remain within the fort. You may regain the lost *SKILL* point if and when you leave. Now turn to **348**.

244

You continue east until you reach a junction, where another path joins from the north. There is a signpost at the junction. The sign pointing northwards reads 'Coven'. To the south the sign reads 'Bilgewater', though no path runs that way. To the east the sign reads 'Testing Grounds'. Which way do you wish to go: north (turn to **191**), south (turn to **57**) or east (turn to **12**)?

245

You search the rough rocky walls for some time but find nothing. Frustrated with your lack of progress, you return to the crossroads. Will you now head north (turn to **354**) or east (turn to **310**)?

246

The charts and maps are no doubt vitally important, but

you cannot decipher them. In the drawers of the desk are papers, books and drawing-equipment. But one drawer is locked and you cannot open it. You grasp the handle and tug. But the drawer is firmly locked and does not budge. Again you heave at it but this time you only succeed in pulling the handle away from the front of the drawer! Your anger mounts and you flex your claws. You will smash up the desk to get into the drawer. The timbers split after your first blow. Turn to **302**.

247

A surge of anger rushes through you. You step over to the nearest head, flex your claws and slash across its face. As your claws fix in the soft flesh, it flies from its perch out of the light and out of sight. You hear no sound to indicate that it hit a wall or landed on the floor. A menacing laugh comes from the voice, which sounds as though it is just over your shoulder. You spin round, but see nothing. The voice simply continues its mocking laugh. You turn back and gasp with surprise when you see that the head has returned to its position! At the same time, you feel a wave of pain spread right through your body. Every muscle is in agony! A few moments later, the pain subsides, but the aches remain. You must lose 2 *STAMINA* points. Will you now leave the room through the secret passage (turn to **79**), or will you attack one of the other heads (turn to **9**)?

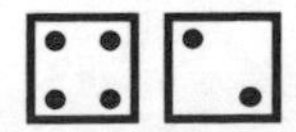

248

You stand up, ready to leave the area. After glancing left and right to make sure you are alone, you turn towards the westerly passage. At least, you *try* to turn. But your body will not respond. Instead it is bending down towards the lifeless Dwarf on the ground. Turn to **399**.

249

You tuck into your meal. The meat is rather tough, as it is no doubt several days old. But while you are eating, something catches your attention. Tied around the human's waist you find a small leather pouch which contains 2 Gold Pieces. You may take these with you; and you gain 4 *STAMINA* points from the meal. Your attention is also captured by two glass flasks lying by the side of the unfortunate human. Though they have been battered in the struggle, they are not broken and each contains a coloured liquid. If you would like to drink the green liquid, turn to **318**. If you would prefer to drink the blue liquid, turn to **350**. If you wish to drink neither, you may continue by turning to **293**.

250

The sack can be used to carry anything you may find during your journey. From now on you may ignore any instructions which tell you that you can only take one item from, for example, a room. Leave the room now by turning to **394**.

251

You step over to the miserable Half-Orc and kick the creature viciously for daring to bump into you. A great cheer goes up from the crowd of onlookers. 'Leave him be, creature,' says the bare-chested villager. '*I* will finish the muck-faced worm off.' But his words are too late. You are locked in battle with the creature:

HALF-ORC	*SKILL 6*	*STAMINA 6*

If you defeat the creature, turn to **367**.

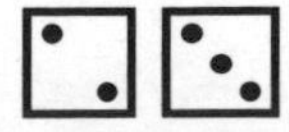

252

You enter the hut and find yourself in a room decorated with intricately woven cloths in rich colours, which hang from the walls and ceiling, making the room itself dark and mysterious. A long, thin stick smoulders in a brass pot which stands on a table at one end of the room and as it burns it gives off a heavy, perfumed smell. There is also a pack of cards on the table, next to a clear glassy orb. You can see the hanging cloths behind the table rustling and a voice breaks the silence: 'Who calls on the powers of Rosina of Dree? Who wishes to know his destiny? Speak!' You wait and watch as an old woman, plump and stooped, shuffles out from behind the curtain into the room. She is dressed in brightly coloured robes and she sits down behind the table. She squints as she tries to focus on you.

'Far from your home you have come to speak with Rosina,' she smiles. 'And much further have you yet to travel. Now you have found me, I may guide you to fulfilling your destiny. But will you pay my price?' She will read your fortune, but only if you have money to pay with. She will charge 2 Gold Pieces. If you have the money, turn to **11**. If you wish to fight the woman, turn to **151**. Otherwise you may leave by turning to **386**.

253

The building has been disused for some time. Long benches have been smashed to provide firewood and there is the remains of an old fire in the centre of the hall. High on the walls, windows made of coloured glass have been broken and there are many holes in the roof. But apart from this there is little of interest. You leave the building and may either return to the stones (turn to **198**), or head on past them into the wood (turn to **261**).

254

An angry sneer spreads across your face and you step over to the Weather Mage, claws poised to strike. He backs away from you and holds his hand up. 'Idiot creature,' he scoffs. 'Do you think one so brainless could possibly challenge one so well versed in the mystic arts? I will enjoy toying with your life. It will be fine sport.' You slash at him as he steps back and catch him across the arm. A red stain spreads across his sleeve, but he has hardly noticed your blow. His head has turned to face the ceiling; his eyes are closed. As you prepare to strike once more his eyes open. They are shining white! Will you continue with your attack (turn to **47**), or will you quickly leave the room (turn to **459**)?

255

'Wait!' cries Grog as you start across the clearing. 'Look at this. Notice how all the footprints *avoid* the centre of the clearing? Perhaps it is unsafe. I suggest we keep to the outside.' You follow him round the edge of the clearing towards the trail you have chosen. Have you chosen the trail to the north (turn to **267**) or the trail to the north-east (turn to **114**)?

256

Breathing heavily, you rise to your feet and stand over the body of the Chaos Warrior. Your attention turns to the Black Elf who is once more blowing his whistle for reinforcements. Instantly another Chaos Warrior appears in the doorway ready for battle. You must resolve your fight with him:

CHAOS WARRIOR	*SKILL 8*	*STAMINA 7*

If you win, turn to **39**.

257

You cannot see a thing. Your feet shuffle noisily through the straw which covers the floor, as you grope around the walls for a way out. If this cavern is the lair of another creature, then you may well be walking straight towards it! But you hear no sounds other than your own and eventually you reach a hole in the rock, which is large enough for you to walk through and leads to a passageway. You continue slowly along the passage, still groping your way, but you stop when a blue light flicks on in front of you. The welcome hue of a glowstone makes you blink and turn away until your eyes become accustomed to the light. When you are finally able to take in your surroundings, you find that you are at a junction where you may turn either to the east (turn to **61**) or to the west (turn to **309**).

258

With bared teeth and claws at the ready, you storm along the passage towards them. They stand their ground, draw their weapons and prepare themselves for battle. The leading adventurer lays a brown sack on the ground and raises his weapon as you approach. You must fight both adventurers one at a time; the passageway is not wide enough for them both to attack:

	SKILL	*STAMINA*
WARRIOR	*8*	*9*
FIGHTER IN LEATHER ARMOUR	*7*	*8*

If you defeat them both, turn to **13**.

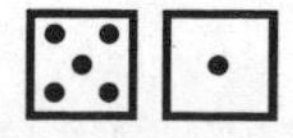

259

You wrench the bracelets from the wrists of your foe. They make a tinny clinking sound as you turn them over in your hand and you admire the intricate carvings which decorate them. Even in the meagre light of the glowstones, they shine in an alluring way. You can make them wide enough to fit around your own wrists, and when you have put them on, you proudly hold them up before you and turn them this way and that. You may discover during your travels that these bracelets have a special ability, which will be revealed to you later. Add 1 *LUCK* point for your find. Now turn to **115**.

260

Some inner instinct of self-preservation takes over from your fury and tells you that this Elf bowman is not to be trifled with. You turn from him and speed back down the corridor. However, you manage no more than five steps before you realize that your attempts to escape are futile.

Ahead of you, four more Dark Elves bar the passageway, all with bows drawn and aimed at your chest. You are confused! Which way should you turn? But your confusion is short-lived. At a signal from their leader, arrows zing from all four bows. Their aim is good. Three of the four shafts pierce your heart . . .

261

The path takes you along towards the trees. You pass a sign on the edge of the forest, which reads 'Knot Oak Wood'. Once in the wood, the going is more difficult as the light is obscured by the tall trees. If you wish to rest by one of the trees, turn to **362**. If you would prefer to keep going, turn to **162**.

262

You step over to the door in the north wall. But as you grasp the handle, a deep creaking sound comes from behind you. You swing round to see the door in the east wall slowly opening. Glowstones in the passage beyond the door flick on to light up your way. You cannot resist this invitation, and you leave through the east door. Turn to **49**.

A bulky creature with a hairy face, razor-sharp teeth and wild eyes

263

The door shudders under your charge but does not open. Lose 1 *STAMINA* point. You try again and this time the bolt is torn from the frame. The door flies open and you step into the room, ready for the creature inside. The room itself has a door in each wall. Scattered around one corner is an untidy pile of bones. In another corner is a half-eaten human carcass. Standing over the carcass – and evidently annoyed that its meal has been disturbed – is a bulky creature with a hairy face, razor-sharp teeth and wild eyes. As you enter, it turns to attack and you must resolve your battle with the Manic Beast:

MANIC BEAST	*SKILL 7*	*STAMINA 8*

The Manic Beast is so called for its tremendous bursts of rage. Each time you inflict a wound on the Manic Beast, its anger will rise for the next Attack Round, and you must add 2 to the dice roll when it rolls for Attack Strength. If you wound it again during this next Attack Round, it will retain the bonus for the *next* Round, but if you do not, its temper returns to normal and the bonus is lost. If you defeat the Manic Beast, turn to **209**.

264

Your final blow passes through thin air and the image of Rosina disappears slowly from view. A smile spreads across the face that you thought was showing the signs of exhaustion from defeat. The smile turns into a laugh, then a cackle and finally fades. You have been fighting a phantom! But your own wounds are real. Startled by this sorcerous trick, you leave the hut quickly and head down the trail back to the crossroads. Turn to **386**.

265

Holding your breath to avoid the awful stink coming from the river below, you step on to the bridge and test its strength with your weight. The bridge seems strong enough. You take a few paces across. Eventually you are forced to breathe again and in the centre of the bridge you take a quick breath. The smell of the river once more hits you and you stagger. Your foot slips on the edge of the bridge and you must *Test your Luck*. If you are Lucky, turn to **418**. If you are Unlucky, turn to **60**.

266

The figure drops to the floor and lies in a dark heap at your feet. Do you wish to investigate the body (turn to **194**), or will you instead search the room (turn to **105**)?

267

You follow the trail as it winds through the reeds. More than once a slippery Swampsnake slithers across your path, but thankfully they have no interest in you. Several types of croaking noises can be heard, but the one that worries you the most is a loud, booming croak which sounds more like a throaty belch. This particular sound is regular, and similar croaks seem to echo it from various parts of the marsh. Ahead of you, the trail is opening up as it reaches a river-bank, where a wealth of colourful plants line the river. But as you stand and watch the river flowing past, you notice a pair of eyes in the reeds! Two large, bulbous eyes blink slowly as you stare at them. When the owner of the eyes realizes you have seen him, he turns and you can see a bulky, rough-skinned shape – rather like a huge stone – shuffle off noisily into the reeds. Will you follow this creature (turn to **53**), would you rather investigate the plants by the side of the river (turn to **380**), or do you want to leave as quickly as possible (turn to **18**)?

268

The door splinters and you stumble forward into a dark room. As your eyes try to become accustomed to the darkness, you hear a high-pitched clicking noise coming from one corner. An instant later, the same sound is coming from another corner. By now your eyes are just about used to the low light and you can make out two shapes, outlined in blue. One is the door by which you entered, lit by the glowstones. The other is the rough shape of another door in the north wall. The light around both these doors is fading. Do you wish to step over to the north door before the light fades (turn to **285**), or would you prefer to investigate the clicking sounds (turn to **383**)?

269

Whiteleaf spits in contempt. 'The ground is cursed where that Ogre-breathed spirit Zharradan Marr treads!' he snarls. 'It is my wish that the wind drops suddenly and he drops with it – to his death! Marr has sailed the accursed *Galleykeep* all his life, with its foul crew of blood-lusting beast-men. Someone should sabotage the floating hellpit, by holing its hull. I know how to get aboard. The *Galleykeep* comes to ground not far from here – just off to the west – when the wind dies down. Nothing would please me more than to see the accursed vessel plummet from the sky and crash to the ground, killing all on board!' The Elf finally picks himself off the ground and dusts down his robes. He thanks you again and leaves. Turn to **414**.

270

You ignore the peasants and sit down in the field. They continue their yelling and the stones still land close by, but you are *hungry*! You grab an ear of corn and put the whole thing in your mouth. The peasants dare not come too close to you, but they will keep up their barrage of stones until you leave their field. There is a chance you may be hit by one and you must roll one die six times. Any time 6 comes up, you have been hit by a stone for 1 *STAMINA* point of damage. After you have rolled the die six times, you can leave the field (turn to **87**) and you will gain 3 *STAMINA* points for your meal. If, before you go, you wish to punish the peasants for attacking you, turn to **421**.

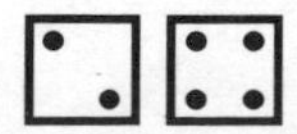

271

Thugruff sizes you up and picks a broad-handled axe from his armoury. You take it and admire its sharp blade. Thugruff himself picks up a smaller axe and begins your instruction. You watch his technique attentively. By the end of the lesson, you have improved your *skill* considerably. Add 1 *SKILL* point. What are you planning for your future at the Testing Grounds? If you wish to continue improving your *skills* until you are chosen for duties on the *Galleykeep*, turn to **43**. If you are plotting the right moment to attack Thugruff, turn to **82**.

272

You follow the path through the woods until you reach a clearing. Here there is a small pond. The water is not stagnant, as a small stream leads from it deeper into the woods, and it is a favourite watering-hole for the woodland birds, although they flit high up into the branches when you arrive. The water shines with a silver sheen and you can see quite clearly the reflections of the tree-tops and clouds. Will you rest here beside the pond and perhaps drink from it? If so, turn to **176**. If you would prefer to pass by and continue along the path, turn to **52**.

273

You step up to the bones and sniff them. A shiver of excitement runs through you: Hobbit bones! In eager anticipation, you follow the passage south until it reaches a point where it turns to the east. You sniff for the scent of Hobbit and can smell something faintly in the air. At the next corner, the passage turns north. Further on it turns west. The smell of Hobbit is now getting stronger and you eagerly follow the passageway round a corner to the south. You reach another pile of bones on the ground. You stop to look, but these are not Hobbit bones. They are the bones of something much larger, perhaps a human or even a Hobgoblin. The passage ahead turns to the east. Will you follow it (turn to **356**), or would you prefer to go back (turn to **227**)?

274

You head west out of the village. The peasants walking towards you gasp when they see your shape and cross over the road to avoid you. You ignore them and continue. Ahead you can hear sounds of excited voices coming from one of the buildings. As you approach this hut, the sounds become louder. You hear a sharp *crack*, the door of the hut bursts outwards and a tumbling figure rolls out of the door and straight into you! As the dark-skinned Half-Orc picks himself up, another figure steps through the doorway. This one is a broad-shouldered human with a bare chest. The small crowd behind the human is urging him to finish off the Half-Orc, but the noise dies down when they notice you. Will you join in the fight? If so, will you come to the aid of the Half-Orc (turn to **291**) or the human (turn to **251**)? If you do not wish to get involved in the fight, you can leave them to it and continue your journey by turning to **107**.

275

The Black Elf realizes he is no match for your strength and he suddenly pulls from his pocket a small whistle, which he puts to his lips and blows. The shrill sound can barely be heard and you take advantage of the Elf's distraction to grab him in your claws. But before you can choke the life out of him, his signal is answered and a larger creature steps through the archway. This creature is covered in heavy armour. Vicious spikes jut out from each joint and a large, dark-eyed helmet reaches down to its shoulders. It carries a two-handed axe, which it now raises to do battle. You must ignore the Black Elf and instead turn to face this Chaos Warrior:

CHAOS WARRIOR	*SKILL 9*	*STAMINA 8*

If you defeat the creature, turn to **256**.

276

You carefully try the door. It creaks on its hinges but opens easily, allowing you into the room. You are ready for the creatures inside and hope to surprise them. But when you enter, it is you who are surprised at what you see. Turn to **161**.

277

You listen at the door and hear slithering noises followed by chomping sounds. You step back for a moment to consider what you have heard. You decide to turn back in the direction you have just come from. As you feel your way slowly along the pitch-black passage, you are again startled by the high-pitched twittering noise that you remember from your last encounter with the small flying creatures. You swat hopelessly at them and manage to hit a couple. But one swoops down and catches you painfully in the left eye! Fortunately your eye was blinking at the time and it has not been permanently damaged, but the bruise swelling up above your left cheek will keep the eye closed for some time. You must deduct 1 *SKILL* point. You may restore this *SKILL* point if at some time in the future you reach daylight. The attacks from the flying creatures continue and you decide to abandon this route and make your way back to the door. Finding it once more closed and barring your way, your jaw tightens and your lips curl back in an angry snarl. Both directions face you with danger and frustration! You step back to take a leap at the door with your fists. Turn to **101**.

278

You try your best to pick the sticky Gluevines from you and back out of the tangled mass of vegetation. But it is hopeless. Eventually you give up, exhausted, to recover some strength before trying again. It is then that you hear the high-pitched chattering of the Forest Imps who have come to check their traps.

Twelve tiny faces peer into the tunnel. Small, green-skinned faces grin excitedly at the sight of such a large catch. Two spearmen advance cautiously up the tunnel towards you. When they are close enough, they jab towards your foot. You pull it away to avoid being hit, but your actions are so restricted that resistance will be hopeless. And as soon as the spears pierce your skin with their deadly poison, the effect will be immediate. Your adventure has ended here.

279

You turn back towards the crossroads. On the way back, you may stop to examine the orb, if you have not done so already, by turning to **155**. Otherwise continue on to the crossroads and you may take either the passage to the west (turn to **213**) or the passage to the east (turn to **50**).

280

A short distance along the passageway you stop and listen. Distant footsteps and the clanking of metal warn you that creatures of some sort are heading in your direction. Do you wish to return to the junction and head north (turn to **371**), or will you continue in the direction you are heading (turn to **342**)?

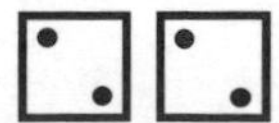

281

You poke around the bodies of the three dead ruffians. Something shining on the wrist of the third adventurer catches your attention. Clumsily you rip at the clothing of all three, eventually exposing three objects of interest. The leading adventurer wore, around his neck, a pendant made of a dull, dark metal on a leather thong. The third adventurer wore two wrist bracelets of a shining yellow metal. The other carried a pouch containing 12 small flat discs of a shiny metal. Which of these is of the most interest to you:

The dull metal pendant? Turn to **306**
The two wrist bracelets? Turn to **259**
The pouch containing the discs? Turn to **412**

282

The walls of the tunnel become damp and glisten in the odd half-light. You follow the passage until you reach a point where it turns sharply southwards. Continuing round the corner, you find that the light has now almost totally faded, and you must feel your way along the wall. Several paces down the slimy corridor, you reach a dead end. The wall is rocky and pocked with many nooks and crannies. There is also a musty smell in the air of animal decay – perhaps simply dead rats or maybe the remains of something larger. Around your feet there are several loose stones. At least you *assume* they are stones, but some are too long, thin and brittle to be shards of rock. Your groping hand touches a length of rope, which may be a clue to a way out of this dead end. Will you pull it? Roll one die. If the result is 1–3, you close your hand around the rope and pull it out towards you (turn to **99**). If you roll 4–6, you ignore the rope, turn round and follow the corridor back the way you came, continuing straight on past the Clawbeast's cave (turn to **372**). If you wish, you may, *before rolling the die*, decide to *Test your Luck*. If you are Lucky, you may *choose* which of the above options you will opt for. If you are Unlucky, you must roll the die to decide in the normal way.

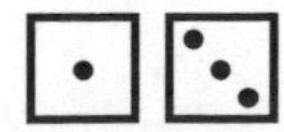

283

You were able to understand the last sentence of the spirit's words as it has passed on its gift. Throughout the book you will find coded speech. Now that you have the gift of understanding, you can translate the code. Otherwise all speech seems incomprehensible to your creature's mind. The secret is this. There are three rules to this code. Firstly, each vowel is replaced by the *following* letter (thus A becomes B, U becomes V, etc.). Secondly, spaces between words are replaced by *the last vowel to have been used.* Thus all vowels mean nothing; they only indicate spaces between words. Finally, the actual spaces between words as they appear are entirely random. They mean nothing and serve only to mislead. With this information you may now continue by turning to **137**. Add 1 *LUCK* point for this discovery. But note this reference as you may want to return to it later to translate code.

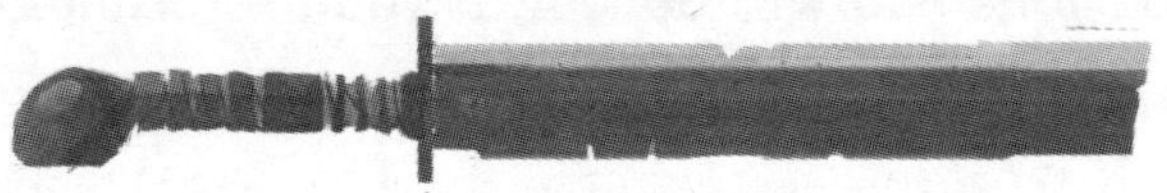

284

Two Goblins and two Elves are whispering secretively to one another. You approach them and find that they are passing something among themselves. You cannot make out exactly what it is, but it is metallic and shiny. You step up to the group, but the four creatures close in to exclude you from their conversation. Will you force your way into their group (turn to **103**) or leave them alone (turn to **348**)?

285

As you move across to the door, the clicking sound seems to dart away from you and travel to the far side of the room. Your sharp claws slide from your fingertips, and you are ready to attack whatever is on the other side of the door. *Something* must have activated the glowstones! You grasp the handle, yank the door open and peer around. But the passage in which you find yourself is empty. It heads on northwards and widens out at a bend where it turns to the east. You follow it slowly until you reach the bend, the glowstones lighting your way. Then you stop dead in your tracks! On the ground ahead of you, in the centre of the bend, is a dark area which seems to be shimmering in the blue light. Perhaps it is a pool of liquid? Or perhaps it is some sort of dark metallic substance? You may investigate if you wish by turning to **445**. If you would prefer to skirt the dark circle, turn to **164**.

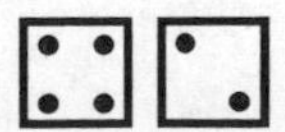

'None may enter the fens of the Toadmen,' he announces

286

Darramouss picks up a jar while he reads from the book. He concentrates his thoughts and seems to focus them on the jar. Then he reaches inside, pulls out a handful of grains of rice and sprinkles them over you. Before you can react, his spell has taken place. The grains of rice have formed into Death Maggots – small grubs with voracious appetites and sharp teeth which will rip even your tough scales to shreds! Scores of the tiny creatures are now feasting hungrily on you and you desperately try to swat them with your hands. Although you do succeed in killing many of them, many more have wedged themselves between your scales and even bored into your flesh. You look up in agony at the undead creature. But Darramouss will show no mercy. His hand reaches into the jar and he tosses another handful of rice over you . . .

287

As the Toadman staggers and falls, you see more of the creatures hopping out from the reeds. What can you do against so many? A stabbing pain in the back reminds you that you will not have much choice in the matter. One of the creatures is behind you, jabbing you with a trident. Another steps forward and speaks to you. 'None may enter the fens of the Toadmen,' he announces. 'Our marsh and our herb gardens are holy. They are for no eyes but our own. There is only one punishment for disobeying this law. That is DEATH . . .'

There is nothing you can do against so many of the creatures. You may fight and you may even slay a few of the Toadmen. But their numbers will overwhelm you. And when they have subdued you, you will be dropped into the muddy Sinkpits of Bu Fon Fen to die.

288

You keep your eyes on the Hobbit and wait for him either to give up his watching or to become involved in the conversation. But after no more than five seconds, the waiting is unbearable! Your mouth is now slobbering in excitement and your limbs are twitching with the promise of the battle to come. Though your mind wills your body to wait for a safer moment, your body will not listen. Turn to **42**.

289

You may add 4 *STAMINA* points for the meal, and then you leave the room by turning to **138**.

290

As you stand against the wall, desperately searching for a way onwards, you almost overlook the strange things happening around your neck. For the pendant you are wearing is beginning to vibrate and is emitting a faint humming sound! When you suddenly become aware of the pendant, you look down towards it to find out what is going on. When you move away from the end of the passage, the vibration fades; when you come closer, it increases in intensity. You cannot understand what is going on! An instant later, the jewel in the centre of the pendant begins to glow. It changes in colour from blue to fiery red. Suddenly a jet of red light bursts from the jewel and lights up a metal rod which is protruding very slightly from the side wall. You grasp the rod and push it. A creaking sound is followed by a deep rumbling as the wall ahead begins to shift. The jewel returns to its former dull blue appearance as the secret door opens . . .

The pendant you have found is in fact a magic talisman which has a special power. It is able to detect hidden doorways. In future, it will warn you of the presence of secret doors but you will have to watch for the warning signs! If you reach a reference which begins: 'You find yourself . . .', then you may look for a secret passage using the talisman's help. Add 20 to the reference you are on at the time and turn to this new reference. If a secret door is present, the new reference will make sense and the talisman will show you its secret (if the new reference makes no sense, then there is no secret door).

Now you must decide what to do. Will you go through the secret doorway you have just discovered? If so, turn to **331**. If you would rather return to the crossroads, you may do so and take either the passage to the north (turn to **354**) or the passage to the south (turn to **212**).

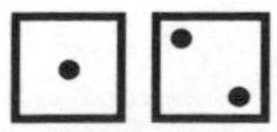

291

Gasps go up from the crowd as you step up to the bare-chested human, your claws poised ready to strike. He has no weapon apart from his bare fists. The other villagers back away and leave the two of you to battle it out. The Half-Oce is still picking himself up, but shouts encouragement to you. Resolve your battle with the human:

VILLAGER	*SKILL 7*	*STAMINA 8*

If you defeat the human, turn to **438**.

292

Your reaction is immediate. The red-robed human is deep in thought and looks an easy target. You step forward and swipe viciously at him with your claws! He screams and falls to the ground, clutching at his face. You look down at the undefended wretch and prepare to deliver the death-blow. But at that moment, you feel a terrible sting in the back, which causes you to bellow and swing round. The remaining adventurer has lunged at you with his sword and succeeded in piercing the scales and flesh on your back! You must lose 2 *STAMINA* points for the wound, and then you can face the Knight in plate-armour:

ARMOURED KNIGHT	*SKILL 8*	*STAMINA 9*

If you defeat the Knight, turn to **446**.

293

You leave the room through a door in the east wall. The door opens into a dingy corridor, which is quite short and ends at a wooden door. When you listen at the door, you can hear conversation rising and falling in pitch as if two or three creatures (or humans) were locked into a long discussion. This is your only way onwards. Will you try the door and attempt to creep slowly into the room (turn to **276**), or will you attempt to surprise whatever is inside by charging into the room with claws drawn (turn to **66**)?

294

She beckons you to follow her into her home. In one corner of her kitchen, shelves hold dozens of bottles of potions. She takes down a bottle containing a straw-yellow potion and pours it into a bowl for you to drink. The smell and the taste are awful, but you manage to force it down. When the bowl is empty, you turn to go.

'But where are your manners? Wait a moment. I must show you round your new home,' chuckles the old witch. You are confused. *New home?* But you are beginning to feel differently about the ageing crone and her hovel. Her voice is calming and tuneful; the hut seems to offer comfort and shelter. 'You will enjoy it here,' she continues. 'For you and I are meant for each other. Now that Shanga is of no use, I *must* have another slave; otherwise how may I keep this home? I will give you chores to do and I will feed you well. Tonight we will feast on Shanga – for he is dying anyway. You will enjoy spending your life in Dree. And every day I will give you another bowl of my special Potion of Obedience.'

295

Moments later, the fight has ended. The white-haired creature lies unconscious on the ground, while the Brigands rise and dust their hands. They grin contentedly at each other. One of them says, 'There – that will teach that puny sewer-snake to send *us* in the wrong direction!' The other nods and they both leave the clearing along a path to the north. You wait for them to disappear from view. Then you step up to the white-haired figure, who is badly beaten. If you are hungry, he will provide a meagre, but tender meal for you, and you may add 3 *STAMINA* points. Then continue by turning to **414**.

296

You step inside the room and look around. All sorts of carefully collected objects of value are in the room and you pick some of these up to look more closely at them. Then the door slides shut with a rumble and leaves you in complete blackness! Relying on your talisman, you shuffle across to the area of the door and hold it towards the wall. But this time there is no reaction. No vibration; no blue light. There is equally little reaction from the other walls. It soon dawns on you why two long-dead skeletons were leaning against the table. There *is* no escape from the tomb you are now in! The next unwitting visitor will find *three* skeletons in the room . . .

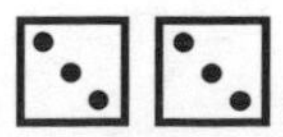

297

You indicate to him that your wounds hurt and that you have a sore head. He invites you to lie down on his bed. The bed is much too small for you, but you manage to keep your balance and lie down while he examines you. The physician rises jerkily from the desk and totters quickly over to the bed. His bony fingers probe the areas around your wounds and rub the side of your head. 'Hmmm. As I thought,' he says, making an uncomfortable rasping sound as he scratches his head. 'Your body has a mild poison circulating within it. I have an antidote.' Quimmel Bone clatters across to a drawer and takes out a small flask. 'Drink this,' he orders. You hesitate, but he is insistent and becomes angry at your refusals. Will you drink the potion as he demands (turn to **228**) or will you refuse and attack the creature (turn to **31**)?

298

You decide to choose the eastward passage, and you follow it to a sharp bend to the right. Almost immediately after the bend you find yourself at the foot of a staircase and you climb the stairs carefully. Then a corridor leads straight ahead southwards until you reach a T-junction where you may turn either east (turn to **373**) or west (turn to **401**).

299

You leave the building and set off west, the rising sun warming your back. Once you have left the area of the graveyard and the ruined chapel, the way ahead looks bleak. The flat countryside is featureless except for the odd flat-topped T'annum tree and occasional boulders which resemble grains of corn on some gigantic field. You stop by one such boulder to rest in its shade.

'Scum! Scum! *Rrrooaak!* Be off with you, scum!' squeaks a tiny voice which makes you jump. '*Rrrooaakk!* Move on, dung-face. Show us yer back.' You look round, but can see nothing. You stand to search around the stone. '*Rrroaarkkk!* The vomit-puddle walks! Go on, sewer-snake! Away!' You are bewildered by the voice, until you catch sight of a small black Jabberwing bird, hopping round on the top of the boulder. It opens its beak and again the voice speaks to you: '*Rrrooaaark!* Make dust, goblin-brain. Go north to Dree. Only Windward Plain out to the west. Not much happening there. *Rrroakk!* Well, what you waiting for, sewage-slime? *GO!*' You have by now had enough of these insults. You cannot catch the little creature and you are sufficiently rested, so you set off. The creature is delighted to see you go. You attracted a swarm of flies while you were resting and the Jabberwing wants to eat some – once you are safely out of the way!

You may add 2 *STAMINA* points for your rest. Which way will you now continue: west (turn to **96**) or north (turn to **433**)?

300

The door opens into a narrow passageway heading north, and glowstones flick on to light your way. Unlike the other passageways you have been travelling along, this one has a cobbled floor. The cobblestones feel smooth and pleasant for your great feet to walk on, but you cannot ignore a feeling of apprehension, since the stones must have been laid by an organized and intelligent creature. You follow the passage for a short while until suddenly a loud *CLANG* sounds behind you and stops you dead in your tracks! You wheel round to find that a heavy portcullis has dropped behind you and sealed off the passage. You step back to test it, but the bars are much too strong for you to smash or even bend. You have no choice: you turn round and continue north up the corridor.

A little further ahead, you reach a crossroads. The glowstones light up three ways onwards, but you cannot see very far down the passages. Will you:

Continue northwards?	Turn to **443**
Try the passage to the east?	Turn to **50**
Try the passage to the west?	Turn to **213**

301

North of the building, the countryside is almost

featureless. After walking for some time, you come across a solitary tree standing by the side of the path. It has a dark brown – almost black – trunk and its leaves are brilliant green. They shine unnaturally, as if they might glow in the night. Among the higher branches, large round fruits hang. You study these, considering how you may get them down. You are certainly not built for climbing trees, but you may be able to shake one down. If you wish, you may *Test your Luck*. If you are Unlucky, you do not manage to shake any fruits from the tree. If you are Lucky, one of the nourishing Chubbley tree fruits falls to the ground. You may then eat this juicy fruit and will gain 4 *STAMINA* points. When you are ready to leave, turn to **45**.

302

Suddenly, you stop what you are doing and listen. Your ears have picked up a sound outside the door. 'Ssshh!' hisses one voice. 'We must surprise the creature, whatever it is. Remember what it has done to the gatherers. Get ready. Earth ... water ... fire ... and *air*!' At that moment, the door cracks, bursts from its lock and crashes back against the wall to reveal a sea of ugly faces, straining to lunge forward at you! 'Take the creature!' comes the cry, and they flood forward, bellowing their battle-cries. You have no chance against this horde of Hobgoblins and your adventure has ended here.

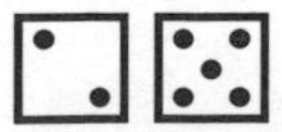

303

You ignore his words and investigate the scientific instruments. But none of them mean anything to you. The Weather Mage is outraged at this uninvited intrusion. 'Get out of here, beast,' he screams. 'Did you not hear me? This is not a playroom!' He holds his head back and closes his eyes. When he opens them, they are shining white. Will you make a hasty exit from the room (turn to **459**), or will you wait to see what he is doing (turn to **47**)?

304

You leave the building and continue past the yard of stones. You join a path which leads east over a stile and through a field of crops being gathered by peasants. Heads bob up over the tops of the plants as, one by one, the peasants notice your presence. Screams come from a couple of the women and the men rush towards you, hurling stones. They keep a safe distance, but their missiles are landing close. Will you quicken your pace and make off across the field away from them (turn to **87**)? Or will you react to their attack by turning on them (turn to **421**)? You may also decide to settle down in the field and eat some crops (turn to **270**).

305

Thugruff recovers from the blow and staggers to his feet. 'So the truth is revealed,' he pants. 'Our quiet friend has ambitions to replace Thugruff. But this can never be. Zharradan Marr will never let a stranger run his Testing Grounds, of this you can be certain. And though you may defeat your ageing teacher, you cannot defeat Marr's legions!' With these words he reaches into his tunic, pulls out a small whistle and blows it. You stop your attack. Within moments, the legionnaires will be upon you! From the castle they come swarming to rescue their battlemaster in numbers that you may not even hope to fend off. Mercifully, your death is swift at the hands of the frenzied legionnaires.

306

You are fascinated by the ugly pendant. You carefully hook the leather thong with a claw and pull it free of the adventurer's head. You turn it over in your hand and can see that it is circular, with a dull blue stone set in the centre. You stare at the pendant for some time, wondering what to do with it. Then you remember how the adventurer wore it. You are just able to squeeze it over your head and you carry the pendant proudly around your neck. The pendant has a secret, which will be revealed in due course. If you reach a reference which begins: 'You cannot see a thing . . .', deduct 20 from the reference number you are on at the time and turn to this new reference. You may add 1 *LUCK* point for this find. Now turn to **115**.

307

A trail has been cut through the bulrushes. Your heavy feet splash along the marshy trail until you reach a clearing. The going seems a little more solid and you can see footprints – not human footprints, but the large webbed footprints of some unknown creature. From the clearing there are two ways on, one to the north and one to the north-east. Which will you choose: north (turn to **132**) or north-east (turn to **163**)?

308

You travel west along a twisting passageway. Several times you bump clumsily into the walls and grunt in annoyance. But your tough scales protect you from damage. The temperature drops noticeably and each breath sends steamy snorts from your nostrils. After narrowing slightly, the passage widens as it leads towards a chamber. A sound from ahead and a flickering light warn you to take care. But rather than making you stop to listen, the prospect of an encounter seems to excite you! You bare your teeth and your claws and stride forward into the chamber. Turn to **205.**

309

The passage continues west, then turns sharply to the right. A few paces along the corridor you reach a junction where you can go either west (turn to **280**) or north (turn to **371**).

310

You cannot see a thing as you grope your way along the passage. Your anger begins to rise and is near to boiling when you reach a dead end ahead. Will you search the dead end for a possible way onwards (turn to **171**), or return to the crossroads and take the northern passage (turn to **354**) or the southern passage (turn to **212**)?

311

The glowstones once more light your way as you plod slowly north up the passageway. After a short distance you see a shape ahead, slumped motionless on the ground. When you reach the spot, you can see that these are the remains of a small furry creature – about the size of the Dwarf you came across earlier. It has probably been dead for some time, but if you are hungry you may wish to feed on it. If so, turn to **363**. If you ignore it and continue, turn to **75**.

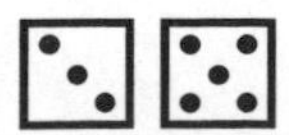

312

The commotion on deck has attracted the attention of other creatures. You can hear the sounds of footsteps and a cacophony of growling voices getting closer. You had better hide! Ahead of you is a door leading from the deck and you step through and close it behind you. You find yourself at the top of a staircase leading down into the ship. You carefully descend until you find yourself in a circular hallway with five doors leading from it. Behind you, the voices are shouting angrily on the deck above. They will soon be following you down the stairs, so you had better choose a safer hiding-place than the hallway! Each of the doors has a symbol on it. To your immediate left, the symbol is a jug from which water is pouring. The symbol on the next door is a burning fire. The next door has the symbol of a crown; the next a delicate snowflake; and finally the door to your right has a battle symbol on it: two crossed swords, painted in blue. Which will you choose:

The jug of water? Turn to **346**
The fire? Turn to **29**
The crown? Turn to **129**
The snowflake? Turn to **158**
The crossed swords? Turn to **111**
None of these? Turn to **302**

313

You lower yourself over the edge and on to the first step. You sway a little, but gradually you become accustomed to the awkward position and you take the next step downwards. Once your head is below the level of the ledge, you find you are able to lean against the side of the chasm for balance and you take the next few steps easily. However, the next step is smaller than the others and is slightly further away. This will be dangerous. *Test your Luck*. If you are Lucky, turn to **65**. If you are Unlucky, turn to **338**.

314

You enter a short passageway which you follow to a T-junction. You consider which way to turn. Turn to **298**.

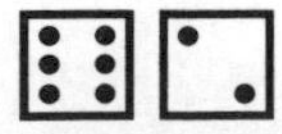

315

There are two ways on from this clearing and while you are deciding which to take, you are startled by a loud croaking noise which seems to come from immediately behind you. You spin round to find yourself facing a creature almost as large as you, with a huge head on a puffed-out body with warty skin. Its feet and hands are webbed. It opens a cavernous mouth and lets out a deafening croak, while its two glassy eyes blink slowly. In one hand it grasps a trident and it seems to want you to back into the centre of the clearing. But having seen the sloshy mud in the centre of the clearing, you are not sure whether you are all that keen to oblige. Will you back towards the centre of the clearing as the Toadman wishes (turn to **68**), or would you rather fight the creature (turn to **145**)?

316

'Be patient!' he says, scratching his head. 'Now what was it to add next? Ah yes, Sculliweed! Now where are those Sculliweed seeds?' Your eyes follow his round the room until they reach a jar which has 'Sculliweed Seeds' on its label. The jar is empty. 'Damn! and damn again!' he curses. 'Now I shall have to visit those scoundrels in Dree to buy more. Blast!' He turns away from his pot and towards you. 'So much for my Potion of Fortune,' he says. 'Not much use having a Potion of Fortune without the luck herb. Right then, what can I do for you. Oh, my goodness!

You're a *beast*! Er, um . . . Do you need a healing balm? Or perhaps you would like me to remove a curse? Ah, just name it! I-I'm sure Euphidius can help.' Will you allow him to use healing balm on you (turn to **426**), or do you want him to remove a curse (turn to **188**)? If you want neither of these, you may leave him and head out of the village by turning to **374**.

317

You step through the door and reach out to feel what sort of a place you are in now. Your scales brush against rocky walls. It seems you are in a passageway, and you step forward, steadying yourself against the walls, and shuffle along the passage. A snort of contempt comes from your nostrils, in anger at your predicament. Your pace quickens as your anger builds, until suddenly you trip over. You spit out the foul taste of a mouthful of the jelly-like slime into which you have fallen head first. Then you raise yourself to your feet and lean against the wall. Something is not quite right. A sharp pain comes from your belly and you grip yourself with a grunt of pain. Minutes later you are writhing in agony on the floor, thrashing around in the slime! Your thrashings are causing the poisonous slime to fly all around you, and you cannot help but catch more globs of the deadly substance in your mouth. There is no escape from this lingering death . . .

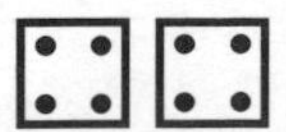

318

You put the bottle to your mouth and gulp down the liquid. Almost immediately, you begin to feel strength flowing through your body. You have discovered and drunk a Potion of Strength, and it takes effect quickly. You may restore your *STAMINA* to its *Initial* level. Now continue by turning to **293**.

319

You poke your head through the hole in the wall and take a deep breath. The foul air makes you cough deeply. You can hear far below the sounds of running water and the smell coming from the filthy river is overpowering. You pull yourself back into the room. Will you now investigate the boxes (turn to **217**), push the boxes into the hole in the wall (turn to **322**) or leave the room (turn to **436**)?

320

As their leader falls, the other two adventurers rush to attack. One is a female warrior and the other is a thief. Both are carrying shields and both attack you at the same time:

	SKILL	*STAMINA*
WARRIOR	*7*	*7*
THIEF	*8*	*6*

If you defeat both of them, turn to **281**.

321

You stand your ground and wait for the undead creatures to arrive. Soon the shuffling stops and a fist thumps the door. Claws raised, you are poised to strike. The door swings inwards and a sea of dead faces search you out with lifeless eyes. You lunge forward to attack! Your first swipe decapitates two Zombies, but the creatures do not die! You lash out furiously, but the struggle is futile. Their numbers are overwhelming. Eventually they will wear you down and tear you apart. Your journey ends here . . .

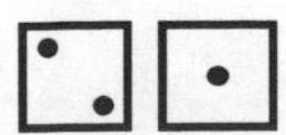

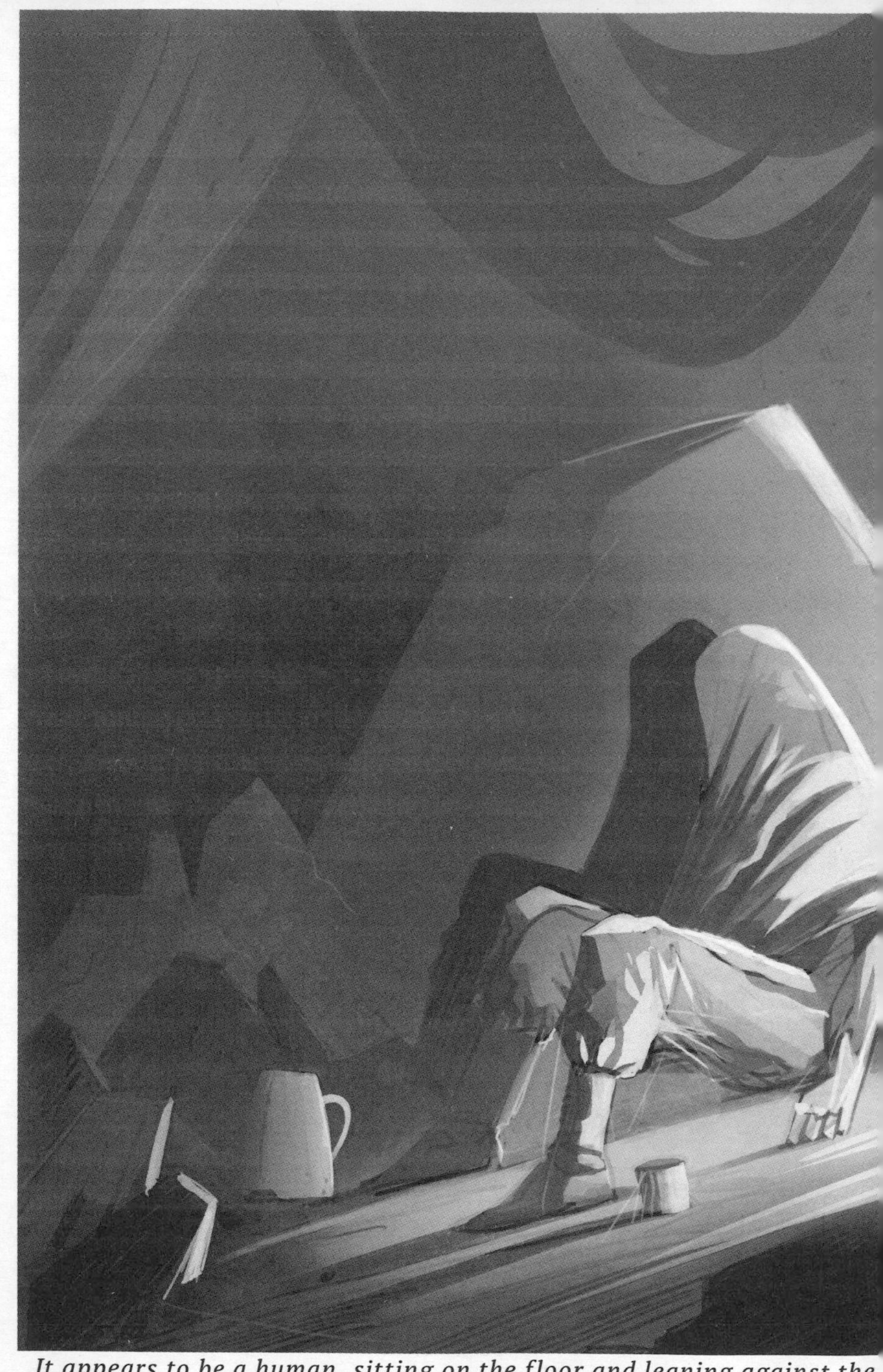

It appears to be a human, sitting on the floor and leaning against the wall, a tattered cowl over its head

322

You pick up the first box. It is quite heavy and something soft and bulky bumps about inside. You fit the end of the box into the hole in the wall and shove. The box slides down what seems to be a long chute and finally splashes into the water below. You pick up the other box and do the same. You may now leave the room. Turn to **436**.

323

You are intrigued by the voice and find yourself strangely attracted to it. It guides you towards one of the central arches in the east wall. 'Come closer, so I may speak to you in private. No, not that arch, this one. That's right. Have no fear. I will tell you of the all-knowing one *and* tell you where you will find some juicy Hobbits. Just a little further. It is so long since I have enjoyed company and I do so love to find out what happens in the outside world . . .' You pass through the arch and look around. When your eyes have adjusted to the light, you can see that you are standing in a short tunnel which ends several paces ahead in a dead end. There are no glowstones, but a glistening sheen covers the ceiling. At the end of the short passage is a shape which you can just make out. It appears to be a human, sitting on the floor and leaning against the wall, a tattered cowl over its head. A leather flagon stands at its feet. 'Come closer,' says the voice. 'My hearing is not good. Can I offer you drink?' Will you approach the figure (turn to **439**), or will you try another arch (turn to **220**)?

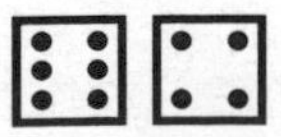

324

As you settle down to sleep in the run-down old building, you reflect on the words of the witches. You must find for them Sculliweed roots, from a plant you have never seen before. However, this task does seem to arouse your interest and you are aware that something of yourself is developing. Your mind goes back to the blind wizard in the room and how you would never have been able to undertake a task such as this if you now felt as you did then. It is almost as if you are developing *wisdom*! This notion occupies your thoughts and you drop into a disturbed sleep. When you awake the next morning, light is streaming in through coloured glass in the windows and you heave yourself to your feet. A fresh meaty meal is lying next to you and you eat it. You may add 8 *STAMINA* points (if you are able) for the rest and the food and 2 *LUCK* points for the encounter.

You may now set off. Will you head north (turn to **301**), south (turn to **95**), east (turn to **304**) or west (turn to **299**)?

325

This plant has mysterious properties. You may or may

not get the opportunity to find out what it can be used for. If asked to present this plant to someone later in the adventure, remember the number twenty-seven. Now you may leave the river-bank by turning to **18**.

326

As you march on eastwards, you reach a bend where the passage turns to the north. A creaking sound from around the corner alerts you and you stop just before the bend. The sound is a slow, repeating creak. You peer round the corner to find out whether you can see anything. But the glowstones are not alight and all you can see is blackness. Will you continue round the corner (turn to **441**), or return to the junction and head west instead (turn to **353**)?

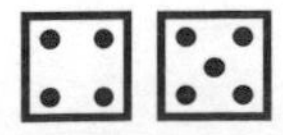

327

As the Demon advances, you stand your ground and prepare to attack. When it is almost upon you, you swing your fist into its chest. Your fist passes right through! You swing again, and the same thing happens. You step forward into the creature and thrash with both hands. Your hands touch nothing, but your foot comes down on a small, soft object which seems to try to pull away but quickly goes still. As this happens, the huge shape of the Rock Demon fades. You lift your foot to reveal a dead mouse, upon which the Illusion spell had been cast.

You are still unsure of what has happened, but the danger has now passed and you may either return your attentions to the parchment (turn to **192**) or leave the room. If you decide to leave, you may use either the door in the south wall, through which you entered (turn to **450**), or the door in the east wall (turn to **365**).

328

The rest of the body is not deeply buried, but when you have finally uncovered the whole skeleton you can tell that whoever lived here certainly died a painful death: the skeleton's rib-cage has disintegrated! You look again at its outstretched hand. The liquid! Is this a warning? Or could the liquid have prevented the disaster? You puzzle over these questions, then leave the ruins. You may, if you wish, take the bottle of green liquid with you. Turn to **126**.

329

At last the pieces of the puzzle fit together. You step up to the mirror and stare into the glass. You are looking not at your own image, but *deeper.* Within seconds your uncertainty disappears, as the reflection of your own shape begins to fade and something gradually takes its place. From the depths of the misty netherworld which the necromancer now makes his sanctuary, the awesome form of Zharradan Marr takes shape before you!

As the mist clears, you can make out that Marr is sitting behind a desk in what seems to be a library of some kind. Books are scattered across the desk, along with mystical artefacts and demonic idols, which also decorate the tall chair he is seated in. Zharradan Marr himself appears to be either deep in thought or asleep. A shiver of fear runs down your spine. A feeling of danger sets your

heart pounding and you cannot help but just *stare* at the necromancer. His very form seems to exude a power which is so strong you can almost feel it.

At once his eyes flick open! You jump back as his fiery pupils, like two burning coals, pierce your soul with their stare. His lower lip curls down to reveal sharp, biting teeth and a sinister hissing sound comes from his mouth. 'So!' speaks Marr, with a voice that resounds in your ears. 'Like the salmon fish, my creation returns to its home, drawn by the forces of nature! Ha! You have done well. And you have brought my prize.' You look puzzled. 'Ah yes, my fearsome friend,' he chuckles. 'It is no accident that you stand before me on the *Galleykeep*. Yours was my finest marrangha and it has been a complete success. Not only have you proved to be a perfect creature to replicate as my personal legionnaires, but your mind is as sharp as your muscles are strong. You have passed every test, from escaping my dungeons to finding your way into the *Galleykeep*. And you have safely returned to me the Vapour!' Marr seems to delight in revealing his plan, rather as a father would to his son . . .

'When we first met, you were my captive. Though you deserved no charity, I was merciful. Rather than have you slaughtered, I offered you a choice. Either you were to serve me, or you were to become a subject for my own marrangha experiments. You chose never to serve under me and thus your fate was decided. As a token of respect I reserved for you my most ambitious experiment.' You dwell on his words. You cannot remember ever having met Zharradan Marr before. And why should he have *respect* for you? Turn to **121**.

330

You follow the path. After a long trek southwards, the trail sweeps round to the east. It begins to widen into a well-used road just as you reach the outskirts of a dusty village. On your left you pass a run-down building which could prove a useful place of shelter for you. But a growing commotion ahead brings your attention back to the road. A number of villagers are beginning to bar the road. As you step forward, one picks up a stone and hurls it at you. It lands close by your foot. A second villager throws another stone, and this one bounces off your chest! Lose 1 *STAMINA* point for the painful blow. They cheer and grab more stones to throw at you. It seems you are not welcome here and you decide to turn back before you are hit again. *Test your Luck*. If you are Lucky, none of the villagers manage an accurate shot. But if you are Unlucky, you must take another 2 *STAMINA* points of damage from their stones. You retrace your steps to the crossroads and this time you may either turn west (turn to **177**) or carry on north (turn to **130**).

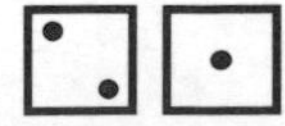

331

You step through the door into another rocky passage. But this one is short, and empty shelves are fixed to the walls on both sides. At the end of the passage is a wooden door. You step up to the door and shove it open. Turn to **15**.

332

You must resolve your battle with the deadly creature. Although not strong, the Giant Hornet has one powerful weapon. If you roll a double while rolling for its Attack Strength, it has managed to sting you and the effects are fatal. You will die unless you *also* manage to roll a double in the same Attack Round. If you do manage to roll a double with your Attack Round roll, then you do not die, but must take 6 *STAMINA* points of damage instead before your Instant Death blow kills the Hornet. Resolve your battle:

GIANT HORNET *SKILL 6* *STAMINA 7*

If you defeat the Hornet, you had better leave the chamber quickly. Turn to **239**.

333

You grasp your crystal club and swing it at your opponent's head. To your amazement the club seems to take on a will of its own! As your opponent ducks, the club follows his movements and comes down heavily on his skull. The force of the blow shatters the club, which now lies in fragments on the floor. But the blow was sufficient to slay your opponent outright. You have won this battle, but you have lost your club. Return to the previous reference and carry on.

A spindly arm rises above your shadow with a sharp knife clutched in its hand

334

You wander around the room, but there is nothing particularly remarkable about it. You stop by the pile of cloth and bend down to pick it up. But, to your alarm, it springs into the air and disappears! Astonished at this strange occurrence, you look round the room for signs of the cloth. The flickering shadows make your search more difficult and in the end you shake your head and ignore the incident. You begin to move off towards the archway, when you suddenly feel a sharp stabbing pain in your back!

You spin round, roaring loudly, to face your attacker. There is no one there! But drops of dark liquid, rolling off your back and dripping on to the floor, confirm that you have certainly been injured. You must lose 2 *STAMINA* points. As you search round trying to spot your attacker, you get your first warning of the phantom you are facing. Your shadow shifts against the wall and, as it does so, it reveals *another* shadow, trying to remain concealed within your own! A spindly arm rises above your shadow with a sharp knife clutched in its hand. You leap to one side as the arm descends. The knife catches your shadow's arm as you jump away, and dark blood seeps from between the scales of *your* arm. You must lose 2 more *STAMINA* points. What do you want to do now? Will you attempt to fight the deadly Shadow Stalker you are facing? If so, turn to **34**. If you want to grab for the torches, turn to **379**. If you prefer to flee from the area, turn to **242**.

335

You are determined to leave. 'If you must leave,' squeaks the little Pixie, 'then so be it. But you should be warned: you will not get far.' He opens the gate and lets you out. Without even looking back, you set off down the trail the way you came. Long after the castle has disappeared from sight behind you, an eerie whistling catches your ears. It seems to be coming from all around you; it is like wind, yet all is still. The whistling turns to soft voices, and you stop to listen. Darkness is closing in, and moments later it is too dark to see far in front of you. When you do peer ahead, you are startled to see a group of *figures* silhouetted against the dark sky in front of you, as if they have been formed from the very darkness itself! Then the spell breaks! All is now back to normal: the darkness, sounds and figures have disappeared. Realizing that something mysterious is going on, you decide to try to make the job of following you more difficult. Turn to **57**.

336

The *Galleykeep* looms closer and your frustration grows. If you had been in a calmer frame of mind, you might have noticed the Whipwood tree, bent over double and held to the ground by a rope passing through a stake and ending in a loop. Your next step takes you straight into the centre of the hidden loop, and your fate is sealed.

The *Galleykeep* duly arrives to hoist its cargo of food on board. You will provide a hearty meal for the crew tonight . . .

337

'Swjnfb fbrd apfo yprf. Ypvuh bvf ebffne fpv ndugvj ltyi pfot hf ecr j mfep fowjlf vlub ndamb lj cjpvs ub rsp no bamps to sfrjp vsupff fncfej n it hfed ryerf gj pnsop fo sblbmpnjs. Bsap vnjsh mf nte ypvu br fesfnt fncfde tpovnd frt bkfebap frjl pvs umjss jpn opfo rfcpvfry. Y pvum vstut rbv flen prthwbrds abndaf ntfreth fev nd frgrpvnd ud pmb j nip fozhb rrb dbnam brra thfr fetpos ffkep vtubn darf cp vfref lbsks a cpnt bjnjng is wjrlj ngivbp pvrs. *Th fsfeb rfeth fevbp pvrs upfost jttlf ewpbd.* Y pvum vstuf jnd i thf ethrff eflbsk sacp n tbjnjngi thfs fevb p pvrsu bnda rftv rn uthf me tpoth jsic pvrt. PNON POB C CPVNT UMVST UT HFYEB FEP PFNFD. T hjs ijsi t hfe sfn tfncfe pfot hf ecp vrtu bnda thfe gfbs a hb sa bf fnecb st. Th jsij si ypvru pvn jshmf nt. Yp vumvs tusvc cf fde jni ypvr umjs sjp noprod jfe jn i thfeb t tfmpt.'

Underneath this writing is more, but written in a different style: 'Vb ppvr upfoknpwlf dgf / – Flb xfnmb nfe p fosj lvfrtpn = / – Wjngfdeh flmft.

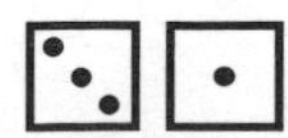

338

Your foot slips on the step. You lose your balance and tumble down, down towards the Bilgewater below. But you never feel the impact of hitting the water. Just before you reach the river, you collide at full speed with a boulder protruding from the face of the cliff. Your death is instantaneous.

339

You stagger round the walls of the room, desperately searching for a way out of the growing furnace. But it is hopeless. The air is now so hot that you cannot breathe without scorching your lungs. Consciousness fades before you are finally roasted in the tremendous heat of the furnace trap.

340

You enter the largest of the caves. It is quite deep and is pitch-black, so you can see very little of what is inside. Straw covers the floor and there is an unpleasant smell in the air. Suddenly your ears prick up! A snuffling noise is coming from deeper in the cave, followed by the dull clang of metal on rock. Your nostrils pick up the smell of animal sweat. Do you want to continue into the cave or will you instead leave whatever is in there in peace? If you want to go further in, turn to **451**. If you want to leave, turn to **386**.

341

As you search through the woods on your seemingly hopeless task, the ship in the sky is becoming larger. It is coming your way! You begin to thrash about in frustration, but just then you see what you are looking for. Ahead of you – appearing much too obvious now you have spotted it – is a tall, slender tree, bent back on itself – a *Galleykeep* hunting trap! You pick yourself up and stare at the device. The tree, a Whipwood, has been shaved of its branches. Its tip is held taut by a rope which ends in a ring. You study it until you are sure that you can understand how it works.

You wait, watching the slow arrival of the *Galleykeep.* At a suitable time, you spring the trap. The tree snaps upwards and you are hoisted through the air until you hang loosely at tree-top level. You are helpless! Your only hope is that the *Galleykeep* crew see you and pull you on board. The ship gets nearer. As the dark shape looms above you, a long pole reaches out over the side and pulls you up through the air. Your plan is working!

Sharp claws scratch at your scales as the hands of dark, foul-smelling creatures pull you up and over the side of the boat and drop you in a heap on the deck. Playing dead, you gather your strength and wait for a suitable moment to spring into action. Two pairs of rough hands grasp your shoulders and hoist you along the deck towards a

guillotine, whose blade is poised and ready to drop. At that moment you make your move! You pull yourself to your feet and fling your two guards over the side of the ship. Two burly Goblins step forward with shorts words. You must resolve this battle. The creatures attack together:

	SKILL	*STAMINA*
First GOBLIN	*6*	*5*
Second GOBLIN	*5*	*5*

If you defeat the Goblins, turn to **312**.

342

The footsteps and clanking get louder and louder. You can feel your anger rising and your lips curl back to bare your teeth. Suddenly the footsteps stop and you hear hissing noises. They have heard you approach! The passageway is rough and twisting and you are straining to see any signs of them ahead. You step nearer and nearer; and they are doing likewise. Finally, you reach a length of straight passageway. Ahead you can see the dull light of a glowstone and picked out in the light are two human faces. Evidently they can see you too, as their reaction is similar: you stare at each other for a few moments. They hold their ground. Do you want to attack (turn to **258**), or will you wait to see what they do (turn to **432**)?

343

You bend down and make your way along the tunnel through the overhanging foliage. You cannot help but wonder about how such a tunnel ever came into existence. It is unlikely that it would occur naturally. But then that only leaves . . .

Your questions are answered when you feel your progress being hindered. You are tugging against sticky vines which have wrapped themselves around your legs and back. The more you tug, the more lengths of vine you pull on top of you. You begin to panic! What can you do? If you wish to make a desperate attempt to break out of the tunnel, turn to 4. If you wish to relax and wait to see what happens next, turn to **278**. If you are carrying a bottle of green liquid and wish to try drinking it, turn to **214**.

344

The passage continues westwards but begins to narrow after a few paces. It bends first to the left, then to the right. At one point you disturb a group of rats feasting on some partially decomposed remains, but they scurry off into the blackness as you pass by. Suddenly, sounds in the distance alert you and you stop. Ahead there is a sharp bend to the southland flickering light and dancing shadows warn you of danger. For a few moments you hesitate. But your emotions take over. A raging storm seems to be gathering within. Your eyes narrow; your lips curl back to reveal your sharp teeth; you flex your powerful muscles and step forward. Fearlessly you step round the corner to face whatever awaits you. Turn to **205**.

345

You stumble down the rocky bank and splash into the river. The dirty water feels greasy to the touch and the stench is *horrendous*. You force your way forward against the fast-flowing current, deeper and deeper into the darkness of the cave. Your presence is noted by a host of fish and other animals living in the Bilgewater. Most are not capable of harming you. But there is one river creature who thrives in vile waters. Known as the Devil's Locks, it is a huge burrowing creature with long stinging tentacles. In rivers it will bury its body in crevices, allowing its deadly tentacles to waft in the current. The effect is rather like seeing a long-haired disembodied head lying on the bed of the river (hence the name). You, of course can see nothing. Nor do you know anything of the terrible creature. The last things you remember are soft fibres wrapping themselves around your leg and a sharp pain as the first sting releases its quick-acting poison . . .

346

The door opens and you step into a dingy room. Dust and cobwebs have begun to settle over the furniture and the curtains over the portholes are drawn. The room itself has an unmade bed against one wall. A wardrobe door yawns half open, rocking as the *Galleykeep* sways and revealing elegant uniforms, now beginning to look a little dusty. You get a sudden fright when you see a creature staring at you, but relax when you realize it is only your reflection in a full-length mirror which hangs to the side of the wardrobe. Further round the room, there is a desk, covered in charts and maps, one of which protrudes from a folder marked 'For Captain's Eyes Only'. A spiral staircase to one side of the desk ascends to another hatchway which is closed. As you are making your way round the room, you get another fright when you bump into a long, thin, brass-trimmed device which stands on three legs and points out of the window. There is no one in the room; nor does it look as though it has been used recently. But you might as well investigate the contents. Which will you start with:

The wardrobe? Turn to **59**
The mirror? Turn to **422**
The desk? Turn to **246**
The spiral staircase? Turn to **370**
The brass-trimmed device? Turn to **225**

347

You try the door but you cannot get a grip without a handle. Your claws dig into the wood and you pull hard, but to no avail. The door is closed tightly and is being held by some catch. You cannot open it. Will you instead examine the figure on the chair (turn to **452**), or search through the bones in the corner of the room (turn to **64**)?

348

As you wander through the multitude of creatures, you start to consider this place. So far your life has been aimless. You have been wandering alone through the land. Here is a place where you will be fed, where you will mix with others, and where you will never be short of a good fight. On the other hand, a voice in the back of your mind is still asking the same questions. Who are you? What are you doing here? Where have you come from? The answers to these questions will probably not be found here. Thugruff comes over to you and asks you whether you would like to stay to train as one of Marr's legionnaires and serve on his *Galleykeep.* What will you do? Do you want to leave (turn to **455**), or will you seriously consider training as a legionnaire (turn to **43**)?

349

The guard lies dead on the ground and you step back to catch your breath. You may feast on the guard's body, but if you do, you will gain only 3 *STAMINA* points, for his taste is not to your liking. The way onwards seems to be through the metal door in the wall opposite your entrance. You step up and try it: it is locked. You strain to see through the small barred viewing-hole set in the door. You can see a stone stairway leading upwards, and a soft cool wind caresses your cheek. Will you look for the key to the lock (turn to **112**) or try to break down the door (turn to **128**)?

350

The blue liquid smells sweet and you sip down the contents of the flask. There is no noticeable effect. But the effects of the Potion of Fear you have just drunk will not be revealed until you enter your next battle. When you do so, you will feel strangely afraid of your opponent and you will never again be able to use the Instant Death rule, unless you find someone who has the power to remove curses. Continue by turning to **293**.

351

The path continues through the undergrowth, but the going becomes more difficult. You soon find it difficult to tell which way the path leads, as the whole area is so overgrown. You peer through the woods ahead and there seems to be little of interest, although an area to your left seems to be unnaturally dark. This could just be a cluster of broad-leaved trees blocking out the light, or it could be something else. Do you want to try beating your way through the vegetation towards it (turn to **381**), or will you turn round, follow the path back to the fork and take the other direction (turn to **183**)?

352

'Enough!' shouts Thugruff. 'I have seen enough.' If you reduced Eleven's *STAMINA* to 2, turn to **118**. If he reduced your *STAMINA* to 2, turn to **431**.

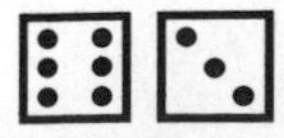

353

You continue west and you notice that the air is becoming distinctly cooler. The walls of the passage become damp and glisten in the glowstones' light. A breeze is blowing against you, as if to persuade you against this course. Your ears pick up the sound of running water and each step brings this sound closer. Eventually you find yourself standing on a narrow rocky bridge which spans a bubbling stream some distance below. You stop to look down at the flowing water. It is not easy to see in the dim light, but your nose twitches at the unpleasant smell which issues from the stream. If you feasted on the Hellhound, you must lose 2 *STAMINA* points for the nausea you now feel. You hurry on over the bridge and soon afterwards come across a passageway leading north. If you take this passage, turn to **172**. If you prefer to continue west, turn to **149**.

354

You stumble off awkwardly up the passage. The ground is rough underfoot and the passage is getting a little narrower, though the ceiling appears to be much higher up. Eventually you reach a dead end. There seems to be no way forward. Will you grope around the walls to see whether you can find a way of progressing (turn to **179**), or will you return to the crossroads and turn either to the east (turn to **310**) or to the south (turn to **212**)?

355

The creature is not the ageing carthorse you expect. Instead it is a powerful stallion and it will put up quite a fight:

STALLION	*SKILL* 7	*STAMINA* 9

If you defeat the horse, you may eat its nourishing meat. Add 5 *STAMINA* points and turn to **386** to leave.

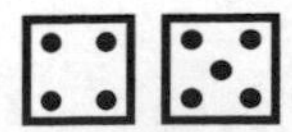

356

You follow the corridor round the bend to the east, then round another to the north. The smell is getting stronger but there are now other aromas in the air. The passage turns west next, and a short distance further on you stop at a corner where it turns to the south. The smells in the air are now quite strong and there are sounds coming from round the corner. You cautiously poke your head round to see what is going on.

The passage ends a short distance ahead. Bones are strewn about the place. Some have remnants of flesh left on them, but not for long. Standing in the centre of the passageway, feasting noisily on the remains, are three Carrion Bugs! They are huge, black beetles with formidable heads in the shape of death's-head skulls. The creatures' heads are armed with razor-sharp mandibles which can strip muscle cleanly from a bone in an instant. You are considering whether or not to turn round and retrace your steps, when your eyes fall on an unmistakable shape – the decaying corpse of a Hobbit! Your eyes widen and your dry mouth becomes moist. Thoughts of retracing your steps fade . . .

You surge through the Carrion Bugs to your meal. They ignore you until you grab the Hobbit. But then they turn towards you: they will not allow you to steal their meal!

You must fight the Carrion Bugs all together:

	SKILL	*STAMINA*
First CARRION BUG	*7*	*6*
Second CARRION BUG	*8*	*5*
Third CARRION BUG	*7*	*5*

If you wish to escape during the battle, you may do so by turning to **240**, but only after at least three Attack Rounds. If you defeat all three of them, turn to **375**.

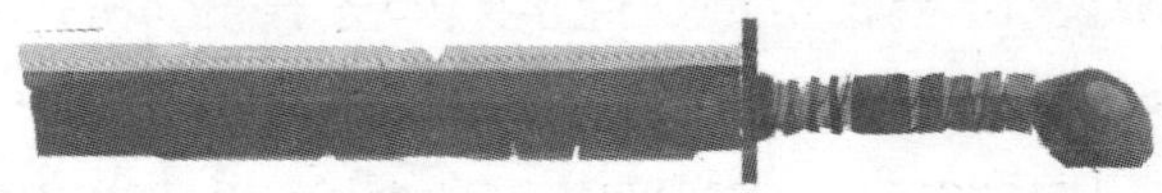

357

You kick the door back and slash out at the Rhino-Man. You must resolve this battle:

RHINO-MAN *SKILL 8* *STAMINA 9*

If you defeat the creature, you may search the guardroom. As the Rhino-Man was about the same size as you, you may wish to take something from the room. If you take a dusty brown sack, turn to **250**. If you take a metal breastplate, turn to **415**.

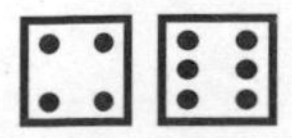

358

A passage leads from the opening into the rock-face, and you follow it. But you find that, as you travel north, the light fades rapidly. There are no glowstones in this passage and you must progress carefully, steadying yourself by running your hands along both walls. The ground underfoot is rocky and several times you stub your toes painfully on protruding stones. Later, you can no longer touch both walls at once. Although you are unable to see anything, you sense that you are entering a large chamber. Turn to **257**.

359

Battered and crushed, the physician drops to the floor. You catch your breath for a few moments. Will you now head for the door and leave the room (turn to **178**), or will you continue looking round the room (turn to **407**)?

360

You have no wish to give the ring back to the blind wizard. It may prove very useful to you in the future. And, apart from that, you think it looks splendid on your finger. The old wizard wants you to lead him away, but your attitude is mixed. He may slow you down and you have learned all his useful information. You stand up, brush him aside, and leave. If you come across Darramouss, you may use the ring as follows. When you are given the option to *grab* him and do battle, add 50 to the reference you are on at the time and turn to this new reference. Now turn to **138**.

361

You pick up your club and step towards the mirror. When Zharradan Marr sees your weapon, his confident manner becomes a little nervous. 'So, my offspring of marrangha,' he says, though perhaps a little too eagerly. 'You choose to turn against your creator. Do not be hasty. Let me first tell you of my plans for us. Whatever future you wish, it can be achieved.' Turn to **460**.

362

After a few moments you find it difficult to keep your eyes open and your head begins to nod. Resistance is useless. You roll over on the ground and fall soundly asleep. But your sleep is disturbed by dreams of dark creatures, humans with sharp swords and magical encounters. In the centre of your dreams is yourself, understanding nothing, for ever wondering *where* you are, and *why*. In one dream you are running from a hideous figure, who is pursuing you in a ship which flies. The faster you try to escape, the easier it is for the ship to catch up. Leering sadistically, the figure drops a net over you! You crash to the ground, trapped in the net, trying desperately to escape . . .

You wake up with a start, arms flailing madly. A breeze has blown the branch of an oak into you, so that its leaves cover your face and chest. You breathe a sigh of relief and pick yourself up. Your eyes narrow to slits as they adjust to a new experience for you. Daylight! You may add 4 *STAMINA* points for the rest and then you set off once more through the wood. Turn to **244**.

363

The dead Hellhound would no doubt have made a tasty meal had you arrived several days ago. But now its rotten flesh gives you severe stomach cramps. You double over and your claws scrape on the rocky walls as you try to support yourself. You must lose 4 *STAMINA* points and wait for a while before you continue. When you are ready, turn to **75**.

364

You greet the Dwarf. At least you *try* to greet the little creature. But instead of any message coming from your throat, it is silent and your hands reach down to grasp the terrified figure around the chest. He screams and makes a strange sound, which sounds like: 'Kff pebw by afrp momf.' You try to answer, but the only sound you are able to make is a grunt of effort as your rough, scaly fingers close tightly around the creature's chest and your sharp claws dig in. Summoning up all its strength, it swipes at you with its sharp sword. The blade digs in under the scales above your knee, but the wound is not too serious – deduct 2 *STAMINA* points. The blow causes you to roar loudly and to increase the pressure on the creature's chest. Its ribs crack like twigs under the force of your grip and the body falls limp. You drop it to the floor where it lands like the sack of bones it now is.

Your thoughts are confused. Will you attempt to hide the body (turn to **218**), will you examine this strange little creature (turn to **399**), or will you leave the area immediately (turn to **248**)?

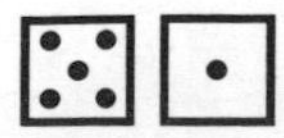

365

The door opens into a straight passage leading east, which you follow until you reach a dead end. You growl in frustration and, as if your voice had acted as some kind of trigger, you hear a click and a sliding sound. Part of the rock-face slides aside and reveals another passage running north and south! You step through the secret doorway cautiously, wary of a trap. When you are through, the door grinds shut again. But at the same time there is another sound, which seems to be coming from *above* you. Just in time you look up to see a heavy portcullis dropping from the roof towards you! You fling yourself forward not an instant too soon. A heavy *clang* sounds behind you as the portcullis hits the ground. You escaped death by inches!

Since you hurled yourself north, the way to the south is now sealed off by the portcullis, and you pick yourself up and set off north. Soon you reach a crossroads where you may turn east (turn to **50**) or west (turn to **213**), or continue northwards (turn to **443**).

366

You step back into the bushes and search the clearing suspiciously. All is quiet, until a shrill cry breaks the silence. This is followed by the sounds of a struggle and finally three figures tumble into the clearing from the undergrowth, locked in combat. Two rough-set Brigands are grappling with another creature. The Brigands are burly humans, with leather breastplates and boots. The belts around their waists hold throwing-knives, but they are using their bare fists in this battle. Their adversary is thin and nimble, with long white hair and angular features. He wears a silky robe and appears to be unarmed. He is putting up a brave fight, but is clearly losing the battle as blow after blow from the brigands thuds into his stomach, ribs and head. He is crying out for help. Will you help him? If so, turn to **429**. If you would rather keep hidden until the Brigands have left, turn to **295**.

367

Only the Half-Orc's attacker is disappointed to see the miserable creature drop down dead. The villagers applaud and usher you into the hut to drink a toast to your victory. If you refuse their hospitality, turn to **107** to leave Coven. If you accept their invitation, turn to **395**.

368

There are all kinds of birds and some rabbits to be found in the wood. To catch some food, you must *Test your Luck* successfully. If you are Lucky, you will catch a small animal for 2 *STAMINA* points of nourishment. If you are Unlucky, you will not. You may try as many times as you like, but you may not gain more than 4 *STAMINA* points in total. Turn to **229** when you want to continue.

369

You step into the passage and your eyes adjust to the green light. You breathe cautiously as you progress, but it seems that the smoke is not harmful, though it smells a little pungent. The passage leads after only a few paces to impenetrable blackness; not even the green light is penetrating the dark. Your eyes strain to see anything of the surroundings, but without success.

Suddenly a light flickers to your left! A small flame lights up something: it is a human face! The face is motionless and its eyes are closed. The skin is old and withered and you cannot tell whether it is alive or dead. Another light flickers! Another sombre face lights up before you. And another! Eventually there are four faces, all dimly lit, around the chamber. An instant later, their eyes and mouths flick open wide and the silence is broken by a sharp voice which cuts through the darkness. The effect is terrifying! 'Ypvruprpg rfss ehbs ab ffne wbtchf def pvlucrfbtv r fep fodf str vctj pn. Spo fbray pv uhbvfe dpn fe wfll ethp vgh uypv uk np won pt ow hyo prow hbt. Bvtay pvo hbvfi cbv sfdatw pipf ath favbp pvrse tpebf ulpst. Zhbr rbd bnam brrah jms fl f ehbsa dfc rffdey pvr udfst jny. Yp vushbl lar fmb jn ijni hjsi dvng fpnso b nd adp omy objd djng. Fp roji bma db rrbm pvs suypv rumbs tfr.' Jfiy pvuc bna vn dfrs tbn dahj mi tv rnut p orff frfn cf enj nfty. 'Y pvru fjrs ti prd frejsi th js. Rf pprtofp rodvt yubta thfe yfl lpwstp nfemj nfs. Lfb vfenpw ob ndahfbdath f rfejm mfdjb tfly. Jiwjllibf ewbt chj ng.'

As the voice ceases, a rumbling sound comes from ahead of you. The same green light indicates another secret passageway, which the voice evidently wishes you to take. Will you leave through the new passage (turn to **79**), or will you step up to one of the illuminated faces and crush it in your hand (turn to **247**)?

370

You climb up the staircase and try the hatch at the top. It is open and you climb through. But instead of entering another room, you find yourself on a secluded part of the ship – evidently the captain's private deck. You look around for another hiding-place, but there is none to be found, and soon you are faced with an angry hoard of Orcs and Hobgoblins who have silently followed you onto the deck. You will get to meet Zharradan Marr all right, but as his prisoner. And when he has finished tormenting you for his pleasure, you will remain aboard the *Galleykeep* as his slave for the rest of your days.

371

The passage runs straight ahead until you reach a junction, where you may continue north (turn to **144**) or turn east (turn to **204**). Alternatively, you may return to the previous junction and turn west (turn to **280**).

372

The passage heads east. The rough stone floor begins to feel different underfoot and you look down to see that it has been laid with flat stones of irregular sizes. The light seems to be better, although with a definite bluish tint, and you look up to see blue glowstones in the ceiling, lighting your way. Mysteriously, their glow appears only as you approach; when you look behind you see the light has faded. There are a number of crevices, and small passages lead off from the main one, but you ignore these as they are far too narrow for you to enter. A sound from ahead catches your attention – the soft thump of something landing on the ground. Further on, you discover that it was a tied-up sack. Something inside the sack is struggling, but cannot get out. In size, the lump is similar to the Dwarf you killed earlier. Will you investigate the sack or continue along the passageway? Roll one die. If you roll 1–4, you will stop to study the sack more carefully (turn to **186**). If you roll 5 or 6, you will ignore it (turn to **440**).

373

The rocky corridor continues for some time and then turns sharply southwards. Ahead of you, at the end of the passage, is a sturdy wooden door; to your left is another door. Will you try the door straight ahead (turn to **15**) or the door to your left (turn to **241**)?

374

On the way out of the village, you pass more huts and more of the villagers, who rush across the road to avoid you. Ahead of you is a figure slumped face down on the ground. When you get closer you can see that it is a dark-skinned Half-Orc, and that it is dead. Do you want to investigate the body (turn to **91**), or will you ignore it and continue (turn to **107**)?

One of the Rhino-Men is boasting that he could easily defeat Thugruff in battle

375

With the Carrion Bugs dead, your thoughts revert to the tasty Hobbit. You pick up the rigid body and sink your teeth into its stomach area. Although irresistible, the taste is not too pleasant, as the body has been dead for some time. Nevertheless, you eat heartily and you may gain 4 *STAMINA* points for the meal. Then you follow the passage north, and later east. As you turn the next corner, your heart sinks. Another of the creatures is arriving for its meal! To get past you will have to defeat the Bug:

CARRION BUG	*SKILL 7*	*STAMINA 6*

If you defeat it, turn to **227**.

376

You thrash about in the woods, becoming increasingly frustrated by the hopelessness of your task. *Test your Luck* again. If you are Lucky, turn to **341**. If you are Unlucky, turn to **336**.

377

One of the Rhino-Men is boasting that he could easily defeat Thugruff in battle. The Orcs are taunting him and the tension is mounting as the other Rhino-Men defend him. A fight may break out at any moment. If you want to stay to see what happens, turn to **124**. Otherwise turn to **348**.

378

You step forward to make your way past the Hobbits. But even as you take the first step, you know that you cannot carry out your intention. Though you may wish to ignore the Hobbits, you cannot pass by your favourite food. Turn to **42**.

379

You reach up for the torch on the wall beside you, but it is just out of your reach. Meanwhile, the Shadow Stalker is once more poised for attack and only by shifting sideways quickly do you avoid a fatal blow. Instead, the plunging knife grazes your shadow's leg. Lose 1 *STAMINA* point. Will you now try to fight the creature (turn to **34**), offer a gesture of peace (turn to **135**), or flee as quickly as possible (turn to **242**)?

380

The riverside is a place of great natural beauty. At least, it *seems* to be natural, but there is always the possibility that someone has planted the colourful plants in their beds along the banks of the river. A tall green-stemmed reed is topped with coiled trumpets of purple flowers which hang down facing the river. These flowers are so beautiful that they have a hypnotic effect on the fish of the river, which are attracted to the water beneath the reeds and can be seen swimming beneath them. Another blue-stemmed plant has no flowers but its glistening colour is quite remarkable and it has a strong herbal odour. Yet another plant has leaves which are perfect circles, red in colour. As you watch, one of the leaves drops into the river. The leaf seems to have some purifying effect: as soon as it touches the water, all cloudiness is gone from the area around the leaf; the water becomes crystal-clear until disturbed by the flow of the current. Another plant, out of reach in the water, has delicate flowers of silver. As the wind blows, the flowers whistle and tinkle together with an eerie, calming sound which makes you feel quite relaxed. You may, if you wish, gather a few of *one* of these types of plant before you leave. Which will you choose: the one with purple flowers (turn to **325**), the one with a blue stem (turn to **106**) or the one with the red leaves (turn to **181**)?

381

You pick your way through the woods towards the shaded area. The thick vegetation makes it impossible for you to travel in a straight line and you find yourself turning this way and that to pick out the easiest route. Eventually you reach the shadowy patch and discover to your disappointment that it is a tight thicket of tall Heavenstip trees, their leaves desperately thirsting for the sunlight from above. You turn back towards the path. But where is it? You have no way of knowing which way you have come from and your eyes scan the wood for familiar signs. There are none. Acting on a hunch, you finally set off towards the spot where – you hope – you left the path. Turn to **57**.

382

The gas drifts from the flask, but rather than spreading out, it pulls itself together into a purple cloud and billows up before you. You watch open-mouthed as a shape begins to form in the cloud, and eventually turns into a face, which stares deep into your eyes. The face is human-like, but thin and with jagged features. The pupils of its eyes are not round, but are instead serpent-like. Its thin-lipped mouth opens and speaks: 'Jib mar flfbsf defr pmo myorf st. Fpv lucrfb tvrf ewhbtadpo ypv uk npwop fothfe fprcfsew jthi w hjchiy pvutb mpfr. Bvt unpnf thfl fssemye pvr ppsfe jsipr db jnfd. Jibfstpwop n oypv uthfe ppw frepfo rfbs pn. Frp monp wo pnoyp vubr fej nicp ntr plop foypvr upwnodfs tjny. Bnd anpw-emby ajir ft vrn utp omyo pfbcf fv lurfste vntj lip ncfem prfethfeh fbv fnsetb kfeth fj ri ppsj tjpns.'

Your anger mounts and you swipe at the cloud. But your hand passes right through the gas without even disturbing it. The mysterious face blinks slowly and the colour of the cloud flashes momentarily from purple to white, and back to purple again. Then the face disappears and the cloud is sucked down back into its flask. Once safely inside the flask, the stopper replaces itself in the neck and the bottle settles into its cradle in the wooden casket. An instant later, the casket and its contents have faded to nothing!

You decide you have had enough of this room, but you may add 2 *LUCK* points for your find. Will you leave through the door to the west (turn to **51**), or the door to the east (turn to **33**)?

383

You turn towards the corner where you last heard the clicking noise and let out a deep growl. As you step into the corner, the clicking starts again! This time it becomes quite frantic. To your complete astonishment, the sound darts across the room in front of you and heads for an opposite corner! As you were virtually *in* the corner, and there was no room for anything of any size to pass you, you realize that whatever is making the noise must be very small. Your head turns to the other corner. The pitch of the noise has increased and there seem to be two – if not three – distinct creatures clicking away. Your curiosity has been aroused and you step towards the corner. Only then, do you appreciate the danger you have been facing. The flashes of light coming from behind

the door before you entered were emanating from a small group of Blinding Beetles. These large insects have the power to emit extremely bright flashes of light, which are powerful enough to blind all but magically protected creatures. Your harassment has finally angered them to their flash-point. Three intense bursts of light explode before your eyes, followed by complete blackness. The Blinding Beetles' attack has been effective: you have now lost your sight. You rub your eyes with your scaly hands to try to wipe away the blackness, but there is nothing you can do. In desperation, you bellow pitifully and stumble around the room as if there were some way out of the sightless world which is now yours. As you grope along the wall, you come across a door. You give it a yank, feel it open and a rush of air hits you. Roll one die. If you roll 1, 2 or 3, turn to **80**. If you roll 4, 5 or 6, turn to **317**.

384

Test your Luck. If you are Lucky, you manage to reach the doorway before Darramouss can react (turn to **79**). If you are Unlucky, Darramouss manages to close the door before you can reach it and you must wait to see what fate he has in store for you (turn to **286**).

385

You consider the little creature's words. What you remember of your life has been somewhat aimless. You may just as well spend some time here. He leads you back to the courtyard and explains to Thugruff your reluctance to stay. You are not keen on the villanous Half-Troll. But you must now decide your future, since you are staying. Do you want to work hard and try to earn yourself a position on the *Galleykeep* (turn to **43**), or would you rather bide your time until you can seize a suitable moment to assassinate the foul-breathed Thugruff (turn to **82**)?

386

You head off back towards the crossroads and turn this time to the north. Turn to **130**.

387

He looks deep into your eyes for several moments. Eventually he grunts and stands aside to let you through into the guardroom. The place is dirty, and smells of rancid ale and stale food. Across the room is another door. This one is made of metal and has a small barred viewing-panel at eye-level. Through this panel you can see steps leading upwards. But while you gaze at the door, you are not watching what the guard is doing. Suddenly you feel a heavy blow on the back of your head. You slump to your knees, dazed by the impact, and turn to see the guard advancing towards you holding a heavy club. Lose 4 *STAMINA* points for the blow and turn to **98** to battle with the guard.

388

The going becomes a little steeper and the river splashes faster over its rocky bed. Ahead you can see that it seems to disappear over a ledge and, when you get closer, you see that the river plunges over a tall waterfall and crashes into a natural pond far below, before continuing along a narrower stream through a gully carved in the rock. The effect is quite spectacular, but it presents a problem to you. How do you get down? Following the path along the river-bank is impossible. You will have to continue through the undergrowth. Turn to **57**.

389

Your foe is defeated and you feel justifiably proud. Your gaze passes from the dead creature to its lair. But there is nothing of interest, and the sickening stench of Clawbeast makes you want to leave quickly. There are three ways onwards: the passage behind you, a cave entrance in the western wall and another in the northern wall. What will your next action be? Roll one die. If the roll is 1–4, turn to **230**. If the roll is 5 or 6, turn to **165**.

390

You head off eastwards. After a few steps, the passage

begins to widen and you can hear distant sounds ahead. As you get closer, you recognize them – and your mouth waters! For the sound you can hear is the unmistakable chatter of tasty Hobbits! Without any consideration of the consequences, you make your way quickly towards the noises. The glowstones light your way to a wide chamber. The passage enters it around a bend and you stop to survey the scene. Marble flooring marks the entrance to this meeting-chamber which is decorated with carvings and dark archways. Three Hobbits, wearing none of that obstructive metal armour, are engaged in a heated discussion in the centre of the chamber. They have their backs towards you, but they are concerned about their safety and one of them keeps on looking around the chamber for any signs of danger. Will you wait until this one is occupied before rushing in to attack (turn to **288**), or will you ignore the advantage of surprise and simply rush in (turn to **42**). Alternatively you may wish to ignore the Hobbits and head across the chamber to a passage opposite which continues to the east. If you wish to do this, turn to **378**.

391

The water is cool and refreshing. However, its silver sheen comes from mineral deposits which make it unsuitable for drinking. Lose 2 *STAMINA* points for the strange 'heady' feeling which comes over you. When you are ready, turn to **52** to continue.

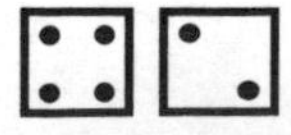

392

Your final blow sends the Knight flying across the chamber to land in a crumpled heap against one wall. You grunt in satisfaction. Your attention is drawn immediately back to the dead Hobbit lying by the fire and your mouth waters at the thought of its sweet flesh. But you have forgotten the final adventurer. The Wizard has now completed his spell. With a final incantation, he delivers his magic, directed straight at you through his two little fingers. You feel no more than a tingling sensation as his spell takes effect. 'Yp v ubr fen pwovnd fre myec pntrpl of pvluc rfb tvrf.' A smile spreads across the sorcerer's lips: 'Bl lamy aw jshfs ebrf e ypvr ucpm mbnds. Gbt hfrem ye cpm rbd fseb n daf pll pwomf!' You intend to step forward and slash him with your claws, but your muscles will not respond. Instead, you step over to the dead Knight, pick him up and carry him over your shoulder. You do the same with the Hobbit. The Wizard then turns and makes his way down the passage. You follow, carrying the rest of his party. And this will be your fate: to spend the rest of your life as a slave to your master, whose Control Creature spell has worked perfectly.

393

You step up to the door in the west wall and tug at the handle. The door will not budge. You grunt in anger, take a step back and prepare to smash the door. But the door is stronger than you thought. You nurse your sore shoulder for a few moments (lose 1 *STAMINA* point), and then return to the centre of the room. Will you try one of the other doors (turn to **405**) or, if you have not already done so, investigate the room (turn to **104**)?

394

Although there are three doors leading from the guardroom, you ignore the one to the south. Will you leave via the door in the north wall (turn to **314**) or the door in the west wall (turn to **116**)?

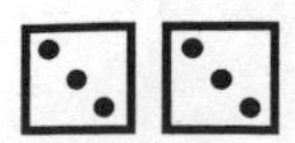

395

Inside the hut is a counter and from behind the counter someone passes you a bowl full of liquid. The bemused villagers watch as you cup the bowl, sniff the liquid, and finally pour it down your throat. The taste is rough and your stomach seems to be undecided whether or not to heave the ale back up again. But instead it decides on a hiccup followed by a great throaty belch which delights the villagers. They laugh at your bewildered expression and the bowl is once more filled up for you to drink again.

Several bowls later you are feeling decidedly lightheaded. The villagers eventually leave the hut and you stagger back out on to the street to continue your journey. You may add 3 *STAMINA* points for the ale, but you must reduce your *SKILL* by 1 until the effects of the ale have worn off. This will be indicated by in the text. Now turn to **107**.

396

The door cracks as you charge it and eventually you break into the room, but not before you take 1 *STAMINA* point of damage for a sore shoulder. The room inside has no occupants. Instead a single desk is surrounded on three sides by racks of parchments, each rolled up neatly and tied with string. A door in the east wall is half hidden behind the untidy racks. Do you want to head out through this door (turn to **365**), or will you pick up a parchment and see what it says (turn to **100**)?

397

As the defeated Warrior slumps dead to the ground, another steps through the archway to take up the battle. You must fight this one too:

CHAOS WARRIOR *SKILL* 7 *STAMINA* 8

If you defeat your attacker, turn to **46**.

398

You pick up a chair and fling it at the door. The chair shatters. By now your anger and frustration are twice what they were before! You try kicking the door with your huge foot. The door seems to shudder a little more than it did before, and a few grains of dust fall to the floor from where the hinges are attached to the rock. But still the door remains intact. You must lose 1 *STAMINA* point for the injury to your foot. If you want to keep trying the door, turn to **128**. If you would rather give up on the door and look for the key, turn to **112**.

399

Your hands relax and the sharp claws retract into your fingers. You clumsily fumble through the Dwarf's dirty vestments. Your fingers will not fit into the pockets, but you do succeed in snapping the thongs of a large leather pouch which the creature has around its waist. As the ties break, the pouch spills its contents on the ground in front of you. It contained several circular pieces of shiny metal and a piece of hide, which unfolds as it drops out of the pouch. It is light in colour and has markings all over one side. You pick it up awkwardly and look at it, but it makes no sense at all. You become quite fascinated by this piece of leather. You turn it round, rub it with your hands and throw it in the air. You place it on your arm and on your head. You decide to take the leather with you. Unknown to you, the message on the hide may be useful later in your adventure. Turn to **337** to examine the message. If you are carrying this piece of hide, you may return to **337** at any time to re-examine it, but you will need to remember the reference you have come from in order to return and continue.

As you may have realized by now, your own wishes have little effect on your reactions as a creature. You have only glimpses of what you are like and what you are capable of. Although this will change as the adventure progresses, at this stage you are at the mercy of your own whims and instincts. You are standing at a junction where you may go either east or west. Roll one die. If you roll 1, 2 or 3, turn to **308**. If you roll 4, 5 or 6, turn to **148**.

Among the debris you find a skeleton hand reaching into the air

400

You step into what is left of the building. Among the debris you find a skeletal hand reaching into the air, the rest of its body buried beneath the ruined walls. In this hand is a stoppered bottle, and within the bottle is a small amount of green liquid. Around the rest of the building there are the remains of various items of furniture: a smashed table, a splintered chair and a wrecked bed, its straw mattress ripped to shreds. But your attention returns to the hand clutching the bottle of liquid. If you wish to leave and take this bottle with you, turn to **126**. If you would rather dig the body out of the rubble, turn to **328**.

401

After a few paces, the passage begins to wind irregularly in a generally south-westerly direction. You follow it for some time, and then it turns south. You arrive at the top of a flight of stairs, but decide against going back down to the lower levels. There is another passage leading east here, and you decide to take this route. Turn to **156**.

402

Your hand closes round his neck. As you tighten it, you can hear the grinding sound of bones being crushed. But Darramouss's expression is unchanging; he shows not the slightest concern. You release the neck and drop the limp body to the ground. But the instant you release him, his body snaps back to life and the incantation continues! You set your claws and bring them ripping across his chest. As soon as you make contact, the body goes limp and it flies through the air, in response to your blow, like an empty sack. But before it lands, it once more fills out and takes shape. As the life surges quickly back into it, the creature flips in the air and flies back to land where it was! This time, the creature opens one eye wide and glares at you. You are caught in a vice-like grip of agony! The pain is overwhelming and you sink to your knees whimpering in front of the desk. You must deduct 4 *STAMINA* points. While you writhe in agony, Darramouss finishes his incantation. Turn to **286**.

403

The tiny face you saw in the distance was unmistakably that of a Hobbit! Unable to control yourself, you climb to your feet and set off in pursuit. Although you are slower than the little creature, it leaves a trail of glowstone light which you can follow. And even though you have just eaten, the smell of the Hobbit sparks off your appetite once more. But you are much too slow to catch it. As you lumber down the passageway, even the glowstone trail disappears. Eventually you reach a junction. Will you continue north (turn to **144**), or will you turn to the east (turn to **204**)?

404

The passage is much wider here and footprints in the dirt indicate that it is more frequently used. But all the footprints seem to be heading the other way! A little further ahead you come to the top of a narrow staircase heading downwards. You consider this for some time, but eventually decide against going down the steps. You turn round and retrace your steps, this time turning east at the junction. Turn to **373**.

405

You may leave by one of the three doors leading from the room. Which will you choose:

The door in the north wall?	Turn to **300**
The door in the west wall?	Turn to **393**
The door in the south wall?	Turn to **6**

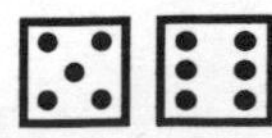

406

One of the Rhino-Men catches your attention and you remember the message. His back is a little stooped and he is obviously past his prime. He looks at you with tired eyes as you approach him; he has seen many young, strong and ambitious legionnaires in his time and he finds them quite tedious. You step up to him and pass him the message. He steps back and looks at you incredulously. 'Is this true?' he stammers. 'Is my sister safe at last? Then I have no need to stay at this godforsaken castle. Thank you for this news, strange creature. I must now make my plans to leave.' Will you join in with his plans to leave the Testing Grounds (turn to **449**), or will you continue wandering through the groups of legionnaires (turn to **348**)?

407

You glance towards the dead creature and move away quickly. But without warning, the skeleton's bones spring together to re-form Quimmel Bone and in an instant it has grabbed the two knives and is once more attacking you. Resolve this battle:

QUIMMEL BONE	*SKILL 8*	*STAMINA 7*

If you win, turn to **178**.

408

The cave leads north to a large tunnel in the rock which runs from east to west. It is large enough for you to walk along. Roll one die. If you roll 1–3, you decide to turn west (turn to **282**). If you roll 4–6, you turn east (turn to **372**).

409

You tug at the door and it opens to reveal a storeroom of some kind, with shelves lining the walls. But there is nothing on the shelves and there seems to be no way through. As you peer into the cupboard, a creaking sound startles you. You swing round to see the door in the east wall slowly opening. Glowstones in the passage outside flick on to light up your way. You cannot resist this invitation and leave through the east door. Turn to **49**.

410

The terrified shopkeeper will give you no trouble as you help yourself to provisions. You feast on the food while he cowers helplessly in the corner. *Test your Luck*. If you are Unlucky, you eat a handful of poisonous herbs and are violently ill (lose 3 *STAMINA* points). If you are Lucky, you avoid the poisons and can add 4 *STAMINA* points for your meal. When you have finished here, you may leave the village by turning to **374**.

Four of the living corpses rise from their graves and surround you

411

You turn to another gravestone, keeping one eye on the grave of Donag Haddurag and listening for warning signs. The next grave is that of a woman, whose inscription reads: 'Here lies Sophia Whiterose. Like a rosebud she blossomed with beauty, but alas she died entwined in her own thorns.' You puzzle over the words – but then a scraping sound distracts you. You look back towards the previous gravestone and a shiver runs down your back! A withered hand is pushing the stone aside! Then you hear the same sound behind you, and again to your left, as scraggy limbs slowly push gravestones aside and long-dead bodies crawl out!

You kick the nearest gravestone closed. It slides back into position, severing the protruding forearm, and a muffled expression of pain comes from the undead creature below. Four of the living corpses rise from their graves and surround you. You must fight them all together:

	SKILL	*STAMINA*
First ZOMBIE	6	7
Second ZOMBIE	7	7
Third ZOMBIE	6	6
Fourth ZOMBIE	7	6

If you defeat the creatures, turn to **226**.

412

You pull at the pouch. As it opens, the twelve discs tumble to the floor. You mutter in annoyance and grovel on the ground to pick up those you can still see in the dim light. Roll two dice. This is the number of discs you manage to find. They are, in fact, Gold Pieces and they may well be useful to you later. Add 1 *LUCK* point for your find. Turn to **115**.

413

The creatures are now at the door of the crypt and entering. You hurry off down the staircase. Pebbles, rocks and even parts of bodies rain down on you as you descend the stairs, thrown by the hideous creatures on the surface. You try a little too hard to get away from them quickly, your foot slips on a loose rock and you tumble over and over down the stairs. Unfortunately for you, this staircase has been designed for unwanted visitors. At the bottom of the stairs a dozen sharp iron spikes protrude from the ground! There is nothing you can do to prevent yourself landing squarely in the centre of the spikes. Your death is instantaneous.

414

A path leads from the clearing to the north, although you can see that it soon forks left and right. Will you go east (turn to **272**) or west (turn to **139**)?

415

You fumble about with the breastplate and eventually it slips over your shoulder and stays in place. It will be a useful defensive piece and while you are wearing it you may add 2 points to your Attack Strength during each Attack Round. But it does not fit perfectly and makes moving your arms awkward. While you are wearing it, you must deduct 1 point from your *SKILL* score. You may now leave the guardroom by turning to **394**.

416

You feast heartily on the creature. Add 4 *STAMINA* points for the nourishment. After resting to digest the food, you pick yourself up and continue downstream along the river-bank. Turn to **388**.

417

Marr casts his spell, but it has no effect. A startled look appears on his face and he searches his memory for a way you could be immune to his magic. 'Of course,' he nods finally. 'The Chattermatter failed to entice you. That incompetent fool Hannicus! His instructions were to keep the Elven Dust walled in. Nevertheless, I am sure that your little act of defiance will be reconsidered in view of the riches I may offer you . . .' But you have other ideas. It is now your turn to attack, and you have decided on your target. You will not go for the necromancer himself, but for his mirror. If you have with you a crystal club, turn to **28**. Otherwise turn to **152**.

418

Your foot slides back over the edge of the bridge, and you tumble through the air towards the river below! You shudder with horror at the thought of landing in the filthy waters. But fate is kind to you. Before you reach the water, your head cracks hard against a protruding rock. You are senseless when you hit the river and you never know the unpleasantness of your death in the filthy stream that is the Bilgewater.

419

You shift your weight and turn your great bulk around. With laboured steps you stomp back the way you came and pass the lifeless body. Turn to **308**.

420

You settle down on the floor and begin to feast on the fleshy legs of the first Blood Orc. The taste is not pleasant, but you are hungry. The bearded human continues to stumble round the room, talking in an excited tone. Eventually he comes close to you and trips over the body of the other Blood Orc. His hand scrapes against your back and he shivers with horror when he feels the scales and spines. He rises to his knees and begins to feel your neck and head. You are somewhat bemused by this and allow him to continue. But when his fingers rub across your mouth and feel your sharp fangs, he cannot contain himself any more. Before he can even utter a scream, he faints and slumps to the ground beside you. You finish your meal (add 4 *STAMINA* points) and leave the room. Turn to **138**.

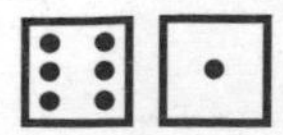

421

You turn angrily towards the peasants as a stone hits you on the shoulder. Lose 1 *STAMINA* point. The men and women are yelling at you, trying to get you off their land. But you are furious and rush towards them through the crops. They beat a retreat, keeping their distance, and hurl more stones. Again you charge forward, again they retreat and again comes the hail of stones. This time another stone hits you in the chest. Lose another *STAMINA* point. After two more charges, you realize that your efforts are futile. They will always be able to move faster than you through the crops, as your greater bulk is slowing you down. You eventually turn from them and return to the path. They follow you, once more jeering and shouting, until you have left their field and are well out of range of their stones.

Ahead of you, a green forest spreads across the horizon and your path is taking you into it. As you enter the forest, you reach a sign which reads 'Knot Oak Wood'. Turn to **244**.

422

The mirror has an ornate gold frame, but otherwise appears to be an ordinary full-sized mirror. You consider smashing the mirror, but it is possible that the noise may alert the crew to your whereabouts. Turn to **302**.

423

You pick your way along the river-bank, following it downstream. The going is not easy. At one point you must climb carefully down a rocky cliff, where the river passes over a waterfall. Eventually you reach a calm pool where the waters slow and spread over a wide expanse. Steam rises lazily from the pungent water and you halt in your tracks as the smell – now stronger than ever – reaches you. Through the steamy mist you catch a glimpse of a creature further along the bank. It stands tall on four legs and is drinking contentedly from the foul waters. You creep closer, keeping hidden in the bushes. The creature stands on long, cloven feet. Its skin is covered in tough scales and its tail ends in a spiky ball. Its head is sleek and serpent-like, with a long, thin tongue that darts in and out as it drinks from the river. It has not noticed you. Will you creep round the creature so as not to disturb it (turn to **120**)? Will you attack it in the hope of gaining a much-needed meal (turn to **238**)? Or will you approach it gently, try to keep it calm, and then mount it (turn to **127**)?

424

You follow the passage until it becomes impossible for you to see in the total darkness. Now you must grope your way along, feeling the walls with both hands. Eventually a faint red glow appears on the left-hand side of the passageway and you realize you are at another fork. To the left, the way seems to lead to some kind of light-source. To the right, the passage is still pitch-black. Will you choose the right-hand passage (turn to **108**) or the left-hand passage (turn to **182**)?

425

The door is decorated with plates and symbols forged in metal. In the centre is a sign which reads: 'Yfl lpwst pnfe mj nfs. Sfrgf bnt sab ndas lb vfs epnly.' The door is locked, so you decide to try breaking it down. You give it a hard shove with your shoulder. It shudders but does not budge. Indignant, you hit it again, but still it will not open. Lose 1 *STAMINA* point. Before you can decide whether or not to try again, a rustling of keys in the lock is followed by a creaking noise as the door opens. A thin, dark face appears at the door and looks at you. 'Npo nffd etpobp jl iyp vru blppd. Whb tajsijt iyp vuwb ntaj nith fe mjnfs. Jfi jts iwpr kothf necpm fe bbc katpmpr rpw. Baf fw epfo thfesl bvf sewjllidp vbtl fss edjfetpdby.' The Black Elf irritates you with his arrogant manner. You do not want to waste time with him. You grunt and smack your fist into the door, knocking it wide open. It clangs into the wall behind and the Black Elf's jaw drops open.

The room inside is sparse. There is a table and chair against one wall and on the table stands a plate with some food on it and a bottle of drink. Behind the table two bunches of keys are hanging on the wall. An archway leads from the room into the blackness beyond. You step inside and the Black Elf pounces. You must fight him:

BLACK ELF	*SKILL 7*	*STAMINA 6*

After two Attack Rounds, turn to **275**.

426

The medicine-man shuffles over to a shelf full of jars and takes one down. 'This healing balm,' he boasts, 'is the finest south of Dree. But I have never had the chance to test it on a creature such as you. Please allow me to try it.' He spreads some of the ointment across your chest and rubs it deep into your scales. He continues until he has rubbed it all over your body. The effect is almost immediate. You begin to feel strong and rejuvenated. His healing balm actually works *better* on you than it does on humans. You may restore your *STAMINA* to its *Initial* level. Then you leave the village of Coven by turning to **374**.

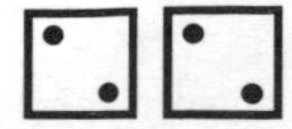

427

You follow the river up the valley until you reach a point where it comes out of a cave in the side of the hill. There is no path into the cave, just the river. If you turn round and follow the river downstream instead, turn to **423**. Otherwise you may either jump into the river and follow it into the cave (turn to **345**), or forget about the river and stomp off through the undergrowth (turn to **57**).

428

The face swirls within the murky mist inside the orb and you watch to see what will happen next. Gradually the face re-forms, but this time it looks larger than before and the sightless eyes begin to glow red like hot coals. Suddenly a small fireball shoots from one eye straight towards you! You jump to avoid it but it catches your leg below the knee and makes you howl in pain. The second eye releases its fireball and this one hits you on your arm just above the elbow. Lose 4 *STAMINA* points for these injuries. Leave quickly by turning to **81**.

429

As you crash out of the bushes into the clearing, the battle halts temporarily and all three combatants stare incredulously at you. You must resolve your battle with the Brigands, who will fight you together. The thin creature is too badly beaten to be of any help and drops to the ground moaning:

	SKILL	*STAMINA*
First BRIGAND	*8*	*9*
Second BRIGAND	*8*	*7*

If you defeat them, turn to **448**.

430

You step forward and cross the cavern, heading for the northerly passage. All is silent from the caves. Perhaps whatever was eating there has now wandered off. You reach the other side without incident. Turn to **41**.

431

'A poor show,' Thugruff sneers, 'for one seemingly with such power. Recover your breath.' While you are picking yourself up, the Half-Troll whispers quietly to the Pixie you met on the gate: 'You know what to do . . .' When you have caught your breath, the Pixie leads you over to a circle in an unoccupied corner of the grounds. 'Wait here,' he says. You wait. Looking at the strange circle, you see that it is not simply a mark on the ground, but a length of rope, arranged in a circular shape. The end of the rope leads off in the direction the Pixie went and is tied to a tree. In fact it is tied to the *top* of the tree, which has been bent right over to touch the ground! It is held by another rope, stretched tight by the tree and fastened halfway up its trunk! You suddenly realize what is happening. At the same time you notice the Pixie, standing by the second rope with a sharp knife! Before you can move, he has cut the rope. The tree snaps upwards, drawing the circle of rope tightly around your leg and taking you up with it until you hang helplessly, suspended at tree-top level by your foot. Turn to **175**.

432

They seem reluctant to advance towards you. Your size and your angry snarl must be daunting to them. They mumble something to each other and turn round. They have decided to leave you and are retracing their steps.

Their glowstone goes out and you lose sight of them. You may now continue safely. Turn to **137**.

433

Following the Jabberwing's advice, you set off northwards. You pause on top of a hillock and survey the area. In the distance to your right you can see a great forest and straight ahead a river cuts through the landscape like a gaping wound. You head on and, a short distance after you have left the hillock, another trail joins yours from the right. Turn to **134**.

434

The Tree Spirits are tightening the circle, moving in closer and closer. You are hoplessly trapped. They are not evil creatures, but they allow no one to pass through their forest without permission. The penalty is *death*!

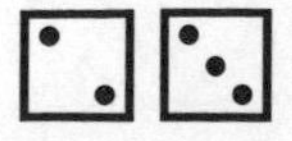

435

The heavy knocker booms loudly on the metal plate. A grunting noise comes from behind the door and you can hear feet shuffling as some sort of creature responds to your knock. The door slowly creaks open and a long snout appears. Small, pig-like eyes peer out at you from behind the single tusk which stands in the middle of the Rhino-Man's face. The door opens wider and you can see the creature's stout, heavily armed torso and legs. It speaks to you: 'Cp mfepn othfn. Whb tabv sjn fsseh b vfey pvu hfrf. B nswfarqvjc kly.' Jfi ypvu cbnav ndfrs tbn d athf ecrfb tvrfetv rnujm mfd jbtf lyet porf ffr fn cfe sjxty itwp. 'Lps toyp vrotp ngvf efh. Th me bfgpnf. Bfe pffow jthiy pv ubff prfe jid fc jd fetpohb vfe belj ttlfebb ttlfepr bct jcf.' He is closing the door without letting you in. Will you shove the door and step in to attack (turn to **357**), or leave, return to the junction and take the northern passage (turn to **144**)?

436

You have four doors to choose from. Will you try the door in the east wall (turn to **49**), the west wall (turn to **409**), the north wall (turn to **262**) or the south wall (turn to **201**)?

437

'No gesture? Darramouss gave you no gesture?' The guard is incredulous. You shrug as if to say that you did not see Darramouss. 'But Darramouss is always in his chamber. Look, wait here for a moment. I must check his room.' The guard grabs a club and rushes off down the passage, leaving you on your own. Will you keep your word and remain where you are until he returns (turn to **38**), or will you step into his room and look for a way out (turn to **54**)?

438

The villagers watch wide-eyed as their champion drops to the ground. Then anger takes over. 'Rog is dead!' cries a voice. 'Let's get that *thing* that done it!' One of them nips back into the hut and produces a pitchfork. 'Quick!' comes a gruff voice from behind you. 'We must leave quickly. Come with me.' The Half-Orc is beckoning you to follow him out of the village. You look again at the villagers and decide that his suggestion is a sensible one. The two of you continue, pursued by the villagers, until you reach the edge of Coven, where they stop and watch you leave, jeering and shaking their fists.

'A foolish thing to do, that,' says the Half-Orc, his sly eyes glancing over at you. 'Getting involved in someone else's fight. If *I'd* been *you*, I would have left you to fight your own battle. Chances are he would have killed me. But then what's that to you? And all because I ate his dog. What does he expect? I was *hungry*! I suppose I *could* have killed it first . . . Would you not have done the same? Well, wouldn't you? Lost your tongue? The silent type, eh? Well I am Grognag Clawtooth. Call me Grog. Which way are you heading? Carrying anything *interesting*? Shall we travel together?'

The creature is shorter than you are. He is dirty and he smells. His jet-black hair is untidy and has not been cut for far too long. His clothes are little better than rags, although he wears a thick leather breastplate and a battered sword hangs from his belt. The two of you will continue your journey together. For as long as he is with you, watch out for reference numbers. If you turn to any references ending in a 7 (e.g. 247), deduct 52 from it and turn to this new reference. Read the two together. Continue now by turning to **107**.

439

You growl suspiciously and step closer to the figure. The spines on your back are bristling and every muscle is tense. You extend one arm just far enough to hook a claw under the ragged cowl and flick it aside. But beneath the cowl is *not* what you were expecting! The sight of the rotten head with its gaping eye-sockets makes you stagger back in fright! An evil laugh resounds through the air, coming not from the figure, but from the glistening Chattermatter hanging from the ceiling. Having snared you into its lair with its ability to speak in many tongues, it now drops from its perch to cover you with its sticky, web-like body. While you struggle in vain inside the living slime, it releases its deadly poison, which will paralyse you. As your struggles subside, the Chattermatter begins to digest your tasty body. You will get no further!

440

Your curiosity has been aroused but not captured by the creature squirming within the sack. You give it a heavy kick as you pass, and send it scuttling across the floor. Whatever is inside squeals for mercy but falls silent after colliding painfully with the stony wall. You continue past it along the passage, your way still lit by eerie blue glowstones. Suddenly, you hear a footstep. You stop to listen hard. A shape forms in the passageway before you! Turn to **63**.

441

You rush boldly round the corner to face whatever is making the creaking. Glowstones in the ceiling blink quickly on in front of you, trying to keep up with your progress. After a few steps, you reach a junction with another passage, which runs from east to west. And on the left-hand wall you discover the source of the creaking – a sign, suspended on a short pole. A cool breeze is wafting through the passage and this is causing the sign to creak as it swings backwards and forwards. You study the sign, which reads: 'Yfllp wst pnfe mjnfs eth jsiwby'. Underneath the letters, there is a large arrow pointing eastwards. You glare angrily at the sign for worrying you and swipe at it with your claw. But it is too high up for you to reach. Will you take the sign's advice and turn to the east (turn to **122**), or would you rather go west (turn to **208**)?

442

The guard draws a bunch of keys out of his pocket and opens the metal door to let you through. You grunt in thanks, and begin climbing the steps. At the top, you find yourself in a cold, stone-walled room with a large stone platform in its centre. Carvings and symbols decorate the platform, which is lit up by a beam of light from a crack in the ceiling. You edge around the room until you reach a door, which you shove open. The sight which greets you makes your eyes open wide …

Space! You have escaped from the dungeon and have emerged into cool night air. Slowly you survey the landscape, your mind filled with wonder at the space all around. You appear to be standing in an open field in which stones have been fixed in regular rows. Some lie down flat on the ground and some are standing up. To your left, near the edge of this field, is a large building with a tall, pointed roof. On the other side, to the right, is a wood, and a path leads straight into the wood from where you are now. Overhead, a huge white orb hangs in the sky giving some light, but this light dwindles when great smoky masses drift across in front of it. You are overawed by your new environment. Would you like to investigate some of the stones set into the ground around you (turn to **198**)? Would you like to look around the old building (turn to **123**)? Or would you like to leave this area along the path into the woods (turn to **261**)?

443

You follow the passage to the north until you reach a junction. To the left you can see that the passage soon reaches a dead end; but on a ledge in the end wall is a large orb of clear stone. To the right you can see that the passage disappears around a bend heading northwards. Will you turn left (turn to **155**) or right (turn to **81**)?

444

The room seems to be uninteresting and you turn to leave. You head back up the passageway until you reach the junction where you continue westwards. Turn to **309**.

445

You retract your claws, so you may feel the strange shape with your fingertips, and you step up close to it. But as you bend down to touch the dark circle, it moves much more swiftly than ever you could. In an instant, it has expanded to engulf the very ground on which you are standing. You suddenly find that you are standing, not on solid rock, but on . . . nothing! Down you fall, through the void, until the journey becomes too much for you. You pass out in the blackness and will never know the gruesome fate which awaits you in the depths of the Blackmouth Floortrap.

446

You deliver the death-blow and the Knight drops to the

ground. With the danger now over, your thoughts turn to *food.* The smell of the still-warm Hobbit reaches your nostrils and your mouth begins to water. You snatch the creature in one hand and eagerly sink your teeth into its sweet flesh. But this will merely provide a snack for you. Inside his armour, the Knight is an impossible meal, but the red-robed Wizard groaning on the floor may be a new taste for you to savour. You silence his miserable whimpers with a single deadly slash from your claws. For the tasty meal you may restore your *STAMINA* to its *Initial* level.

After you have eaten, you rummage through the adventurers' belongings. Their packs have little to interest you. The Hobbit carried a miniature sword and you find a rolled up piece of thin parchment in the Wizard's robe. All three humans carried odd-shaped lumps of a doughy substance – perhaps food, although it smells of nothing to you. They all also have small hide pouches containing round, flat objects of shiny metal. You cannot think what these may be for, so you toss them aside. You must now continue your journey. Passages lead off from the chamber to the north, east and west.

You decide to take the passageway to the west. You leave the chamber, your way ahead lit by the flickering fire. Eventually, the fire's light becomes too distant to help and you are groping your way in pitch-blackness. Suddenly

You have disturbed a group of flying creatures

a high-pitched twittering sound comes from above you, followed by others. You have disturbed a group of flying creatures, which are now squeaking in alarm as they dart about around you! You swipe at them blindly and catch one or two of them as they dive at you and scratch you with sharp claws. But your scales protect you from any serious harm and you are soon further along the passage, where these creatures evidently do not venture. The passage turns north. You follow it around the bend to the right and stop in front of a wooden door. There is no other way forward. Will you heave at the door with your shoulder or is there something else you wish to do? Roll one die. If you roll 1 or 2, turn to **277**. If you roll 3–6, turn to **101**.

447

Your eyes widen as three scrawny creatures form before you. They are thin and angular and move in quick, jerky motions. Although their bodies are covered in a scraggy dark fur, their bony faces are bald, with tiny eyes. In the centre of each face is an oversized, protruding mouth, rimmed with sharp teeth. These vicious little Flesh-Feeders live on carrion. While feeding they make themselves invisible to avoid being caught unawares. But in between meals they are both visible and quick-tempered. They now face you, furious that their meals have been interrupted, and you must battle with the creatures. They attack together:

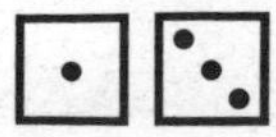

	SKILL	*STAMINA*
First FLESH-FEEDER	6	6
Second FLESH-FEEDER	6	7
Third FLESH-FEEDER	6	6

If you defeat them, turn to **89**.

448

Exhausted from your battle, your attentions turn to the white-haired creature lying moaning on the ground. Seeing that the battle is over and that you mean him no harm, he turns towards you. As he speaks to you he winces in pain from his beating: 'I offer you – *aaaaah!* – my thanks for your aid. My name is – *oooh!* – is Whiteleaf. I am – *unnngh!* – an Elf. Home for me is the village of Ethelle Amaene.' He turns over on to his back and continues: 'Aaahhhh, that's better ... I know these woods well. Perhaps I can be of service to you in return?' What would you like him to tell you:

Anything he knows about Stittle Woad?	Turn to **58**
What he knows of the *Galleykeep?*	Turn to **269**
More about himself ?	Turn to **167**

449

Old Twenty-nine – the legionnaires proudly refer to themselves by their numbers – has been at the fort for some time. He knows everything that happens and all the ways to escape. The two of you spend the evening together and he is happy to talk about his own past, though his stories do tend to ramble. He and his sister were recruited into the service of Zharradan Marr many years ago. Rhino-Men are particularly suitable as guards and Twenty-nine can remember being a member of Marr's personal guard during the sacking of Salamonis. But he disliked Zharradan Marr.

The turning-point in his career came when he was caught drinking in Salamonis with another Rhino-Man who was known to be engaged by Marr's former colleague, but now arch-enemy, Balthus Dire. This incident marked the end of his progress in Marr's army. From then on he was watched, imprisoned and punished regularly by Thugruff. His sister was held prisoner in Marr's dungeons in case he should decide to try escaping. Now that his sister is safe, he can at last be free from the Half-Troll's tyranny.

Later that night, under cover of darkness, he leads you to an area in the wall where the stones have been loosened. With a little work, you are able to clear a hole large enough for the two of you to get through. You leave the Testing Grounds and continue through the woods all night. He promises to lead you to someone who can tell

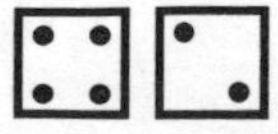

you more about yourself, someone who he knows lives in a clearing in the woods. But he will be recognized if he goes with you. Finally you reach a trail which heads north. Twenty-nine tells you to follow the trail, while he sets off to the west. But a short time after he has left, you hear a cry coming from his direction. Will you rush after him to see if you can help (turn to **10**), or ignore him and continue (turn to **174**)?

450

You leave the room and find yourself once more in the east-west passageway you entered from. You remember the noises you heard behind the door ahead to the east. But there is no other way forward. The door is locked, so you must once again charge it. Turn to **263**.

451

You creep slowly into the blackness, your claws ready to strike. You can now hear the heavy breathing of a large animal close by. In an instant, the creature strikes! Two heavy blows crash down on your back and send you sprawling into the depths of the cave. The attack is accompanied by a shrill whinnying and you spin round to face your attacker. Silhouetted in the cave entrance you can see that your opponent is a frightened horse, which is balancing on its hind legs, ready to strike again! Lose 2 *STAMINA* points for the blows you have already taken.

If you think the creature might make a tasty meal, you may fight it by turning to **355**. Otherwise you may avoid the horse, leave the cave and make your way back to the crossroads by turning to **386**.

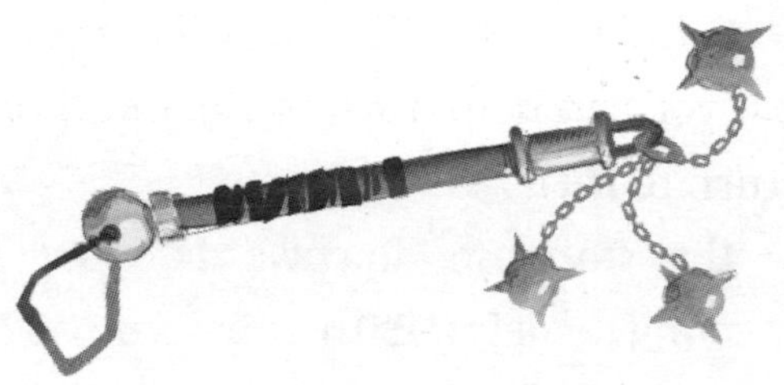

452

You step up to the chair and look at the figure. An ugly face protrudes from the red cape. Its strong jaws have sharp biting teeth, but the dark skin is stretched tightly over the creature's lumpy skull. The eyes bulge beneath its closed eyelids as if they were trying to burst out. You take the cape in your claw and slowly lift it. At that moment, the creature's eyes flick open! It springs from its chair and fastens its teeth into your neck before you have time to react! Lose 2 *STAMINA* points. You must now resolve your battle with the Blood Orc:

BLOOD ORC	*SKILL 7*	*STAMINA 5*

If you defeat the creature, turn to **207**.

453

You spend some time watching insects scuttling about on the surface of the pond and enjoy the twittering of the birds in the branches high above. Eventually you decide to press on. Add 2 *STAMINA* points for the rest and turn to **52**.

454

You follow the staircase downwards, your huge feet desperately trying to maintain their balance on the narrow stairs. *Test your Luck*. If you are Lucky, turn to **37**. If you are Unlucky, turn to **413**.

455

You slip away from Thugruff and make your way round to the front of the building, where the gates are locked shut. Once more the little Pixie appears. 'What is this?' he smiles. 'Leaving us so soon?' You grunt and nod your head. 'But you surely cannot wish to go already. You cannot refuse our hospitality.' There is a hint of menace in the little creature's voice, although there is surely nothing any creature so puny can do to harm you. He is leading you back into the Testing Grounds. Will you pull away from him and assert your wish to leave (turn to **335**), or let him persuade you to return (turn to **385**)?

456

The pitiful figure whimpering on the ground puts up no resistance as you end its miserable life. You may feast on the body and, if you do so, you will gain 4 *STAMINA* points. Then leave the village of Coven by turning to **374**.

457

You regain your footing and hurry across the bridge to the other side. Shaken by your near accident, you continue until you arrive at a side passage on the right. You do not like the look of this side passage, so you continue eastwards. Turn to **122**.

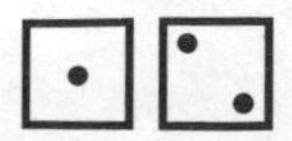

458

You crouch low and squeeze through the narrow gap. As you pass through the doorway, a single glowstone flicks on to reveal the contents of the small chamber which you are now standing in. The room is completely bare except for a large chest against one of the walls. You step over and examine the chest. You push it, shove it and bash it, trying to break it open. Finally, a lucky push opens the lid. Inside, you find two mysterious objects. The first is a large circular plate made of strong metal. It has a sharp spike which protrudes from the centre on one side and two leather straps on the other. On the same side as the straps is attached a leather pouch which may be useful for carrying things. The other object is a piece of rough, coloured rock, about the size of your forearm. One end is wide and the other is much narrower. It is a dull green colour and glistens faintly in the light. But it appears very brittle. It may make a useful weapon gripped by the tapered end, but it would no doubt not last long in battle. You may take one of these items with you. Any metallic discs may be placed in the pouch on the plate if you choose this object. If you choose the plate, turn to **197**. If you choose the rock, turn to **110**.

459

You turn back towards the door. 'I see you got the hint,' mocks Nimbicus. 'Don't bother apologizing for the fact that you have just ruined my concentration. I shall have to start reading my tome again. But don't let that worry you. Oh, no. Close the door on the way out. We probably won't meet again. Leastways, not if *I* see you first. Bah!'

You leave the Weather Mage and return to the hallway. The noise outside is spreading, as more of the crew join in the search for you. You must now choose another room. You quickly study the symbols again. Will you try:

The jug of water?	Turn to **346**
The fire?	Turn to **29**
The crown?	Turn to **129**
The crossed swords?	Turn to **111**
None of these?	Turn to **302**

460

'Our partnership will be supreme in Allansia. Together we shall rule. If it is riches you desire, then you shall have all the wealth you can use. If your lust is for power, then I shall give you western Allansia as your own empire.' His words are spilling out with mounting anxiety. But you are not listening. Instead you are preparing to swing your club. 'Do I waste my words?' he screams. 'Then think on this. If I should be lost, how will you regain your former self? Will you be content to remain a beast for the rest of your days, constantly feared, hated and even hunted by your own kind?'

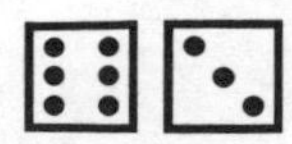

This time, his words stop you. You consider them. Should he disappear for ever, perhaps you will spend the rest of your days banished from civilization, an enemy of your own race. But then what guarantee do you have that Marx's experiments are reversible? None! You glance back up at him just in time to catch him wiping the smile from his face. He has been playing for time! His image is disappearing! Furiously you grab your club. Your eyes narrow; you grit your teeth. A low growl comes from deep in your throat. As Marr's image fades you move quickly. In a trice you have grabbed the club and swung it. The room is filled with the sound of breaking glass as the mirror shatters into tiny fragments before you. The portal from his land of limbo has been destroyed! He may never return to your world!

You turn towards the door. A bolt of pain shoots up from your foot! You have cut yourself on a splinter from the glass. But this should not be! The thick scales on your feet should not be scratched by such tiny fragments. You look down. And then you realize what has happened.

Your greeny-brown, scaly foot is no more. Instead the foot is pale-skinned and vulnerable. The claws have gone too! Your hands have returned to their human form and, when you look at your reflection in a fragment of mirror left hanging in the frame, a familiar face stares back wide-eyed at you! Marr's experiments were performed by sorcery, not surgery, and when he disappeared, the spell was broken!

As your memory returns, you remember the bitter struggle high over the Moonstone Hills, when Zharradan Marr and his winged Tooki forces bore down on your *Galleykeep* in overwhelming numbers. Like a raging stormcloud, the dark Tooki – a specially bred race of War Griffins – swooped down on the ship, their mounted Blood Orc archers raining arrows and killing many of your crew. The surprise attack was so quick, and so deadly, that you had no option but to surrender. As Zharradan Marr stepped down off his own richly adorned Tooki on to the deck of the *Galleykeep*, you swore you would avenge this defeat. But Marr had other plans for you . . .

The tables have now been turned. You are back in your position as Commander of the *Galleykeep.* Marr's brainless creatures will respect your authority. Though Marr may have shown you a mercy of sorts, you in turn gave him the mercy he deserved: *none!*

HOW TO FIGHT THE CREATURES OF TROLLTOOTH PASS

Before embarking on your adventure, you must first determine your strengths and weaknesses. Use dice to find out your initial *SKILL*, *STAMINA* and *LUCK* scores. On page 360 there is an *Adventure Sheet* on which you can record the details of an adventure. You will find on it boxes for recording your *SKILL*, *STAMINA* and *LUCK* scores.

You are advised either to record your scores on the *Adventure Sheet* in pencil, or to make photocopies of the page to use in future adventures.

Those who are familiar with the Fighting Fantasy rules should note that there are some new rules in this book.

SKILL, STAMINA AND LUCK

Roll one die. Add 6 to this number and enter this total in the *SKILL* box on the *Adventure Sheet*.

Roll both dice. Add 12 to the number rolled and enter this total in the *STAMINA* box.

There is also a *LUCK* box. Roll one die, add 6 to this number and enter this total in the *LUCK* box.

For reasons that will be explained below, *SKILL*, *STAMINA* and *LUCK* scores change constantly during an adventure. You must keep an accurate record of these scores and for this reason you are advised either to write small in the boxes or to keep an eraser handy. But never rub out your *Initial* scores. Although you may be awarded additional *SKILL*, *STAMINA* and *LUCK* points, these totals may never exceed your *Initial* scores, except on very rare occasions, when you will be instructed on a particular page.

Your *SKILL* score reflects your general fighting expertise; the higher the better. Your *STAMINA* score reflects your general constitution, your will to survive, your determination and overall fitness; the higher your *STAMINA* score, the longer you will be able to survive. Your *LUCK* score indicates how naturally lucky a person you are. Luck – and magic – are facts of life in the fantasy kingdom you are about to explore.

BATTLES

You will often come across pages in the book which instruct you to fight an opponent of some sort. An option to flee may be given, but if not – or if you choose to attack anyway – you must resolve the battle as described below.

First record your opponent's *SKILL* and *STAMINA* scores in the first vacant *Encounter Box* on your *Adventure Sheet*. The scores for each creature are given in the book each time you have an encounter. The sequence of combat is then:

1. Roll the two dice once for your opponent. Add its *SKILL* score. This total is your opponent's Attack Strength.
2. Roll the two dice once for yourself. Add the number rolled to your current *SKILL* score. This total is your Attack Strength.
3. If your Attack Strength is higher than that of your opponent, you have wounded it. Proceed to step 4. If your opponent's Attack Strength is higher than yours, it has wounded you. Proceed to step 5. If both Attack Strength totals are the same, you have avoided each other's blows – start the next Attack Round from step 1 above.
4. You have wounded your opponent, so subtract 2 points from its *STAMINA* score. You may use your *LUCK* here to do additional damage (see over).
5. Your opponent has wounded you, so subtract 1 point from your own *STAMINA* score. Again you may use *LUCK* at this stage (see over).
6. Make the appropriate adjustments to either your opponent's or your own *STAMINA* scores (and your

LUCK score if you used *LUCK* – see over).

7. Begin the next Attack Round (repeat steps 1–6). This sequence continues until the *STAMINA* score of either you or your opponent has been reduced to zero (death).

INSTANT DEATH

As you learn more about yourself during the adventure, you will realize that you are an extremely powerful creature, capable of killing most opponents with a single blow. If you *roll a double* when rolling for your Attack Strength, then you have landed such a death-dealing blow. Your opponent will die instantly, without the need to resolve the particular Attack Round you are in.

FIGHTING MORE THAN ONE OPPONENT

If you are involved in a fight with more than one opponent, you must choose at the start of each Attack Round which of the opponents you will be directing your own attack towards. Roll the dice for each of the combatants. Resolve your own attack against your chosen opponent as normal (if you win he loses 2 *STAMINA* points, if he wins you lose 1 *STAMINA* point). Then you must compare your own Attack Strength (i.e. the one you have just rolled) against that of *all* the other opponents. Anyone with a *higher* Attack Strength than yours will score a hit against you. You cannot score hits against anyone except the opponent you chose at the start of the round, even if your Attack Strength is higher than one or more of the other opponents.

LUCK

At various times during your adventure, either in battles or when you come across situations in which you could either be lucky or unlucky (details of these are given on the pages themselves), you may call on your luck to make the outcome more favourable. But beware! Using luck is a risky business and if you are *un*lucky, the results could be disastrous.

The procedure for using your luck is as follows: roll two dice. If the number rolled is *equal to or less than* your current *LUCK* score, you have been Lucky and the result will go in your favour. If the number rolled is *higher* than your current *LUCK* score, you have been Unlucky and you will be penalized.

This procedure is known as *Testing your Luck*. Each time your *Test your Luck*, you must subtract 1 point from your current *LUCK* score. Thus you will soon realize that the more you rely on your luck, the more risky this will become.

Using Luck in Battles

On certain pages of the book you will be told to *Test your Luck* and will be told the consequences of your being Lucky or Unlucky. However, in battles, you always have the *option* of using your luck either to inflict a more serious wound on a creature you have just wounded, or to minimize the effects of a wound the creature has just inflicted on you.

If you have just wounded the creature, you may *Test your Luck* as described above. If you are Lucky, you have inflicted a severe wound and may subtract an *extra* 2 points from the creature's *STAMINA* score. However, if you are Unlucky, the wound was a mere graze and you must restore 1 point to the creature's *STAMINA* (i.e. instead of scoring the normal 2 points of damage, you have now scored only 1).

If the creature has just wounded you, you may *Test your Luck* to try to minimize the wound. If you are Lucky you have managed to avoid the full damage of the blow, and need not deduct any *STAMINA* points. If you are Unlucky, you have taken a more serious blow. Subtract 1 *extra* *STAMINA* point.

Remember that you must subtract 1 point from your own *LUCK* score each time you *Test your Luck*.

RESTORING SKILL, STAMINA AND LUCK

Skill

Your *SKILL* score will not change much during your adventure. Occasionally, a paragraph may give instructions to increase or decrease your *SKILL* score. A Magic Weapon may increase your *SKILL* – but remember that only one weapon can be used at a time. You cannot claim 2 *SKILL* bonuses for carrying 2 Magic Swords. Your *SKILL* score can never exceed its *Initial* value unless you are specifically instructed otherwise.

Stamina and Provisions

Your *STAMINA* score will change a lot during your adventure as you fight monsters and undertake arduous tasks. As you near your goal, your *STAMINA* level may become dangerously low and battles may be particularly risky, so be careful!

Your backpack contains enough Provisions for ten meals. You may rest and eat at any time except when engaged in a battle. Eating a meal restores 4 *STAMINA* points. When you eat a meal, add 4 points to your *STAMINA* score and deduct 1 point from your Provisions. A separate Provisions Remaining box is provided on the *Adventure Sheet* for recording details of Provisions. Remember that you have a long way to go, so use your Provisions wisely!

Remember also that your *STAMINA* score may never exceed its *Initial* value. Drinking the potion of Strength (see later) will restore your *STAMINA* to its *Initial* level at any time.

Luck

Additions to your *LUCK* score are awarded during the adventure when you have been particularly lucky. Details are given in the paragraphs of the book. Remember that, as with *SKILL* and *STAMINA*, your *LUCK* score may never exceed its *Initial* value unless you are specifically instructed otherwise.

HINTS ON PLAY

There is one true way through *Creature of Havoc* and it will take you several attempts to find it. Make notes and draw a map as you explore – this map will be invaluable in future adventures and enable you to progress rapidly through to unexplored sections.

Not all areas contain treasure; some merely contain traps and creatures which you will no doubt fall foul of. You may make wrong turnings during your quest and while you may indeed progress through to your ultimate destination, it is by no means certain that you will find what you are searching for.

It will be realized that entries make no sense if read in numerical order. It is essential that you read only the entries you are instructed to read. Reading other entries will only cause confusion and lessen excitement during play.

The one true way involves a minimum of risk and any player, no matter how weak on *Initial* dice rolls, should be able to get through fairly easily.

May the luck of the gods go with you on the adventure ahead!

ADVENTURE SHEET

SKILL

STAMINA

LUCK

EQUIPMENT

MONSTER ENCOUNTERS

MONSTER:
SKILL =
STAMINA =

MONSTER:
SKILL =
STAMINA =

MONSTER:
SKILL =
STAMINA =

MONSTER:
SKILL =
STAMINA =

MONSTER:
SKILL =
STAMINA =

MONSTER:
SKILL =
STAMINA =

MONSTER:
SKILL =
STAMINA =

MONSTER:
SKILL =
STAMINA =

MONSTER:
SKILL =
STAMINA =

MONSTER:
SKILL =
STAMINA =

MONSTER:
SKILL =
STAMINA =

MONSTER:
SKILL =
STAMINA =

ADVENTURE SHEET

SKILL

STAMINA

LUCK

EQUIPMENT

MONSTER ENCOUNTERS

MONSTER:
SKILL =
STAMINA =

MONSTER:
SKILL =
STAMINA =

MONSTER:
SKILL =
STAMINA =

MONSTER:
SKILL =
STAMINA =

MONSTER:
SKILL =
STAMINA =

MONSTER:
SKILL =
STAMINA =

MONSTER:
SKILL =
STAMINA =

MONSTER:
SKILL =
STAMINA =

MONSTER:
SKILL =
STAMINA =

MONSTER:
SKILL =
STAMINA =

MONSTER:
SKILL =
STAMINA =

MONSTER:
SKILL =
STAMINA =

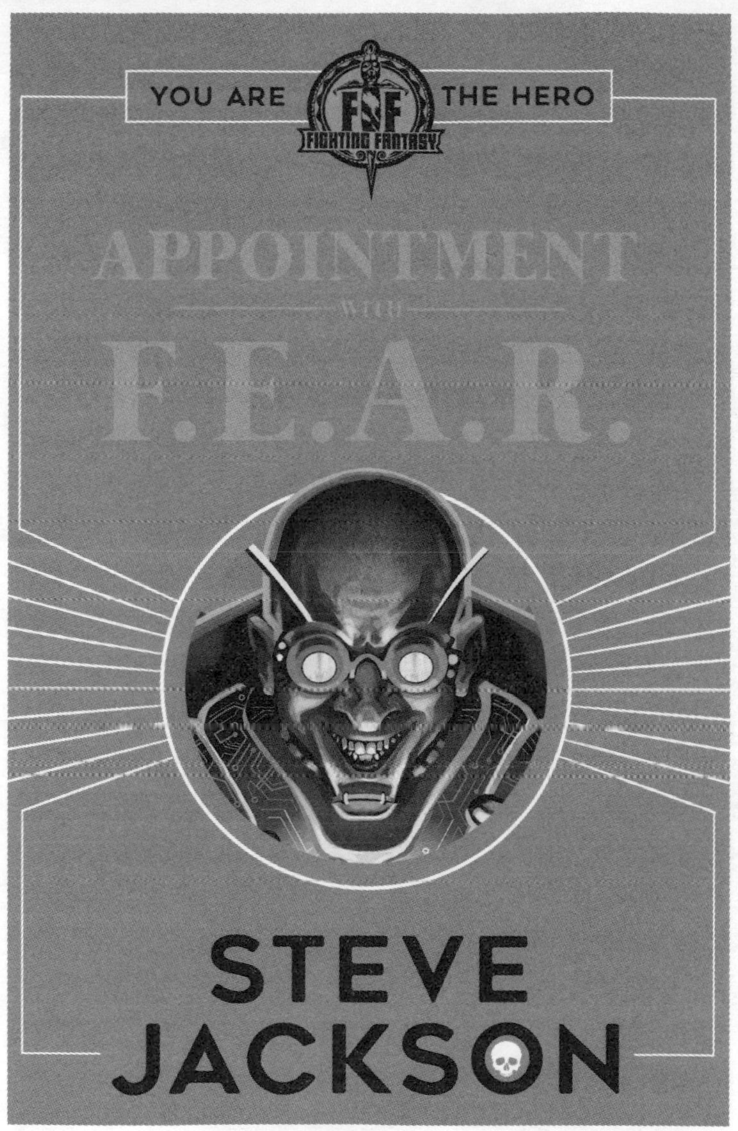

YOU ARE
FIGHTING FANTASY
THE HERO
APPOINTMENT
WITH
F.E.A.R.
STEVE
JACKSON

YOU are the Silver Crusader. YOU use your superpowers to discover the location of a top-secret F.E.A.R. meeting, capture the Titanium Cyborg and his gang, and bring them to justice and save Titan City. Can YOU complete this difficult quest?

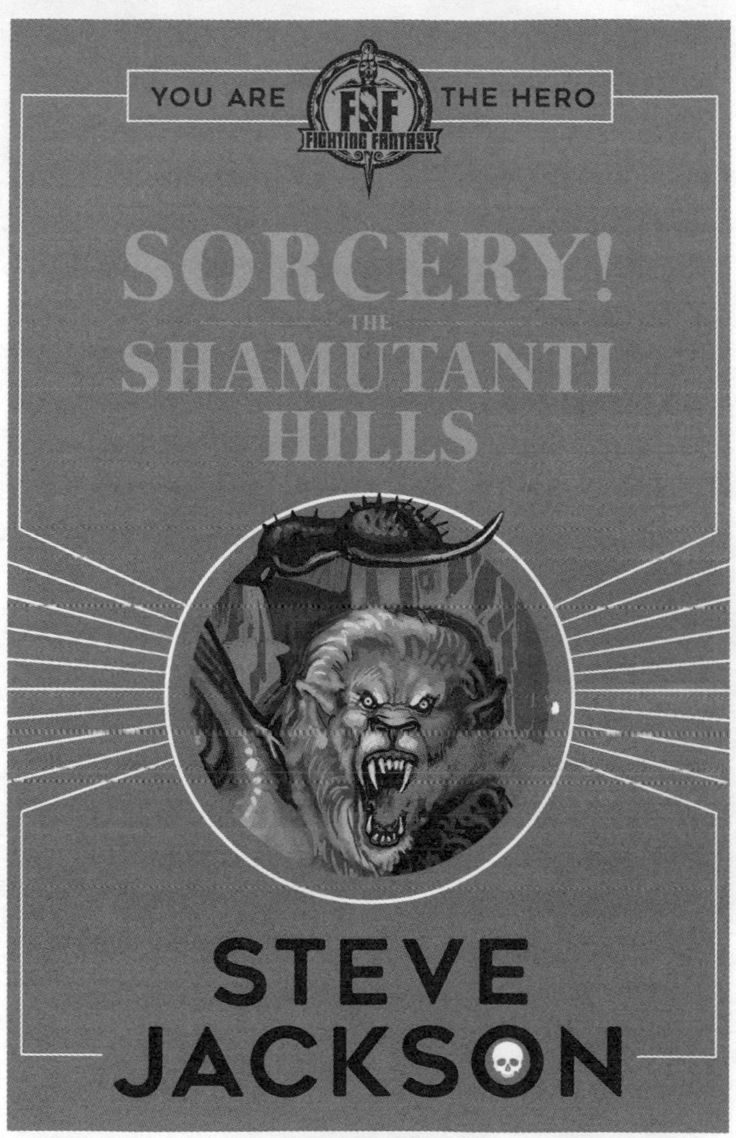

YOU, the hero, must search for the legendary Crown of Kings, and journey the Shamutanti Hills. Alive with evil creatures, lawless wanderers and bloodthirsty monsters, the land is riddled with tricks and traps waiting for YOU.

Will YOU be able to cross the hills safely?

COLLECT THEM ALL, BRAVE ADVENTURER!

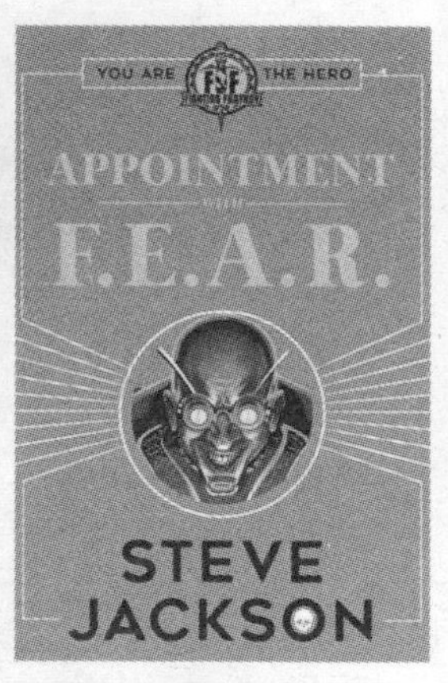